Trifocals: One Man's View

"Just Shadows of Shadows, But It Is All I Got"

Short Stories and Musings

Ron Stultz

Dedication

"Dedication?" As in acknowledging all those that helped form "the who he is" in this moment? A list of names would be several hundred, if not a thousand, long. His parents, who gave him "life" and his ancestors, who were made of stern stuff.

Volunteers who taught and encouraged. Mentors that made him question and think. Co-workers who shared their lives and knowledge.

The Virginia Military Institute that added the honesty and integrity disc to his backbone.

Priscilla, his wife, the love of his life, who has endured, encouraged, and added for over 50 years.

The 4 children (Candy, Zooey, Julie, and Jeff), whom God gifted him to raise, that have the stern stuff of their ancestors.

So many and to all, he hereby proclaims that he is dedicated to someday, somehow, becoming a "real boy" like Pinocchio wanted

About the Author

Ron Stultz: born at the start of the "baby boom" (old); 20/400 vision (trifocals) and an electrical engineer (computer hardware and software design).

He creates YouTube videos of do-it-yourself repairs and muses, doodles (more than one band CD album cover artwork), and "can fix" just about anything.

Interesting to him, he finds writing fiction or a muse much harder than writing computer code. Computer code either works or it doesn't and can be edited until it does "work." But with just words,

"Does it work?" is much harder to determine.

This book is his first compiled fiction and musing effort, and it is his hope that "some of his "modules," will "work" for the readers.

Table of Contents

"The Voices"

He stands on the platform with all the others. He sees, but he really does not notice, and he hears, but he really does not recognize. He is just another piece of cargo to be loaded onto the next subway train.

Time goes by, but he is not aware of it. The train is the only clock that matters and will come when it comes.

He feels the rush of the air come down the tunnel, and he steps forward towards the track to make sure he can get on and find a space.

The train pulls into the station, and he walks on. He does a quick scan of the seats; none are available, never are, and he walks to one end of the car and grabs a handrail to brace against the erratic movements of the train once it begins to move again.

He is there, in the car, but not really. This is nothing more than a step up a flight of stairs, a thing to be done before other things can be done, and nothing more. The train pulls out of the station and begins to accelerate down the tunnel, and then it is completely dark out the car windows except for the train signal or tunnel light.

His slender frame rocks back and forth with the rhythm of the car. He is no more than a large wooden crate stamped for delivery to "Union Square" or "Central Park West" or some other destination. Then the lights in the car flicker once and then again and then go out completely. The train begins to slow to a stop, and for the first time since he entered the subway, he actually has a thought: "Power failure."

After a moment or two, the emergency lights in the car come on, and once again, stares out the window. "It will not be long, never is." But as he stares out the car window, his eyes begin to register that the emergency lights are dimming and then go out completely. For a few moments, there is nothing but silence, but then the voices begin.

"Mommy, I'm scared!" No response. "Come on. I have a meeting. I have to be there in 5 minutes. Why today?"

Then, voices ring out all over the car, and in his mind, he begins to imagine what the voices look like. "My boss is not going to be happy; I can tell you!" A middle-aged secretary wearing tennis shoes she will change out of at work. "Got a client waiting!" A mid-to late-20's businessman in a nice conservative suit and tie, still trying to make it so he does not have to ride the subway.

Again, "Mommy, I 'm scared!" and then a "Shut up your punk ass, kid! We ought just to take us some easy ass money with all these lights out," a male teen voice from the far end of the car.

Voices. Just voices in the dark, but he sees them now in his mind and begins to think about their lives and who they might be.

"What is taking so long?" A teenage girl with some anxiety in her voice: a college student, perhaps.

He thinks about speaking up and assuring everyone that it will be ok and that the power will be back on soon, but then wonders what his voice would sound like, in the darkness, to the others in the car.

"Shit!" a middle-aged woman.

"I got a doctor's appointment and need to get there" another woman with an accent.

"Can we sue the subway system for this?" an older man, perhaps even elderly.

The lights flicker on for a second and then off again. "That is a good sign, perhaps just a moment or two more."

In the darkness, he can hear and feel the breathing of all on board the car, and their closeness is amazing and disturbing at the same time. He has never noticed the closeness of all the other cargo on the train before, but now, they all have voices and are people with directions, needs, and frustrations.

The lights of the car snap on, and this time, a voice from an intercom informs that the power has been restored and the train will now begin running again.

Once more, he stares out the window of the car but his eyes; his mind is drawn back into the car. He turns to look inside the car to find the people behind the voices he has heard.

It is easy to spot the gang of teenage boys with their idle threats of robbery but he is surprised to see the 5 or 6, dressed in soccer uniforms. Plenty of businessmen in suits and briefcases, so he is not sure which one was the complainer. The scared child is easy to spot, but he wonders why her mother did not comfort her.

But as he looks at each, either sitting or standing, he loses sight of what he has been trying to do: match voices to actual faces and gets lost in the people he sees before him.

The Hispanic couple sitting side by side, he thin from obvious daily manual labor and she much too heavy from daily cooking and eating most of it, the elderly gray-haired lady with way too much makeup and cheap jewelry. The college or high school student, with her arms and legs all pulled in, taunt on herself with an open textbook on her lap. Obviously, she is not comfortable so close to those sitting beside her. "She one of the voices?"

The tourist couple, large fancy camera and bags standing close to each other for comfort and safety in the middle of the car: looking lost and confused. Those he cannot see, hidden by newspapers. "Wonder what they did when the lights were out?"

The tall blonde: pretty face, nice-looking legs, great figure that seems so out of place here. "Should be riding in a limo somewhere or at least a taxi cab, a hooker perhaps? 'No': just someone new to the city, trying to break into some business or another. I wonder if she will make her appointment on time."

The black teenage girl with the headphones on her head, rocking back and forth in her seat, lost in her music. "Wonder if she ever even noticed when the lights were out. Did it even matter to her?"

The elderly man with the cane from a different era wearing a hat, threadbare suit, and tie that went out of style 20 years ago. The cane is black and appears to have a silver head on it. Shoes are shined bright, and his face is shaven, clean, and crisp. "Who could he be, and where could he be headed: a mystery."

And then, suddenly, without any warning to him at all, the train pulls into the station but this time, he hangs back and watches the elderly man, the soccer team and camera couple, all head towards the doors and he joins them: people now and no longer just cargo.

Once out of the car, he is behind the camera couple and he can hear them talking about the lights being out and that from now one, they are using the taxis to get around. And then he catches up to the elderly man with the cane and they glance at each other and he hears himself say, "Nice cane. Old?" The old man is a retired police captain headed to a police reunion, "His 20th so far."

A street level, he finds himself overcome with all the people he finds, headed this way and that, alone or in pairs or groups and he can hear their conversations and quickly identifies 2 bankers talking commodities and sales and a young woman carry what is obvious a cello in a case. And a man, pointing to a storm drain and telling a tourist, "His car keys fell into the drain and if the tourist would give him $20, he could take a taxi to his home and get his other set of keys."

He knows they have been here all along, but he has just never seen them, like the cargo on the train but now, it is as if the "lights" have finally come on in the city for him to see, hear, and feel.

"Torn"

He likes the feel of the rock under him, this boulder, his boulder, and as he sits, he can hear the wind making its way from tree top to tree top down the mountain behind him, towards him: wave after wave washing him clean. He likes it here alone.

For a moment, he does not think about why he is here, what he should be doing, or what should happen next, and he likes the feeling.

He lays his back against the sun-warmed boulder and looks up at the sky. The stars are beginning to come "out" and the memory of that night so long ago, laying in the cold and darkness with a friend staring at these same stars.

On the mountain above him, an owl hoots, and the sound, mixed with the wind, is lonesome. For a moment, he misses her and the children, and the thought makes him move, sit up.

Looking at the valley beyond, the lights of a town begin to come on, and he watches as an octopus with tentacles of light reach out into the now darkening countryside, and he is torn, torn between the sky and the town, between some silent mystery he cannot name and his kind and torn between being alone on the mountain and her and all that is back there.

He lays back again on his rock and closes his eyes, and at once, he is walking along the ocean. On one side is the sea and the sky; on the other, his family, other families, and all he and mankind have achieved. Again, he feels torn between the two, and it seems to him that although he prefers the sea and the sky and being alone, he has been told and taught that he should prefer his own kind. Her.

Torn: he always seems torn and wishes he was not, but he again sits up and looks out on the valley below. "Why has he come here? Why did he bolt from her and drive to this mountain again?"

Feeling the boulder under him, he realizes he cannot remember how he has come to this spot, this place, this boulder outcropping on this mountain, and he wonders if it matters or not, and he feels something within him let go, give way.

He is here, just here, and he likes it.

"Radioman"

He sits in a cramped, windowless, metal-walled room, headphones on, bent over a small shelf attached to one wall. The room is lit only by the dial of the receiver, the meters of the transmitter, and a few pilot lights.

A pad of paper sits in the small space in front of the receiver, a pen always in his hand to decipher Morse code or write down any words he hears.

Here, in the dark, he listens for distress messages out of the darkness of a vast ocean.

He is only ears, listening for a sound, any sound that is not hiss, white noise, static, that might be a call for help. Constantly, he is moving the receiver frequency dial slowly from one end of the emergency frequency band limit to the other and back again over and over.

Sometimes, it is a slow scan, and he plunges into the depth of the hiss and 'swims' down through layer after layer until he can go no further. Sometimes, when he is diving, a depth charge of a nearby lightning strike will almost deafen his mind, but he must do the dives to search for the faintest of calls for rescue.

Over the years, his listening has also turned into seeing as he dives deep down. Each layer of noise coming from a further and further away source, and he can see the universe emitting chaos from millions of years ago, and its signal finally reaching and flowing down the antenna wire, into the receiver, and finally into his ears.

Five years. For five years now, he has sat and listened, and only once, three years ago, did he catch a fragment of a distress call and using various filters to extract the faint from the layers, he got enough of the call to rebroadcast it to all those within range of his ship. Three ships responded, and one managed to save the crew and fix the stalled main engine.

Sometimes when he has been on duty for hours and hours, he will think he hears, down deep in the noise, the faint trace of a message, some character, maybe even a word, but then it is gone, lost to the sound of an exploding star or stuff being sucked into a black hole. "Just a trick of his mind, but then again," he wonders. "Could it have been a distress call, someone in need of help? Was someone calling me? What did they need?"

As he turns the receiver dial and waits and waits for coherence, sometimes, he will switch the transmitter to standby and 'send out' messages to various people he knows, thinks of, and cares about, and he wonders if his messages will make it into their dreams or awareness. He knows the message will not be received as he sent it, but perhaps as some phantom on the edge of a dream or maybe just some strange light wind that stirs the hair of that woman he knew once and has never forgotten.

He sees a friend's backyard in the layers and sends out a message to her to be careful of the rake covered in leaves.

Then he 'hears' an old friend and can clearly decipher a call for help somewhere, far off, in a hospital bed.

He sends his old friend a message of "distraction." Hoping a light will go out in the hospital room or something suddenly fall and the distraction will, for a moment, free his friend of pain.

And sometimes, when his mind receiver does not discern anything, he will switch on the ship's transmitter and send out a call on a frequency just outside the emergency band, hoping someone out there in the darkness is listening just like him and wants to talk for a moment. But no response ever comes.

Listening, waiting, and focusing. He has become nothing but listening and waiting. If a fragment, and, if not sharp enough with filters and his plunge into the depths, he might miss a desperate call.

When his midnight to 8 am shift ends, he gets some food and then sleeps for a while. Sometimes, he dreams of someone he has "sent" a message to, only there is something different, like a face or the place, but the message received is clear as if she does not understand his obsession with her, but then again, neither does he.

Then, after sleep, he relaxes sitting out on the sun-lit deck, thinking of nothing at all, and sometimes, his mind will deep dive as if his mind is constantly tuning some unknown set of frequencies and still listening for the sound, a signal, a message, out of some ether which surrounds us all.

He is a radioman.

"This Way or That?"

The drizzle streaks down his glasses as he holds out his thumb, hoping for a ride away, just somewhere away. His heart is pounding in his chest, still distraught from the argument and the raging emotions. "How had everything gotten so bad, so tangled up, so quickly?"

He watches as the speeding cars go by. An interstate: he is on an interstate and does not have much chance of a ride here, and may even get picked up by the police, so he begins to walk South away.

And then, although he does not see the car slow down, he sees a car pull on the shoulder just up ahead of him, and he runs to keep the driver from waiting on him. A rear door opens, and he jumps in. Three men about his age, all drinking beer, ask about him and where he is headed, and for the first time, he is confronted with that decision: "Where to?" All he has been thinking and feeling is away, run away.

He tells the three, who seem to be having a good time drinking beer and telling private jokes that he is just heading south and might spend a night with some friends a hundred or so miles down the road. "No problem," the driver says as they are headed all the way out of the state and pulls the car back on the interstate and floors the accelerator.

He really cannot see the speedometer but can tell, sense, that they are flying now, maybe 80 or 90 miles an hour, weaving in and out of slower traffic, and if they get pulled over with all the beer in the car, it is going to be bad, but it's a ride. He settles into the seat and sips on the beer he has been handed.

The heat of the car begins to dry his clothes, and he closes his eyes and begins to relax. He has a while until he needs to say anything about getting out and realizes his heart is no longer pounding away.

After a while, he looks about to get his bearings, where he is, and can tell it is not much further. The car has been quiet for some time now, and he is reluctant to break the silence, but the driver has to be warned of the impending stop. He leans forward towards the driver and says the next exit. The driver only nods his head, and he thanks the driver again for the ride.

It is still raining when he steps out of the car, says goodbye to all, and wishes them luck.

It is 8 miles to the house and he sticks out his thumb but once off the interstate, traffic is sparse, and none seems interested in picking up the soaked stranger beside the road.

He knows the house will be unlocked, and at this time of night, his friends will be sleeping, and he should be able to slip in, get some sleep, and get out in the morning before they even wake up. He does not want to talk to anyone or explain anything.

After a while, he gives up on hitching a ride as no cars come by anyway, and he wraps his arms about himself to keep warm. The rain has slowed to nothing more than a mist, but his hair and clothes are wet, and he shivers from the dampness.

Finally, he turns up on Willow Street and sees the house. It is dark except for the one light in the living room, and he sighs in relief.

With no explaining to do, he trudges up the porch steps and, on the porch, in the dark, strips off all his wet clothes, opens the unlocked door, and goes in. Quietly, he makes a circle downstairs, looking about to see what has changed since he was last here. Then he hears someone on the staircase and says in a low voice, "It is just me," and his friend responds, "You, okay?" "Yeah, sure," and he hears his friend turn around and head back up the stairs. It was always like that between them. His friend knowing when to ask and when not to.

He sits down for a moment on a couch in the living room and collects himself. It has been a long night and journey, and tomorrow will be a big day. He will head out tomorrow, but he does not have a clue as to where he will go: just away.

He climbs the stairs, opens up the bed, and crawls in. The sheets and blankets are so dry after his long walk into town, and he pulls himself into the fetal position to warm himself. After a while, he finally begins to get the chill out, and he relaxes and turns on his side, and drifts to sleep. He does not dream: too tired to dream.

It is the strong light which wakes him early in the morning, and at first, he simply turns away from the window and the sunlight and covers up his head. He thinks there is no need to jump out of bed; it is early yet, and he drifts right back into a dreamless sleep.

Then, he awakes and looks about, remembering where and why he is here. He turns onto his back and places his hands behind his head, feeling free. "He can go anywhere and do anything he wants now, anywhere he wants, and anything he wants."

Staring at the ceiling, where he should go from here just does not seem to materialize. He waits for some writing to appear on the ceiling, like some directions written there from God, but nothing appears. "Where would he like to go, to do next?" Nothing! Nothing comes to mind. "What is wrong with him? This can be a clean break, a chance to start all over again, to go out there somewhere and become who he is supposed to be rather than what 'they,' she wanted." He turns towards the window. "Where is there to go?" He searches himself for an answer and comes up empty: nothing. No passion for a specific place or specific thing to do. "Perhaps if he packs a bag and just heads out, his direction, path, will evolve on its own."

It isn't his style, really, but maybe that was because of what all the "others" wanted and demanded of him.

This Way?

Outside the window, he can see birds flitting about, and a crisp morning breeze is blowing the curtains inward. Lost in thought, he does not hear her open the door and come in.

He is startled when her body touches his, and he turns to find her there beside him. She has driven through the rainy night to talk and be with him. "She needs him. She loves him."

He holds her tight in his arms, and out of his mouth comes, "I love you," and he realizes that love for her is the only passion, the only place he really wants to go, and the only thing he wants to be: in love with her.

They lie quietly together, looking out the window, and then, as if God really had written on the ceiling for him to see, he knows his direction is with her.

As he has no passion or direction, he will simply follow her, do what she wants him to do, and go where she wants to go.

"Why not, his only passion is his love for her."

Or That?

He holds his arms tight across his chest, trying to keep the cold out, and as he enters the parking garage, he can feel the heat rising out of it, and it is so welcome.

As he descends the ramp of the parking garage, he moves close to the right wall and slowly makes his way closer to the parking toll collection booth. Most nights, it is empty, but he is never sure, so he peeks around a curve in the wall to check it out. Empty. He moves away from the wall and down the ramp, past the tollbooth, and down to the lower level.

His arms are down at this side now, and he begins to warm up as the heat of the garage makes its way through all his layers of clothes and socks.

No one is around, and as he walks along; he looks at all the fancy new cars and wonders who drives them and where they live. "He only owned one new car in his life: never will happen again, now."

Around another corner and still deeper into the underground he goes. Now he can hear the roar of the huge fans pushing the air about to keep it from becoming stale from car exhaust and injecting heated air. "Funny, heat for cars but no heat in the city for someone, like him!"

Finally, he reaches the very bottom of the garage and walks past many empty parking spaces until he comes to the large fan roaring away just above all sorts of metal electrical boxes mounted against a wall.

Looking about one more time to make sure he was not followed and no security guards are roaming, he steps up on one large metal box and then another and lifts himself into a large, rectangular hole behind the air circulation fan. "Home, once more", and moves the blankets he has stored there around to make his bed for the night and takes off one of these many jackets.

Pulling a tin can out of one of his pockets, he opens it and, pulling a fork from a paper bag he keeps in one corner, he begins to eat slowly, looking out of his hiding place, home, at the empty garage beyond and below.

He likes it here, his concrete cave, his home. What a sweet find, this place, this home for the night. High up off the ground and out of the line of sight for all but the most conscientious security guard or car driver.

He finishes off the can and places it near the outer edge of his place so he will remember to dump it in the morning. Then, he straightens his blankets one more time and lies down for the night. It is warm and just enough light to make him feel secure, yet not enough to keep him from sleeping.

The large fan roaring just beyond his cave is such great company. Somehow, it gives him some feeling of constancy that things are okay and drowns out any city noise at night. Laying back with his hands behind his head for a pillow, he closes his eyes and drifts to sleep.

He dreams, once again, of rain falling on him in the middle of the night and him standing by the road, hitch hiking a ride that would take him away but never to anyplace.

As always, he wonders about her and what became of her, but then he turns on his side, and she is gone, and he can only hear and feel the large motor of the fan running constantly outside his doorstep.

Or the Other?

When he awakens, the car has stopped and he finds he is at a gas station, the driver filling the car with gas. "Where are they?" he asks. "Tennessee." He has slept through where he was intending to get out and spend the night at his friend's house. "Tennessee", he has never been to Tennessee: "a new world."

Musing: "You Will Never See It Coming"

On a Greyhound bus traveling, outside the window, only countryside and inside, only impatience, and on the shoulder of the road stands a large black crow.

No sooner has the bus passed the crow, but I am him, there, standing, totally oblivious to the tons of steel streaming and screaming by only a foot or inches away. Then I snap back to my seat, inside, traveling once again, and I begin to wonder how much is rushing by me all the time, only inches, or millions of an inch, or seconds, or some other measurement I do not even know and oblivious to it all?

Cosmic rays from distant star explosions, radio waves from the local country music station, the gazillion neutrinos passing through my body every nanosecond, bacteria, viruses, the tectonic plates shifting of parallel universes, some misshape of the space we are traveling through, some mutation of a single cell deep within the brain or lung or, fate, or destiny or, of course, the will of God.

"Be careful, watch out," I am told, and how exactly do I do that when any single move, any one action, any step, may put me out on that "road," directly in line for the next "Greyhound" and not even aware the road exists or the "Greyhound?"

In the end, it appears that one will never see it coming, no matter how sharp our eyes might be, how much we know, or how good or bad a person we may be. It is there, right there, all around us, and there is no safe way to turn or place to be.

We are all on some "shoulder" somewhere, oblivious, and we "will never see it coming."

"The Treatment"

He lies on his side, facing a light yellow, stained, dirty wall, eyes half open, empty-headed.

It is quiet, other than a constant low moaning coming from nearby.

Suddenly, he is gasping for air. He knows he is only 100 feet from the summit; he can see it through the driving, blinding snow, but he knows he cannot make it.

A spider crawls across the wall in front of him, turns, looks straight at him, and whispers, "You are a sinner," and then moves on. The laughter of his 5-year-old daughter comes echoing down the second-floor hallway of his first home, "He has a daughter?"

He is running, has been running, but the wolves are almost on him, and he is filled with terror. Faces go flying by, some of which he thinks he knows somehow, but others are complete strangers, and all are throwing some sentence or phrase at him.

"Dogs are not tin cans," an old woman spits with no teeth. "Hide under the bridge," a well-dressed businessman. "All you have to do is quiet your mind and then crawl inside the hole that is always there," says an old maid schoolteacher with her gray hair in a bun on top of her head. "There is no sense in fighting it: you can't win," a little boy hanging upside down on a swing set monkey bar. "Don't worry, this is not going to hurt a bit," a woman nurse, dressed all in white with a huge needle in her hand.

"M word chunks multiplied by N chunks of time, taken to the square root of the number of snake tongues in Arizona, and you get exactly nothing of interest or value of any kind," Einstein says, walking by. And then he is inside a cave, the walls and ceiling dripping with moisture, close, tight, about him, and he yells, "God, let me out." "Shut up," comes as a response.

Igloos and snow forts, skinning out dead rabbits and the smell their guts give off, rain pelting him as he lies buried under a pile of leaves, machine gun ready to stop the enemy's advance. "Where is he: machine gun?" He tries hard to remember being in the Army but cannot. "No, it was not him hiding in the leaves, but it was from some movie he had seen once," or so he thinks, but he is just not sure. Lightening hits a tree near where he is standing, and he feels the current through the soles of his shoes. "Stop it," he says, but in a quieter voice: no one hears. "The summit, what summit? I have never been a mountain climber."

He leans forward into the microphone, strumming his guitar, looking at the thousands in the crowd listening to him. Mashed potatoes move about on a silver dinner plate, spelling out words: "Freak, loser, crazy."

He closes his eyes, but it is no good. Now, he hears crickets on a clear summer's night wind, rolling thunder, and bullfrogs calling around a dark, no-moon Lake. His hands: burning, from picking up a campfire coal. His hands: freezing from being too high, outside, too long. The skeleton of some large animal scattered about on the ground, its hide still intact, more or less. A tree falls as he bangs his stone axe. "Stone axe?" A man, with a white cane walks by, stops, and stares at him: "Can't you see you are blind all the time you are learning to see?"

Then, flashes of hundreds of objects: old Egyptian vases; miniature wood horses; old misshapen gold coins from the bottom of the sea; deer antlers; a neon sign spelling out "Jesus Saves" in the shape of a cross; a Chinese bamboo flute with intricate carving; a space alien's face, all mashed in with a big nose and huge nostrils; jars of honey; jars with still borne babies in them; jars of things he does not recognize and does not want to recognize; used condoms laying on a dirty bathroom floor; a bloody knife on the floor next to a pretty young woman, naked, raped; a South American Indian holding up a severed head and grinning from ear to ear; a red, orange, yellow, ugly, mushroom cloud off in the distance and he feeling the rays from it hit him and knowing he is going to die.

Someone groans, and for a second, all the images, feelings, and thoughts are gone. He is so confused and dazed. Most of what he has seen or felt does not feel like him, nor seem to be his memories. "Wolves have never chased him. Perhaps a book, a story told to him?" But all feel like memories, and then again, don't, or not his anyway.

A gravestone with the phrase, "He had too many clues," written across it. Sunlit clouds below him at 35,000 feet, feeling the plane going down, about to crash and burn, and feeling so helpless. "Not supposed to be like this," now extremely agitated from all his thoughts. "Are they really his?" He reaches for a ringing phone, "Hello." There is no one on the other end of the line. Egg salad drips down his chin onto the enormous belly he is pretty sure he does not have. Watching the Aurora Borealis as a kid; holding an egg in his hand and feeling its perfection, the economy of shape, his pushing the button releasing the bomb on all those innocents below, a huge pile of raw, bloody meat. He wants to throw up.

Moving, he finds his arms and feet fixed to some form of restraint. "What? Where is he? Why is he here?" A speedometer reading 189 miles per hour and out the windows of whatever kind of vehicle he is in, the landscape perfectly motionless; giant white numbers 1 and 2 arguing over who is more important while 3 sits on a street curb polishing her nails. A coconut glances off his head, and he rubs it where it hit. Hurts like shit. A woman with huge tits cuddling his head between them and saying, "Poor baby," A slot machine blinking lights at him and calling out, "Hey chump, want to play?" a winner every time." His mouth is so dry, and his temples hurt like crazy.

"Focus," he says out loud, and turning his head, his eyes find a very large open room, two rows of beds with a center aisle. With perhaps 20 beds in all, one wall has floor-to-ceiling frosted windows between each bed. Down the aisle, between the rows of beds, hang five bare light bulbs, but none are lit. All 20 beds are full of what look to be men, all covered from their feet to just under their chins with a plain white sheet: all flat on their back, all looking about his age. "His age, how old is he? Why can't he remember that? "His name, my God: what is his name?" He can't remember.

The floor of the room he is in or thinks he is in is the color of mud, or it is just incredibly dirty; he is not sure which. Other than the beds and men in them, there is nothing else of any kind in the room. "Where is he?"

His focus slips: touching a woman's nipple, an erection; the smell of sex on sheets; a downed electrical wire snapping and popping; throwing up after seeing the victim of a car crash all crushed and bloody; tennis shoes hanging from a telephone line in a back alley of some big city; sitting in a tree waiting for the lions to go away, scared he will fall asleep and tumble to a horrible death; wrapping his hands around her neck and squeezing and squeezing, and so revolted by it; drinking water out of a drainage ditch as he so thirsty and no other water to be had; alone on a raft out on the ocean for days and days and thoughts of just walking away on the surface of the sea; laying on a hillside, alone, leg broken, miles from anywhere and not able to think of a thing to do to save himself.

***

"CZE1287!" Oh, I say, "CZE1287."

He snaps back to his eyes and sees a man standing beside him, all dressed in white with a heavy frame, black-rimmed glasses, and thinning gray hair.

"CZE1287, ah, there we go. I am your therapist, and I have come to tell you that the treatment went exactly as planned, and now we see no reason why you cannot be released tomorrow. Isn't that good news, CZE1287?"

"What?" He struggles to understand but is not sure that this man in white is not just another thought, hallucination, dream, or memory he is having. "What?" he manages to say.

"Come come, now CZE, if I may call you that. Is it all right if I call you that? After all, we are all friends here, aren't we CZE?

20

According to our calculations, your mind should be clearing moment by moment now. Don't you find it so?"

He stares at the man in the white lab coat, white shirt, white pants, and white shoes. "I have been having these strange thoughts, ideas, and memories, whatever. They don't seem like they belong to me. What is the matter with me? Where am I? Why am I here? What have you done to me?"

"Oh, CZE, you really must try to focus more. Of course, all our patients experience a little confusion after the treatment, but more than enough time has passed, and you should be well on your way to a full recovery. Tell me, don't you feel much better now than before?"

"Before what?" beating back the image of a hog's head in a butcher shop storefront window, its tongue hanging out one side of its mouth and its eyes wide open and staring right at him.

"Now, CZE, you know I cannot tell you that. It was on all the forms you signed when you entered here. You may not remember signing the forms or what they said, but CZE, you cannot hold me accountable for that. After all, I am just your therapist. It is not like I run the whole place, you know."

Some turnips pop out of the ground and begin doing the can-can, kicking dirt this way and that, and he begins to shake his head, trying to clear it.

"Why am I strapped down?" "Oh, purely for our benefit: we are so understaffed these days; it would be impossible to let everyone move about as they please. No, that would not do at all. Certainly, you must see that!"

"I see all sorts of stuff, but none of it makes any sense to me. All sorts of things all jumbled up in my head. What has happened to me? Tell me where I am."

"Now, CZE, I must insist, enough of this dazed and confused charade of yours. According to every medical book known, you should be clearing nicely by now. CZE1287, if you insist on pretending you do not know about the treatment and where you are, I am going to have to order up a hyperbaric, and believe me, CZE, you would not like a hyperbaric. No, you would not like a hyperbaric at all: so messy and all. It gives me the shivers just thinking about it."

He takes his hands and rubs his face, and then he sees himself in a mirror, but he does not recognize the face he sees. Along one side of the mirrored face is a long, deep scar like a knife might have cut him, and his hair receded way back off his forehead. "That is not me," but every time he moves his head, the mirrored face moves. He closes his eyes again.

"So, what will it be, CZE? Should I schedule you for release tomorrow, or should I call for a hyperbaric?"

"I want out of here," he hears himself say.

"Oh, I am so glad. I knew you were pretending all along, you funny man. So good, tomorrow it is. You have a good night, and I will see you bright and early."

"Release to where," he fights to wonder through feelings of intense love for a dog he never had; jail bars and a cell that reeking of urine and shit; sitting on the ground under a railway bridge, watching the rain, cold and damp, sirens blasting away in the distance; standing in line with other men, waiting to get something to eat that smells awful as it is poured into bowls and handed out.

***

"Ah, CZE, I see you are awake. Good. Can't waste time now, we need your bed. We are so busy here these days, and you know how the state is about such matters. Waste not, want not, and all that. Personally, I hate all the state slogans and signs, but that is just me. So, are we ready for release CZE?"

He struggles to focus but is able to put on his shirt, pants, and shoes as the therapist hands them to him.

"Well, CZE, just follow me. I don't want you to take this personally, but I do hope I do not see you again for another treatment. We have such a high success rate here, and I just know you are going to do well."

The lab-coated therapist leads him past all the beds, and as he struggles to walk along, he turns his head this way and that, looking at the men all cocooned, but he can tell nothing about them.

Finally, double doors open, and he is standing in a lobby with other closed double doors off it.

Before he even realizes it, his therapist is gone, and a gorilla dressed in some sort of security guard or military-type uniform motions him towards a turnstile door. As with the windows in the room he has been in, the turnstile door has frosted glass, and he cannot tell what lies beyond it.

Entering the door and moving forward, he is immediately hit by brilliant sunlight, and he is forced to close his eyes tight shut and then only slowly open them to adjust to the light. He is in a city. A big city, from the looks of it, and standing just outside the door, he sees he must descend some ten or more steps to get to the sidewalk.

Slowly, he makes his way down the steps, but as he reaches the next to the last step, he stops and sits down.

Still not knowing who he is, he has no idea where to go or what to do next; he sits and watches. At least his visions of canoes on a mirror-perfect lake are gone, at least for the moment.

***

"Hey, buddy! You just get out? Better come with me. They don't like releases hanging around right outside. Ok? You coming?"

He looks around to see who the man on the sidewalk is talking to and then realizes it is him: "Releases?" At least it is not a gorilla this time. He stands up and moves down the final steps until he is on the sidewalk, standing next to the man who has spoken to him.

"Come on, come on with me. There is a nice little park nearby, and nobody will bother us there, or at least not during the day."

They walk along for a while, and he tries to remember the city, anything familiar, but nothing comes. Still images of things he knows he did not do, or see, or feel. Finally, they come to the park, find a bench and sit down.

"Just out, huh, been for the treatment three times myself. Once in that place, you were in and then twice in the place on the other side of town. Real kick in the head, ain't it?"

"I really, I mean, I can't remember anything, and I keep having these strange thoughts, visions, feelings, I…" his words trail off as he sees himself standing alone on some harbor pier.

"Oh sure, real jumbled mess, ain't it. Well, for a while, anyway. Say, do you have any idea of what happened to you? You got any money? Check your pockets. They are supposed to give you 100 bucks when you leave. What? No! Crap! They must have forgotten, or more likely, your damn therapist just took it. Damn, therapist: crazy bastards, the whole lot of them. Shoot them all if I could, but don't tell anyone I said that, ok?"

The man sitting beside him is shorter than he is, has not shaved for several days, smells, and has on a dirty T-shirt that says "Homeless Are Humans Too!"

His hair, uncut and unkempt, is all over his head, in his eyes, and over his ears. He wonders if this man is just another one of his memories or hallucinations or something he was told about.

Shaking his head to somehow get things to fall back into place, he looks out on the park and listens to the man talk and talk and talk some more.

"So, it goes like this. You are a homeless guy, and a ways back; the state decided to start using shock something or another, I forget, treatments on the homeless. Said that studies proved this shocking thing could so scramble your brain that afterwards, homeless folks would become like normal people with jobs, a house, and all that stuff. Might be right, but ain't worked on me yet. How many times have you been in for the treatment?"

"I can't remember any treatment. Shock, you say? What is shock, something or another?"

"Yeah, shock, you know, tape these wires to either side of your head and the back of your neck and like to throw the juice to you. Almost bit my damn tongue off one time, those worthless therapist bastards. Let me see your left arm."

He raises his left arm, and the man on the bench beside him rolls up his sleeve. "5. Man, oh man, you've been through some shit. I can't swear by it, but there have been rumors that each time they 'treat you,' the more juice they give you. I don't think they even care if they cook our brains or not. What is the difference to them? I mean, according to the law, homeless people without like brains, well, the state owns them, and you know what that means? They can cut you up for your parts, like heart and stuff. Yep, cut it right out of you and give it to some rich guy. Ain't life a bitch?"

"5 times: you mean I have been in that place five times and had my brain shocked?" "Yep, that's right. Well, that place or another one somewhere else in the city or state. Sure, you ain't got no money: damn, bastard therapists."

He lifts his eyes off the ground and looks around him, really looking for the first time since he left the turnstile doors. It is such a pretty place that, for a moment, he has no strange visions or confusion. "And this treatment, this shock, is supposed to help me, so I am not homeless anymore?" "Yep, that is what they say. Bullshit if you ask me, but ain't nobody asking me. Say, you hungry? Damn, I wish you had some money; we could dine in style. Sure could use something other than that stinking slop they serve up at the mission, but something hot is better than nothing. Say, you got any kids? I got 2. They live right here in town but don't like me coming around. Say that I embarrass them with the neighbors. Can you believe that? Their own father, an embarrassment! Ain't life a bitch? So, you got any kids that we could maybe visit?"

He tries to wade through the mud of his thoughts, memories, and feelings. "Maybe a daughter, but I'm not sure." "Oh, that's ok. I thought you might have someone who cared about you; that's all. So, you ready for some food, big guy?"

He turns and looks at the man beside him. "Sure, why not? Where else am I going to go? Oh, do you know my name?"

"Oh, sure, says it right there on your left arm: CZE1287. "

"You know, you ought to get yourself a vanity name. You know something classy, like maybe George."

"George?" "No." "Not George." And turning away sees pigeons gathering around his feet, and then a penguin appears out of nowhere, waddles up to him, and cocking his head, "George. What is wrong with George?"

"Ah, Jesus………….."

"The Three Little Pigs"

They are all asleep, and for the moment, I think we are safe.

Being on the run this past year has not been easy, but what else could I do?

Perhaps, someday, you will read about "The Three Little Pigs" in the newspapers, but not today. Only a handful of people know about their existence, and they are not going to tell.

"Three Little Pigs": it is not a long story, but an amazing one in many ways, and I want to share it with you in case something bad happens to me or my 3 little pigs.

It began when I finished my PhD in genetic engineering and was hired by a new startup company in Maryland. The company's goal was for a client, a wealthy client, to use his or her DNA to genetically create various animals from which organs could be harvested for client transplant. Having been altered, the transplanted organ would not face transplant rejection. In my case, my focus was the heart. A client genetically matched pig heart.

At first, it was all computer work, and although the tools I got to use were way beyond anything I had ever seen in college, I quickly became used to them and settled in working through the differences in the genetic make-up of a pig's heart and the heart of my client. My goal was to create a template that could be used over and over again.

To me: being able to work on such a meaningful project right after college felt like a great honor and opportunity, and I poured myself into my work.

Once I got to work each day, I would seldom leave until midnight or later, and then Saturdays and Sundays only became another day to build models on the computer and have it run through the sequences and coding. After a while, the job felt like more of a mission, something I had to do. Real people with bad hearts were waiting for me to engineer the perfect replacement, and it drove me night and day.

It took me over 9 months, but finally, my computer model was perfect. I knew which genes had to be replaced or modified, and I shipped the model with all its definitions and coding instructions over to the Embryo and Nursery laboratory of the company.

***

A week went by, and each day, I would go to work and document or, organize and reorganize my computer files. Some days, I would chat with some other engineers on their projects, but eventually, every day, I would go to the lab to check on my engineered pig.

In the third week, after I had provided the engineering details of my perfect heart pig, when I entered the Embryo Lab to check on things, there was a crowd and great excitement around one small incubator and joining the group, I found myself staring down at 3, well-formed, small pigs. My engineering had worked, and there in front of me were living, breathing infant pigs. I was so happy, and as I watched the three little pigs wiggle this way and that, with their eyes closed and short little legs, I could not but feel pride in what I had done.

I returned to my work and once again set about looking over my design, my template, thinking proteins and the interaction of genes, but late one night, running my design through a new Monte Carlo simulation-based program, I stumbled onto a gene I had ignored in my original design as little was known about its functioning. It did not seem related to what I had been doing, but somehow, my engineering of other genes had changed the protein makeup of this one gene. I checked and rechecked, and every time I applied my change to the genetic code of an ordinary pig, gene 1A345M got changed somehow. How and why, I could not explain it, and what would be the effect of that change? The 3 little pigs all seemed healthy enough.

Once more, I made my way to the Nursery and, looking about, found my three little pigs in a small cage in one corner, but something was not right. Oh, the pigs were all right, perfect in every way except they stood no more than 2 1/2 inches tall at the shoulder and were only 5 inches or less long, and all seemed fully mature. Their eyes were open, and they moved about like real pigs. Looking at their lab charts, what I had begun to fear was there in pencil and ink. The pigs had not grown in height or length in weeks now and were beginning to be called "The Three Little Pigs" by all the lab workers.

What a disaster. My first genetic engineering assignment and I had come up with these 3 miniature pigs, which could not be used for heart harvesting or anything else.

I went home. How would the bosses take it once they learned of my failure? My efforts had cost the company plenty of money, and I could only assume I would be out on the street soon, looking for another job, but who would hire me after this disaster?

Bought a bottle of gin and began to drink. Not sure if I was angry, confused, a 'failure,' or all balled into one.

Asleep on my couch, a ringing phone woke me up, and a woman's voice, identifying herself as Mr. Samples' secretary, said, "Mr. Sample, the Chief Executive Officer of my company, wanted to see me right away." Oh, crap, I knew what was coming: the lecture, the outrage, and finally, the dismissal.

***

I made it to work in about 15 minutes, skipping the usual shower and shaving. I knew I looked like a mess, but I did not care. "How nice does one have to look to be fired anyway?"

I had never met Mr. Samples or his secretary or even been on the floor of the building that housed his office, but when I got there, I was impressed that it was not as gaudy or fancy as I had expected and Mr. Samples' secretary was not some eye candy in a tight skirt but a serious, proper, middle-aged woman.

"Mr. Samples had waited on me, but he had moved on to some other business, and now I would have to wait."

"Good", time to compose myself and perhaps prepare a defense. I had not known that one gene would mutate like it did. No one would have guessed that, and the software did not flag it as a potential runtime error.

Finally, the door to Mr. Sample's office opened, and a tall, well-groomed man in a well-tailored business suit invited me in. He was not alone, for as I entered, Mr. Samples introduced me to Mr. Edge, and we all sat down.

Mr. Samples spoke first. "Your little experiment and excuse my pun, you know it is not going to benefit the company, but Mr. Edge has proposed a way that perhaps the company can recoup our investment in your efforts and you. As you were the designer of the pigs, I thought you ought to hear it from him directly."

Mr. Edge was a rather large man with the ruddy face of a butcher, and I could picture him, in my mind, behind a butcher counter someplace, chopping and slicing. Anyway, Mr. Edge proceeded to ask me if I knew who he was, to which I responded, "No." "Well, not unusual, most people do not, but I am the third richest man in the world, owning significant uranium mines on all continents, but perhaps of more importance to you is that I am a gourmet. For years now, I have tasted the best the world has to offer and have eaten at least one of just about every mammal, reptile, insect, fish or bird that exists, and some that no longer exist, I am sorry to say. The point being is, that I have made a deal with your company to buy your mistake, your 3 little pigs, and have them cooked, one at a time, for a very special meal for myself. As I am told by Mr. Samples that you are the engineer who designed them, I would like to know if eating them will harm me in any way. Other than their miniature size, are they perfect in every other way?"

I was stunned. All my work so this rich jackass could eat my 3 little pigs!

I looked at Mr. Samples and then back at Mr. Edge. Mr. Samples piped up, "Mr. Edge has proposed to cover the entire cost of the project up to this point, which, I might add, would be very good for you, as there would be no reason for us not to continue to use your services." Mr. Edge spoke again, "I assume you have not named them, have you? It can be so much harder sometimes when the boy or girl who has raised an animal has given it a name. I, myself, never name the animals I keep on my ranches. I just enjoy the taste of the exotic and can pay for it."

I sat, not knowing what to say or if I needed to say anything. Mr. Samples did not need my permission to do anything with the 3 little pigs, but then I remembered the whole point of the meeting and, turning to Mr. Edge, "Sir, as far as I know, and I have researched it extensively after discovering the mutated gene, that other than their size, the 3 pigs are otherwise perfect." And then I stopped. I just could not bring myself to say the words, "To be eaten by a bastard like you."

"Well, that's it," said Mr. Samples. "Thanks for your time. Someone will be in touch about what you should start next."

I was stunned. Of course, the pigs belonged to the company, but somehow, the fact that they would eventually be opened up to extract their hearts for human transplant had not ever bothered me, as a human life was going to be saved, but this! Eating, my, 3 little pigs to satisfy some rich guy's desire to have eaten every kind of flesh on the earth? It was just too much, but I had no idea what I could do about it.

I returned to my lab and fired up the computers, but it became obvious I could not work; I was too upset, so I left work early and headed home for a shower and a little more gin.

The shower did help, but the gin, not so much, as the more I drank, the more I became angry until finally, I realized I just had to do something. That rich bastard was not going to eat my 3 little pigs. I could see him in some large mansion dining room, at some long table, napkin tucked under his chin and knife and fork in his hands, and him just cutting away at one of my little pigs and then stuffing his fat face.

***

"No, Mr. Edge was not going to eat the 3 little pigs! I had to do something, but what?" I tried to think of all sorts of actions but could see that only by stealing the pigs and moving far away with them, was there a chance to save them.

I packed up what little I had in a suitcase, took it to the bus station, and bought a ticket to San Francisco. Then, I made my way to work, past the security guard with a wave of my badge, to where the pigs were being kept. As I entered through the door, a sudden panic attack overcame me. "What if Mr. Edge had already taken the pigs?" But there, right where they had been for weeks, were the 3, waiting for my rescue.

Funny, they never made a sound as I picked each in my hand and slipped them into the side pocket of my jacket. "Could they know I was rescuing them?"

Then, back out of the lab, I passed the security guard and out onto the street. A quick cab and I was on a bus to San Francisco with my 3 little pigs all warm and settled into my jacket pocket.

In the ensuing days, I expected to read about the theft of the pigs in the newspaper or hear about it on the news, but apparently, my company had decided that my failure would be bad press for them, so I saw or heard nothing.

But it was only a week or so after I moved to San Francisco that a man came to my apartment building inquiring about me while I was out. He said he was an old friend trying to find me after years of not seeing me. But I knew better. Dear old, rich Mr. Edge was not going to give up that easily, and so began my constant movement from city to city, always watching behind me, taking minor jobs so I would not get noticed.

It has not been easy, and I am not really sure why I did it, but I do have to tell you that I have named my three little pigs. One is called "Straw," another is "Sticks," and the last and my personal favorite is "Bricks."

***

Maybe someday, you will open a newspaper or, watching the evening news, learn of some new miniature creature created in a laboratory somewhere, but until then, you will just have to be satisfied with what I have told you.

"Straw" "Sticks" "Bricks."

They are so cute; I wish you could see them.

Musing: ",Pilot"

I stare down the runway through the turning prop, my left hand on the yoke, my right hand on the throttle control knob, both feet smashed down hard on the rudder pedals. It is January and 30 degrees outside the cockpit but my shirt is soaked with sweat.

Solo. I am about to solo an airplane for the first time.

Twice before, I have driven the long ride from my home to find the airfield covered in morning fog and nothing flying under visual flight rules. Today, in the car, driving to the airport, I am not sure if I want to find the field fogged in or not. Anxiety is not something I am familiar with, and it bothers me that I am so full of it today.

Solo. Although I have taken off and landed the training Cessna 172 at least 60 or more times over the course of my instruction, this time will be different. No instructor beside me to provide vocal support. No instructors to remind me: to check some gauge, watch my airspeed, or lower the flaps. No instructor to turn, push, or pull the yoke just as I cross the landing threshold to correct for a crosswind that has suddenly appeared out of nowhere. Solo. I am to go up, around, and down alone.

Few things I have ever done have required that I get it all correct or 99% on the very first attempt, but this is different. The nose of the plane held too high, and I will stall. Being below 1200 feet, I might not have time to correct and could crash. A turn for landing too high and I might have to go around instead of landing, embarrassing myself and disrupting the very busy airport take-off and landing schedule. A sudden burst of wind on landing and a wing tip could hit the ground. Not enough yoke pulled back at touchdown and the prop could hit the runway.

I stare down the runway, waiting for myself to let go. The tower has cleared me for takeoff and so here I am, out on the runway, ready to push that throttle in all the way, release the rudder brakes, and go speeding down the runway until I reach take-off speed and pull back on the yoke and am airborne.

Pilot training: why did I start pilot training? I did not need to be a pilot for my work and will never have time to rent a plane and fly somewhere for a vacation. "No." I simply wanted to add "pilot" to my name, resume. "Pilot": the rare air of "pilot." How many people know how to fly? The risk, the skill set, the command of a machine that defies gravity. Like my "Extra Class" Amateur Radio License with the difficult 21 words per minute of Morse Code requirement, "Army Lieutenant", "college graduate", "Electrical Engineer."

I like being 5,000 feet above the earth. All that is below shrunk in size and significance, and I can hear none of it and hardly see much of it. I like being there, just not in charge.

Seconds have gone by and I know the tower is watching me and wondering what I am waiting for. Other traffic is waiting to take off or land or soon will be, and they are going to need the runway I now sit on.

I tighten my left hand around the yoke in what one instructor has called my "death grip", as my knuckles are white from the pressure, grip of terror. 'No', not comfortable being here.

Suddenly, the hand on the throttle control knob begins to push the knob into the cockpit firewall and the prop begins to spin up. Then the feet relax on the rudder pedals, releasing the wheel brakes and the Cessna begins its roll down the runway.

Faster and faster, I go, as the throttle knob is now flush with the cockpit firewall, feet moving with the yoke to keep me on the centerline of the runway. Easy, easy, until at about 60 knots, I can feel the plane wanting to lift off the ground. I wait another couple of seconds and then pull back on the yoke and I am airborne.

***

After my first solo, I was given a certificate by my flight school as a form of encouragement, and I continued with my pilot training.

Other than some additional lessons like landing at night, a couple more solo flights, and a few more log book flight hours, I was ready to take the Federal Aviation Administration's (FAA) written examination and then fly about 100 miles, navigate, no GPS, non-stop, to another much larger airport. Land, refuel and return or my license required 'cross country.'

Every solo was anxiety but nothing compared to my first, and now and again, I felt that I could do it, get my pilot's license, and include 'pilot' in my life's resume.

Took the written FAA exam and had only one wrong answer. Again, I got a certificate from the flight school, but although I was doing it, my anxiety would not go away.

Obvious to me then, that some people are just borne flyers. They feel the air in a way I will never feel. Instead of anxiety, I think they must feel exhilaration. I am not a natural-born flyer.

Interesting to me: I actually did my most low anxiety flying when I only used the instruments and gauges in front of me. No view of what was outside the plane. Called 'under the hood,' with just gauges, the plane was more just a machine and I sitting in a garage.

Finally, everything was checked off the requirements list except the cross-country flight, which I could plan for and do anytime.

I was not ready. The requirements for my license may have said I was ready, but I wasn't.

***

Not ready to do the cross-country, I continued to go to the airport and take the plane, fly a few miles out, and then return and land. Or I do what is called 'touch and go', where the plane touches the runway, but I immediately apply power and take off again.

Building confidence: I thought, the more I flew solo, the more confidence I would have and less anxiety, and to some extent, it did help.

Then, on another practice, solo flight, the tower cleared me to enter the 'pattern' around the airport for a landing, but not the actual landing.

I approached the airport and preceded the downwind leg or the parallel path along the runway's boundary, waiting for clearance to land.

When I was well beyond the end of the runways, there was nothing from the tower, so I continued flying straight out, looking around for any sign of an approaching aircraft.

This was not normal. Once in the pattern, the usual way was to be given clearance to land about halfway down the downwind leg, and at the end of the runways, I would make a 45-degree turn and then another 45-degree turn and line up the plane with the intended landing runway. But this time, I continued to fly further and further away from the airport and after a while, I called the tower for landing clearance and got it.

I scanned the air space, up, down, all around, but could not see another aircraft. I began the first 45-degree turn and proceeded to cross the end of the runways in preparation for my 45-degree turn to line up the runway for landing.

Just as I began my last 45-degree turn, I caught a glimpse of something out of the corner of my left eye, and over my shoulder, there was a much larger, jet-powered aircraft bearing down on me. Panic! I had been cleared. I had not seen this aircraft when I had visually scanned the air space, but it was coming straight at me.

I completed the turn, pushed the aircraft into a very deep descent down to the runway, touched down, applied full wheel breaks, and took the first exit to a taxiway.

When I parked the plane and shut down the engine, I was shaking.

***

In a college Psychology class, the term paper was to pinpoint the source of my 'code of conduct,' my morals and ethics. Most in the class simply wrote that the source of their conduct was their parents plus some religion, but for me, the assignment seemed to be, what is 'my code of conduct?' my 'morals and ethics?' and I got lost. Turned in a cardboard box full of definition attempts and pleaded for mercy. I got an "A" for my effort and the questions I had pondered for the very first time. "Solo'. Making decisions with no parent in the "cockpit" and no road with edges, white lines and directions well marked, to follow.

Not sure where or how or when it became embedded, but one element of my 'code of conduct' is that you never quit. No matter how hard, how tough, no matter what, you do not quit. This was followed up by being told, "Quitting the first time is the hardest, but after that, each time you do it, it gets easier and easier."

My 'code of conduct' says never quit, but I was not comfortable with my flying skills. I knew I could make the cross country and get 'Pilot' attached to my name and resume, but, in my mind, I would never be a real pilot or a safe pilot, and am convinced we need more safe, competent everything but not one more unsafe or incompetent.

If I got my private pilot license, wouldn't I eventually, someday, need a break from my reality, drive to an airport, rent a plane, and what? Cause an accident? Be killed because I forgot one simple thing? Kill an innocent on the ground?

'Pilot,' just another accomplishment that is to be added, like a medal to my chest: another medal that defines me?"

In America, when you meet someone, "What do you do for a living?" As if your work defines you.

Do I regret not getting my license to fly? No. I got what I got out of my training and lessons learned are now all tangled into the body of my knowledge and awareness and have added subtle aspects that someone, who has never hard banked or landed an airplane will never have.

Takeoffs were a thrill, with an instructor on board.

Landings were also amazing, a miracle, with an instructor onboard.

Flying in a commercial airliner, all strapped in my seat 'miles' back from the cockpit, I sometimes think to myself, "I could land this plane if I had to."

There is no ', Pilot' after my name, on my resume or medal on my chest.

"The Test"

Mary stares out the subway car window. Although it is only 10 in the morning, she is already tired from the long trip and they still have many subway stops to go.

"The 'test,' the damn 'test,' it's just so unfair," wiping her nose with a tissue and continuing to stare into the darkness of the subway tunnel. "Darkness, yes, she is lost in some darkness like she has never experienced before," and pulls her arms in around herself.

She was stunned, almost as if she had fallen and hit her head hard. "Yes, Mary," the doctor goes on, "you must have heard about the new law?" "No," she struggles to get out, "We do not use the HIS other than for the post and information searches." "Well, it is the law now, and so before you become pregnant, you and Joseph have to be genetically tested to ensure any child you have will not have a predisposition to certain diseases. If your offspring carry genes or markers of certain diseases, then the government will not sanction the pregnancy for government health care and you and Joseph would be financially responsible for your son or daughter's health care their entire life."

Mary shook her head to try to clear it. It was as if she was numb and could not think. Here she was, in for a simple cold she could not shake and only in an offhand remark, had mentioned that she and Joseph were ready to start a family, and now this: this law, this 'test,' this genetic 'test' business!

"Mary, I don't think the law is 'just' or right, but today, it is the law. Without government health care, I am not sure who will be able to have a baby these days except maybe the very rich. I'll bet you don't know how much this office visit costs the government today, do you?"

"No," Mary says, looking out the only window in the room.

"One thousand credits! Can you imagine the hospital cost of having a baby, Mary? 100's of thousands of credits, and then if the child became sick with a serious disease, potentially millions of credits. You and Joseph would be in debt to the government for the rest of your lives with no way to escape paying. No, you and Joseph will have to be tested, and if your genes are 'clean,' there will be no problem. However, if there is a problem, you must consider it long and hard. I mean, besides the economic burden, what if you find out your genes could result in a child prone to some serious disease sometime in his or her life? Would you still want to conceive?"

Mary could not speak. This 'test' business was all too much for her. Finally, she composed herself, "Do you do the testing here?" "No, you will have to go into the city to a special clinic. Mary, I don't have it in your records. Have you ever been genetically tested? If a prior test revealed something, then there is no reason for you and Joseph to make that long trip into the city." "No, never tested and neither has Joseph, to my knowledge. There has never been a need for testing." "Doctor, I have to go".

All the way home, Mary cannot stop thinking about the 'test.' "What if she or Joseph did have some bad genetics that meant their child might develop cancer or MS or some other horrible disease? Would she want to conceive anyway? Who was the government to tell them they could not have children? They were not telling them they could not, but they might as well be if the government was defining who got health insurance and who didn't."

When Mary gets home, it is still early and hours before Joseph returns from work. She thinks about accessing him but then thinks better of it. "Talking about the 'test' is something they had better do together, here at home, and not via access."

Trying to forget the test or at least put it out of her mind, Mary gets busy, but no matter how hard she tries, the 'test' keeps crawling back into the bright spotlight of her mind's central focus. "What will Joseph say? Does he know about the test?" Although they did not use the HIS to keep up with the news, he was at least out and about and perhaps had heard something at work. "Why would he keep it from her if he knew? If, after the test, they were not sanctioned to have a child, would he agree to go ahead anyway and for them to shoulder the child's health care cost?" She knew Joseph loved her, and she did want a baby, but this might be asking too much. "What if he says no?" Her heart sinks. She wants a baby so much, and now there is this damn 'test.' Then, the idea of not telling Joseph about the test and getting pregnant crosses her mind. After he got used to the idea of being a father, she could pretend to learn about the test then. But no, she cannot do that. She will just have to tell him straight up and they will decide together what to do. In the meantime, she fixes herself a cup of tea and tries to calm down by sitting out on the porch. Although her nose continues to drip from the cold, she does not care.

Around 7, Mary sees the bus coming down the road and stopping in front of their home. Joseph steps down and out, and seeing her on the porch, throws up his hand and waves. Mary sees this gesture of affection, waves back, and leans forward with her elbows on her lap. "Put a smile on for Joseph," brushing down her hair with her hands.

"And how was your day?" Joseph coming onto the porch and kissing her forehead. "Ok, I guess. Another long one and I'm tired and hungry. What's for dinner?" reaching down and getting a hold of one of her hands. Dinner! Mary has completely forgotten about fixing dinner. Either it is the 'test' or the cold medicine, but either way, she should not have forgotten dinner. "Oh, I am sorry, Joseph, I forgot. It must be the cold medicine the doctor put me on today. I will fix it right now. What would you like: something in a hurry or something that takes a little longer but is better? Still have two venison steaks that your uncle gave you."

"Oh, the steaks, yeah, go ahead and fix me one of those and I will take a shower and lie down for a bit. Tough day, damn new right-hand programming has a lot of bugs. New kids think they know everything and then forget the simple stuff. Cold medicine working, other than the fog you are in?" "I am ok, I guess. Sorry about dinner."

As she begins preparing the steak, she tries hard to come up with the proper wording so that Joseph will understand the test and how much she really wants to have a child. "What if he says that if they fail the 'test,' he just cannot support the health care of a sick child? Will he even go to be tested with her?"

When the steak is ready, Mary turns the heat down and goes into the bedroom, where Joseph lies naked across their bed. He is asleep. "Just for a moment," and crawls in beside him, curling up against his body. A few minutes pass until she begins to stroke the middle of his back. "Time to wake up, your steak is ready, and there is something we need to talk about."

There it was, all of a sudden, slipping out like she could hold it in no longer. Joseph arches his back where she is still touching, stroking him, opens his eyes, and turning his head, smiles at her. She smiles back. "Something to talk about?", taking one hand to his eyes and rubbing the sleep out of them. "Oh, it can wait until after dinner. Steak is ready." "No, what is it? You brought it up, and I want to know. Steak can wait," taking his right hand and moving it down onto her thigh, just above her left knee, and then slowly sliding it upward under her skirt.

With Joseph asleep again, Mary rises, gets dressed, and heads to the kitchen. "Steak is going to be like leather. Better get out here," she calls out. Mary prepares his plate, then hers, and sits down at the kitchen table. Joseph is not long in joining her.

"So, what is there we need to talk about?" taking up his knife and fork and cutting his steak. Mary pauses, takes a deep breath, and begins. "Joseph, you know how we have been talking lately about having a baby, a son for you?" "Yes," in between chews of steak and potato. "Well, when I was at the doctor's office today, I mentioned it in passing, and he told me there is this new law."

Joseph listens quietly as Mary tells him all she knows about the test. When she finishes talking, Joseph stands up, goes to the sink, leans forward, and stares out the kitchen window to the darkness beyond.

After what seems like forever to Mary, Joseph turns and, in a loud, steady, emotionless voice, "Query."

"Yes", comes a response, from one of the functional panels in the kitchen ceiling.

"All information related to government-sanctioned pregnancy and genetic testing."

10,000 references found. Shall I create a synopsis?

"Yes, and display in the kitchen, the usual place."

Government Order WAU-1287, announced in July of last year, is a new government healthcare initiative to hold down consumer costs. Prior to a pregnancy, a genetic test must be completed, and if no predisposition to a serious disease is found, the pregnancy will be sanctioned, and the cost will be covered by the government health insurance pool. Any pregnancy that is not sanctioned will be ineligible for health insurance.

The new initiative is opposed by various groups around the country and in the most recent protest, four were killed and more than 100 arrested.

Shall I continue?

"No. Store current search results and synopsis," and Joseph sits down. Neither says a word until Mary can stand their silence no longer.

"Joseph, what are we going to do?" "I don't know. Take the test, I guess." "But what if the government does not provide the baby with health care?" Mary reaches out and places her hand on Joseph's shoulder, but he is stiff and does not respond.

"I know you want a child, Mary, and I love you, I really do, and you know that, but to pay the health care costs of a child for his or her life, it could make me a slave, Mary, a slave."

Mary withdraws her hand, and Joseph picks up his fork and knife and begins eating again. Mary knows this conversation is over. She will get in touch with the doctor in the morning and have him arrange an appointment for the test.

Brilliant sunlight blasts Mary back inside the subway car and away from her thoughts. The city: she had only been to the city a couple of times and never cared for it. There is too much of everything, from buildings too close together to, too many people, but here she is, and they are almost at the subway stop where they need to get out. It is 10:30, and their appointment for the test is at 11.

"Must hurry," she tells herself and in a whisper to Joseph. "What?" not hearing her over the rumble of the subway car. "Once we get off, we need to hurry. The building is still about 4 blocks away and we cannot be late." "Oh, ok, sure. You do have all their information in your PDA in case we get lost, don't you?" "Yes, I have it."

The subway train comes to a stop, the doors open, and as many people try to jump into the car as there are trying to get out of it. "No, she could never live in the city."

Up the stairs and then on the street, looking for signs to help direct them. "That way", Mary pointing towards a huge building off in the distance: "That's the building."

It does not take them long to walk the 4 blocks to the building, but once outside, Mary stops and just stares at the entrance. "What's wrong?" asks Joseph, taking her hand. "Just scared, that's all. Seems so cruel to put us through this; I just want a child." Joseph pulls Mary close to him and wraps his arms around her. "Like I said, let's take the test and see what happens. There's no way to tell how your and my genes will combine unless we take the test." Mary looks at him with a stern, hard look: "Dam engineer, so damn logical about everything."

Joseph glances up at the building and all its many floors towering above them. "Mary, it is almost 11. We had better get inside and find where we are supposed to be. You ready?" "No, not really, but I guess we better." As they finally step forward to climb the set of steps, a voice rings out. "You taking the test? Hey, you all taking the test?"

Mary and Joseph both glance to their right, and there beside them is a woman about Mary's age standing almost on top of them.

"It's just plain wrong what the government is doing with this new law," handing them a pamphlet. Mary glances at the front of the paper in her hand. Women Against Government Required Pregnancy Testing. "Did you all know about the new testing law when it was announced? I bet not. Insurance companies in the government health insurance pool must have paid some big bucks to someone. You know how the government is these days. Don't get tested. They got no right to require testing. What are they going to do, deny health care to a child?"

Mary glances at Joseph. She does not know what to say or what to do. "Thank you for the pamphlet. I agree with you that the law is wrong, but we want a child, so we are going to take the test and see what happens."

"You got any idea what they are testing for?" the woman beside them says, handing out pamphlets to everyone walking by.

"No." "That's my point. They can test for anything they want, and who knows if the test is even fair. Maybe rich people or government types, well, their test results are always just fine, and they get child health coverage, and maybe the poor or me or you, don't: just no way to tell right now. Don't get tested."

Mary glances at her watch. They have to get inside and find the office they are supposed to report to. "Look, I agree with you, and I will read your organization's pamphlet, but we are going to get tested."

Mary steps forward, surprising Joseph and almost pulling him off his feet. "Ok, suit yourself, but it is wrong. You getting tested is just telling them that what they did is ok!"

Mary climbs the stairs quickly, unable to stand that woman's voice. "No, she does not agree with the law, but they are here and going to get tested, and that is all there is to it."

Once inside, they find themselves in a huge atrium with several information desks and many, many people moving this way and that. A sign right in the middle of the atrium says: Testing in RM 1001. "That's it," again, pulling Joseph along behind her.

Room 1001 is only two rooms down one of the main corridors of the entrance atrium, and as they approach, they see many couples standing in a line. "Oh no, we're late," but as they approach the room, a man wearing a white shirt, tan slacks, and a black bow tie calls out their name. "Yes, here, we are here," Mary, waving her hand in the air. "Good. Not good to be late: must keep to schedule. There are many, many tests today. Please follow me," and with that short introduction, bow tie leads them down another hallway, to a small room, where he tells them to go in, sit down and wait. "It will not be long," closing the door behind him.

Mary and Joseph look around their tiny room. No windows, only one door, two chairs, and a small medical equipment cabinet on one wall. "Sure is homey," Joseph, trying to break the bleak mood. "What was it with that lady out front? I mean, I understand handing out pamphlets against the law and all, but trying to talk us out of getting tested? What gives her the right?"

The door opens and in walks a white lab-coated woman in her mid-thirties. "Hi, I am Lucy, and I will be administering your test today." "There is nothing to worry about, as I have done this test a hundred times or more. I do know folks are a little upset about this new law, but I am just like you. I did not make the law. I am only a nurse." Mary looks at her and manages a small smile. "She is a woman and thus must understand about having a child."

"Will you please state your name for identification purposes?" After each speaks, a voice from a ceiling panel confirms they are the people they say they are. "Good," Lucy says, "You know, early on in testing, some people paid others to take the test. Before genetic test results were shared among qualified medical and the government health insurance company pool. People would find out they had good genes and get paid big money to take the test for others. Not anymore, as we have too many identification checks now. Did you notice a scanner in the atrium? No, well, one is there, and it matches your face with our databanks. You would not have even gotten out of the atrium if you were not scheduled for today and who you say you are. No, no fooling the system now."

"A lady approached us outside," Mary says, looking into the eyes of this talkative nurse, "Say that there is no way to ensure tests are not rigged for Senators or rich people!"

"Oh, I wouldn't know about that. I just administer the test." "Ready?"

Joseph, quiet the whole time Lucy has been talking and moving about their tiny room, turns and smiles at Mary. "Yes, we are ready."

"Ok, all done," Lucy says, straightening the cap on her head.

"But you did not do anything?" Mary blurts out. "Aren't you going to take a blood sample or something?" "Nope, don't have to. Laser scanned you when you sat down. Just needed your identification to be correct and you to confirm you wanted the test done."

Joseph looks at Mary. "I don't know. I have never heard of laser scanning for DNA before, and I keep up on engineering and science as part of my job."

"Oh, it has been around for years apparently, but only used by the military. Now we have it and a select few other government agencies. Honestly, your DNA has been scanned and is currently being placed in the queue for computational analysis."

"From what I understand, it might take several weeks before we get the official results," Mary standing up, still not happy about blood not being drawn or the nurse not even touching her.

"Yes, that's right. You will get a post. If the test confirms that you have the kind of genes the government approves, then you will receive a certificate to conceive and have exactly one child."

"One child: only one child?" Mary has never thought about it. She just assumed that if their genes were found to be "clean," they could have as many children as they wanted.

"What do you mean, only one child?" Mary asks, stopping her movement towards the door. "Oh, a lot of people do not seem to have gotten that aspect of the new law. Must get tested, and a couple can only have one child covered by the government-sponsored health care pool of insurance companies." Joseph shakes his head and says in a very loud and irate voice, "Are we done here?" "Yes, all done," Lucy smiling.

Neither Joseph nor Mary speaks all the way home. When they reach home, Mary turns to face Joseph as they enter the house. "Joseph, I want you to get the results of the test. As I understand it, there are two parts: sanctioned or not sanctioned, and if not sanctioned, genetic disease disposition markers are defined. Joseph, I don't think I want to know what sort of diseases our child might eventually suffer from, so no matter what, never tell me, please."

"Of course, I understand. I will get the post when it comes, I promise." Then, leaning down, he kisses her slightly on the lips, and they go inside, both tired from the long day.

***

A week goes by, but nothing on the test comes into the HIS queue of messages.

"Said it could be 3 weeks," but Mary anxiously asks for message queue posts each morning.

It was just after noon that the HIS announces an incoming video chat request from a Ms. Herrod.

"Herrod? I don't know any Herrod. What is the call about?"

Ms. Herrod says there is a way Mary can have a baby and full medical coverage for life.

"Start chat," and projected on the living room wall is the image of a woman about Mary's age sitting behind a blue background, smiling. "Who are you, and how do you know about babies and insurance?"

"Mary, I represent a certain country that is willing to provide you, your husband, and any children you might have full medical care at no charge to you. How does that sound?"

"How do you know about our desire for a baby? A certain country, you say. Which country and why would they provide us with such an offer? Who are you?"

"Mary, I am correct that your husband works in the field of robotics and artificial intelligence?"

"Yes, he does, but how do you know that and what does that have to do with our wanting a baby? Is this some scam? What do you want?"

"Mary, your husband's skills, my country needs his expertise."

"I don't know. This is all so sudden. I must talk with my husband. How do we get in touch with you?"

"You cannot. I will place a video chat request at this time each day. If you do not desire to discuss the matter, do not accept the request and delete the message from HIS queue."

"What country? Where would we live?"

"You will be provided with your own home at no cost. Your husband is very important to us."

"This is some sort of scam. We are supposed to just take your word for all you promise?"

"If you agree to leave your country and move, we will provide government-approved documents and arrange all travel."

"Who are you?"

"I am just like you. I wanted a child but was afraid to take the genetics test, it being so new and all, and was given the offer I am now offering you. I wanted a baby and now have a young boy. We are happy here, and you can be too."

"Enough. I understand you will video chat request each day. Cannot say if I will ever accept another chat or not."

"A technical point: If you agree to come to my country and have a child, you must stay here for five years. After that, if there are no more children, you may leave. If you have more than one child, you must stay another five years. Reasonable, I think, considering the cost of healthcare."

"Goodbye," says Mary, calling out, "End Chat," and the HIS wall display goes dark.

***

When Joseph walks in the door that evening, dinner is on the table, and Mary is waiting, sitting at the table for him.

"What is this?" taking off his coat and dropping his briefcase.

"How was your day?"

"Oh, come on, what is going on, Mary?"

"Joseph, I got this video chat call today."

"Ah, about moving to another country and getting free medical care for a family?"

"Yes, you got a call, too?" "I did, but not video, just a voice. I wanted to hang up on her but could not help myself. I think it must be some scam or perhaps part of the test. You know, if we accept the offer, the government denies us a certificate, but if we turn down the offer to move, we get a certificate. I don't know, I did not like it at all. How could some country know about us getting tested? It might even be some intelligence agency checking up on my loyalty. You know I work on classified systems."

"I know, Joseph, I know, but what if the offer is real? What if we could get free healthcare for a baby just by leaving the country?"

"Mary, I know how important this is to you, but we must be careful here. Scam or no scam, it's a big decision. And who is to say we might get a birthing certificate anyway and not need to move."

"Remember, one child, only one child? "This offer is for all the children we want or have."

Joseph says nothing.

"Joseph, will you at least think about it? We do not have to decide right now. Did you hear the part about 5 years for each child?"

"5 years? 5 years for what?"

"If we move and have a child, we must remain in the country for at least five years. If we have a second child, another five years, but there is a way back if we decide we don't like it there."

"Five years! What if I don't like where they place me to work? Mary, I got a thousand questions. This whole thing has to be part of the test, has to be."

Mary knows the discussion is over for tonight and starts eating.

***

The next day, as she said she would, right on time, the HIS announces a request for a video chat.

Mary does not accept chat.

Then, the chat request comes in each day for a week, but Mary does not respond.

There has been little discussion of the move and healthcare offer, but as the days go by, Mary has become increasingly anxious. No posting of test results. "Is there some time limit on the offer? What if the video chats request just stop coming?"

That night, Mary has to discuss the offer but waits until bedtime.

Settled in bed, Joseph has his light on and is reading. Mary begins, "Joseph, I got another video chat request today, but nothing from the testing people. Has that woman contacted you again?" Joseph closes his book.

"I did speak to her the second time she called to confirm what you told me about the 5-year requirement, but other than that, 'no.'"

"Joseph, I am worried. What if there is some time limit on the offer? What if the video chat requests stop? Have you given the offer any more thought?"

"Mary, I can't figure out if the offer is real or simply part of the test for a birthing certificate or something else. The work I do is important to our country, and honestly, leaving feels wrong. Even if the offer is genuine, what if the offer is from some country that is our enemy? What then? We move, and we are traitors who can never come back no matter what that woman says."

"What do we do, Joseph? Day after day, nothing from the testing people and that video chat request every day; it is driving me crazy. Please understand, I do not want to force you into doing something you might regret. Oh, I am sorry to put you in this position. I still want a family, a baby, but I am beginning to wonder if it is a good idea after all. I thought having a baby would be easier than this."

"I read more riots going on against the new law, but apparently, the government is fixed in its position. God knows our taxes are already high enough. No one wants them higher just to cover health care. At work, some are saying health care should only be for working people and not those who do not contribute. Hard to argue against that point of view, but perhaps that is because I have a job the government needs. Mary, we have to just wait."

"And if we get denied?"

"Maybe the offer will still be good, and we can decide then?"

Mary turns her back to Joseph.

***

The days go by, and each day, another video chat request comes in at the appointed time.

On the 16th day since the test, Mary can no longer stand it and accepts the chat request.

"Mary thanks for accepting my chat. Are you well, your husband?"

"Yes, we are well, thank you for asking."

"And what can I do for you today, or are you perhaps ready to do something for yourselves?"

"Your offer, how long does your offer last? I mean, could we accept your offer if we are denied a birthing certificate here?"

"Mary, I want to help you and your husband, but the offer extends until the test results are posted. If the results are opened and read, our offer is rescinded."

"Oh."

"I want to remind you that in your country, a birthing certificate is for one child only. My country will cover the healthcare of any and all children you might have as long as you stay another 5 years for each."

"I want to accept your offer; I really do, but my husband is very concerned. His work: his work is very important to us, and he thinks he might be branded a traitor if he were to suddenly move to some other country. You, your country, are you an enemy country?"

"Enemy country: one day, an enemy, the next, an ally. You know this yourself. What if I say friendly country, but tomorrow, we no longer go along with what your country wants us to do? Then we are an enemy. I do not mean to make it more difficult on you than it already is, but no matter what I say, enemy or friend, who can predict world politics?"

Mary is silent.

"Mary, I wish you well, no matter the decision you and your husband make, I really do. I am a mother and I understand."

HIS announces, "Chat Ended."

Mary wants to talk with Joseph but knows she cannot. She will wait until tonight.

She gets up to go outside for a while and get some sun.

HIS announces, "Post: Test Results."

"The Clothesline"

She sits at the kitchen table in one of the two chairs and stares out the back screen door across the fields that once grew corn and wheat to the woods beyond. She is not thinking or feeling, only staring. Now and then, smoke from her lit cigarette comes curling, swirling up into her field of view and she is once again back in their kitchen.

The boys have urged her to move, but this is her home. Oh, it did take some getting used to, to start with when they moved here, all alone out here in the country with not a house for nearly a half mile in either direction. But after a while, there came a certain peace and quiet she had not known when she lived in the city. No, she will not move.

Sipping down the last of the current cup of coffee, she gets up and heads outside, stopping on the porch for her wicker clothes basket and then heading on to the clothesline.

It is a lovely spring day with a clear blue sky, a light breeze, and a temperature in which she could bathe all day long.

At the clothesline, she starts with the sheets, removing a clothespin at a time and then taking down the entire sheet in a folding motion.

She loves that the sun and breeze have dried her clothes. Monday wash. There is something constant about Monday wash, like it provides an order to her world.

Once, years ago, he had suggested they get an electric clothes dryer so she could dry the wash even when it rained on a Monday, but she would hear nothing of it; it had to be the sun and the breeze.

Folding and refolding the first sheet, she finally pats it between her hands one last time and lays it in the bottom of the empty wicker basket along with the 4 clothes pins that have been holding the sheet to the clothesline.

At the other end of the line, a blue jay has come to make his presence known. She looks down the line at him and welcomes him to the day.

Another sheet is off the line, and again, careful folding and patting is done. As she lowers this sheet into the basket, she remembers when they bought them on that trip to town. He had wanted plain white sheets, but she had insisted on small little blue flowers and he had given in, as he always did.

She begins to take down her clothes. First, her Sunday dress, which is the best one she owns and then her everyday dresses and under things. As she folds the last of her things, she begins to feel a sense of dread and anxiety but moves on quickly to his clothes.

Dress shirts, work shirts, and then a rag. Every shirt he ever bought had the same life: dress to rag.

As she pulls down the first dress shirt, she puts it to her face and smells it. Although his smell is gone from the shirt, she can still smell him, showered, shaved, and lying beside her naked in the cool of the evening. Constancy: Monday wash lets her hold on when sometimes she is not sure she can.

***

Lost in his Cadillac, Cassidy comes to a fork in the road. "Oh, hell," turning left, not sure which way to go.

The road is empty of cars, and it has been a while since he has seen a house or even a sign of human life, but then, coming over a small hill in the road, he sees an old woman outside of a small, single-story house, at a clothesline taking down clothes.

"Clothesline, he says out loud to himself. "Why would anyone still use a clothesline? God, he really must be lost. Maybe I should stop and get some directions? No, would scare the crap out of the old lady," and he passes the house and woman in the yard and continues on lost.

She is taking down his shirts when she hears a car coming down the road. "Odd time of day for any traffic on this road as locals, are always either early morning or late evening, but not now." And pausing for a moment, she sees a giant old Cadillac going by, a man driving. "Lost" "Has to be," watching the car go on by the house. "Lost: I suspect he is no more lost than I am," taking down another shirt.

"Silly," she thinks and suspects that if anyone ever sees her washing and drying his clothes and they know her, they will think she has gone mad but she does not care. Taking his clothes out of the drawer and washing them with the rest of the clothes does no harm other than perhaps moving each shirt one step closer to rag.

He has been gone for almost a year now, but he is not gone. Every Monday, he is on the clothesline with all the other clothes.

With the clothesline empty and the car now long gone, she returns to the house and makes her way to 'their' bedroom.

Opening his chest of drawers, she places his pants and shirts away until next Monday, when she will pull them out, wash them, and hang them on the clothesline to dry.

As she puts away his things, she sees the clothesline as a sort of mirror of how her life has progressed, gone until now.

A single line of clothes, then diapers and baby sheets and blankets, boy's clothes, dual bed sheets, more sheets, two lines of clothes, more boy's clothes, and then three lines of clothes as the boys constantly changed clothes 2 or 3 times a day.

And then back to two lines of clothes as Jeff went off to the Army and then one line, when George left for college. Now, there is just one line, and that is hardly full.

She misses him.

"Rabbit Hole Tether"

It had begun happening more frequently, and it scared him: his powers of visualization.

Whenever he had a problem to solve, a step process to develop, an assembly or disassembly, the practice of a speech, or just for mental exploration and meditation, he visualizes.

The first time it happened, he was more amazed than frightened.

He had gone deep inside a visualization on a particular problem and somehow, from there, had gone onto another problem, thought stream, and then another and another, and it was only a very loud sound that pulled him out of his visualization, and he returned to his body. "A tether: a rabbit hole tether." He had never thought about it: his mind was tethered to his body. "What if he went so far down into a visualization, a thought stream, that he got lost and could not find his way back?"

At first, the tether was reassuring and let him continue to go deeper and deeper down through a series of visualizations of realms and worlds that only his mind could have thought of. But recently, the alarm of his body reality had become harder and harder to hear, to alert him that it was time to return, like some watch on a deep-sea diver. "What if he went too far and could not get back to the 'surface'?"

Although a struggle, he began to be able to keep some element of his physical with him as he moved through visualizations and thought streams, and when the physical became tense and tight, he would back out slowly and return to his body.

Then, one day, the pain came and stayed and stayed: cancer. Operations, chemotherapy, drugs, none of it helped much, and so he began once again going down the rabbit hole of his mind.

Deeper and deeper into strange places that did not resemble his body's reality at all and in which his body and its pain were not a part. But in the end, he was still pulled back up via the tether and to the pain of his body.

Then, one day, while asleep in a dream, out walking in a large, open, grass field, he comes across an actual, very large, 'rabbit' hole and looking down into it, expecting only darkness, he sees years of his life, each a film strip playing, orbiting around the Earth and without a moment's thought, jumps in, feet first.

Down and down he went: into and out of the center of stars, past numerous galaxies, looking out through the eyes of a seagull down upon an empty, timeless ocean beach, deep dark green water crashing, a pale yellow sky overhead; dreams, all the dreams he ever had, all overlaid like multiple layers of paint on the wall of some old, old house; into the consciousness of a barnyard door; feeling the mind of the hive, a part of and not separate and then somehow, he could feel the tether was stretching, becoming very, very thin and it seemed all right to him, and without a warning and hardly a whisper, the tether simply pulled apart like taffy stretched too far and he was gone.

The alarm sounded at the nurse's station, but it was too late: his heart would not start no matter what they did. He was gone.

Yes, he was 'gone', but not the way they thought.

"The Horse"

"The Horse" came to me in a dream. It was a very strange dream as it was not about something I did yesterday or had ever done or even a place I had ever been to.

I was in Cairo, lost in a centuries-old bazaar filled with small shops that had all manner of Egyptian tourist reproductions, giant rugs, brass lanterns, restaurants, and many other items, large and small. It was a maze of alleys and avenues, some even underground.

In the dream, I was really there; I had no idea why, but I was simply amazed. The place was so real and full. As I walked along, sometimes I would stop and look or maybe even enter a shop and browse. My interest seemed to be in ancient items, of which there were many. "Not 'fake,' every shopkeeper claimed as this or that was 500 BC or maybe not as old as 400AD.

Alabaster carvings: amulets, cartouches in gold and precious stones, and lots of King Tutankhamen, even with his likeness on dinner plates.

Mostly, I simply walked and marveled at the place as it seemed endless, stretching in all directions.

I came across a coffee shop on an avenue or wider thoroughfare and sat down. Ordered tea and lit a cigarette. "Please, sir, tea will be free If I can have one of the cigarettes." I gave him 2: big mistake.

Apparently, everything is watched by everyone in the bazaar, and upon giving the waiter 2, a stream of people offered this or that for just one of my American-made cigarettes. I gave and gave until I had only two left for myself.

After I had hand signaled no more, I sat quietly for a while, watching the stream of people moving back and forth with only a few tourists, but then a man approached from around the corner of some alley ahead and came directly to me. "Sir, I think you should see this. Come with me." "No, that is OK; I'm not really sure why I am here and don't need anything." "Sir, my shop has many fine old pieces, not fakes like you see here: very special, very old." "Yes, I am sure you have a fine shop, but no thanks." He walked away.

I finished the tea and began walking again in the direction of the man who had the very fine shop. When I reached the alley, he had come out of; I turned and started down it. More shops offering the same and more: kitchen faucets, cabinet handles of all shapes and sizes, and even robes, hats, and T-shirts. I walked on.

Then, one shop had locked glass cases in the front, and inside the case were various Shabtis or small clay figurines. These figurines were a common item in any tomb, and there must have been thousands of them in Egypt over the centuries. But I was drawn to the multitude in the case, with each having a date associated with it and all 1000 BC or older. I went inside the shop.

The man who had come and asked me to follow appeared from behind a curtain, "Ah yes, you come anyway. Good. You like the figurines? All old, I guarantee."

"I don't know. I'm just looking. Thank you." "I open the case for you? I show you whatever you want." "No, not necessary but thanks." The shop owner turned and went behind the curtain again, leaving me alone.

As I looked at the figurines, I also began to look about the shop.

Every available inch of the small shop's walls had shelves holding some item or another and then I noticed a small horse high up on one shelf. For some reason, it seemed out of place or as if it did not belong in the shop. It appeared to be brown clay, very well-formed, with many small holes in it.

I moved to the shelf and gently picked up the horse. It was light, obviously hollow, but then as I moved my two hands to turn the horse to see it all, I began to hear blowing winds, The strangest winds, old winds, if there is such a thing, and as I moved my one hand or the other, the winds would strengthen or subside as my hands covered various holes in its body and I felt as if I was those winds blowing across the expanse of the Egyptian desert thousands of years ago. I was only wind. A chill went through me. 5000 BC.

"Sir, you want to buy?" I was startled. "Did you hear that, the winds?" "Very fine piece. I just got it in the shop, very old. You want to buy?" "Did you hear the winds?" "Sir, you want to buy?" I put the clay horse back on the shelf and walked out.

I was in a daze of some kind, and it took a minute, a year, or a century for me to physically return to my body and head back to buy the horse.

I retraced my steps and found the shop quickly. "Ah, you come back." "Yes, I want to buy the horse." "Oh, most sorry, I just sold it." "What?" "I just sold the horse." "Was it an American?" "No sir." "But I have many fine figurines, come, you look, I'll show you." "No, the horse; who did you sell it to?" "Sir, I do not know."

Gone! The horse was gone.

I stood outside the shop looking for anyone carrying anything, but nothing.

The horse was gone.

I woke up out of the dream.

***

I have now visited Egypt 4 times, looking for the brown clay horse with small holes in it.

Of course, I visited the Cairo bazaar every time, but even after four trips, I am not sure I have actually seen all the shops in the bazaar, but I continue to look and ask about the horse. Sometimes, when I am in the bazaar, I ask myself, why didn't I simply respond to, "You want to buy it?" With, "Yes. Why did I turn and leave?"

Oh, just a dream, you say, but that clay horse is more than a dream. It is real and out there somewhere. I seem compelled to find, have, and own it more than anything I have ever desired.

Alexandra, Giza, Luxor, Aswan, and most of the smaller cities and all museums, large and small, but no brown clay horse with holes.

"Oh, you are the man asking about the horse." I have become known through much of Egypt.

Once in Cairo, I mentioned "my horse" to my guide and the next day, he took me to a pottery shop where overnight, the owner and his staff had made 30 or 40 different clay horses of various sizes. "But, no, sorry, this was old, had holes, made sound."

I felt bad about all the work that had been done and told my guide that he had misunderstood. There was only one clay horse with holes in it, and it had winds, ancient winds, in it.

*****

I am old now, too old for another Egypt trip, and my hope of ever seeing, holding, hearing, and feeling that clay horse is fading. Oh, I can be there in that small shop so long ago, any time I want in my mind, and even now, there is an afterglow of what I felt holding the horse: the ancient winds of 5000 BC.

In searching for the horse, I rode river boats down the Nile for miles and miles; climbed my way up inside the Great Pyramid and sat on one of the base stones for a long time; went underground to visit a Coptic Church and was very spiritually touched; visited a Mosque; Valley of the Kings; learned that all the stonework was done by various teams from rough to fine. Hieroglyphs; rode camels and, like a bird, rode the thermals on the high desert plain overlooking Giza; saw mummies of all types, including crocodile in the Cairo Museum and even King Tut's linen condom; met many nice people, some tourists but mostly Egyptians with many recognizing me and commenting I was at least 3000 years old.

I own a large alabaster lidded jar from 400 AD or so, which is not very old and which contains 3 smaller lidded jars. All the smaller jars are filled with windblown sand and dust from my travels in Egypt.

Own it? I have wondered over the years where the horse dream came from. Why even has such a dream? Was it all about 'Owning'? I experienced the horse, and it left its imprint on me, but perhaps the horse could never be owned by anyone: just some artifact popping out of the afterlife now and again. 'No,' never owned, like the wind. But why do I want to own it so badly?

"Own?"

To "own": as to have a piece of magic? Can I own it so I can use it anytime I want? Own, as to show off to friends? Own, as to constantly worry about it being stolen or simply dropped and broken? Could it have been mine 5000 years ago? Could I have been its maker?

Own. And what do we ever really own?

Pharaohs owned everything and even tried to take a lot with them to the afterlife, only for most to be looted, sold as scrap or to some tourist, or put in some museum in England or elsewhere.

I saw a movie once, where this tribe, somewhere far from what we call civilization, had no concept of "ownership;" everything was communal. And when 'ownership' came to the tribe, it resulted in conflict.

'Own'. I own my dream. I own the experience I had with the brown clay horse.

I know, you say, just a dream, and perhaps you are right: it was just a small, clay horse with holes that had ancient winds in it somehow.

If you ever see it, experience it, please let the man asking about the horse know. I no longer need to own it. I just want to confirm what I felt, know to be true: ancient winds of an ancient time.

Musing: "West Point of the South - Parade Rest"

Friday.

On the field.

Parade Rest.

Down the line,

Voices.

I cannot hear.

Here. Here I stand.

Clean, starched, pressed, shiny,

silent.

Alone and yet a part of.

Parade Rest.

I only stare straight ahead,

nothing moves,

and then,

from my right

it begins.

The Japanese planes coming down

out of the sun,

to strafe the troops, the line.

The mini-ball whizzing by my ear,

the mortar landing nearby,

the call to "charge."
Parade Rest.

I am so clean, motionless

while others

far away,

low crawl away

from bullets and bombs

and a hell of horrors.
Parade Rest.

While I stand in the bright afternoon sun,

I can see and feel others in a war far away,

fighting and dying

and I feel guilty.

The chaos of fighting so stark,

in contrast

to me

here now.

Parade Rest

Beyond the "current war,"

so many other wars.

All those islands and jungles.

All those beach landings and hedgerows.

All those mini-balls and fields of honor.

All for me

to stand here,

silent,

in the sun.

Parade Rest.

Guilty, but I will stand silent.

I will not move.

My time will come.

Parade Rest.

Then

the call,

and I respond

with 1000 others.

Privileged, Guilty.

Musing: "Lost in the Mixture's Black Hole"

Everything fades so quickly now, so I must try to capture its essence before it disappears completely.

2 + 2 = 4. Actually, 2 apples + 2 apples = 4 apples. 2 apples + 2 oranges do not = 4 apples or 4 oranges.

High-speed jet, needle valve, idle speed jet, intake manifold.

Recently, I was presented with the opportunity to explore the world of carburetors. Again! Although I have had to work on "carbs," as I call them, several times in the past, I thought perhaps I was done forever with them.

Apparently, I did not learn all I could or should have out of my other carb experiences, so I was given another chance. This time, I think I got it.

You do not see real carburetors much anymore, only on small engines. The particular carburetor I was presented with this time was on my 5-year-old lawn tractor.

Several weeks ago, the lawn tractor engine began a surging action where it would run and then try to die out, only to speed up again and then try to die out again. I could stop this "surging" by choking the carb almost closed, telling me I had to enrich the fuel-air mixture.

Mixture? 2 apples + 2 apples = 4 apples. But 1 gasoline + 10 air + 1 spark = burn, power, and exhaust.

Mixture.

I began my effort to repair the carb by taking it completely off the tractor, inspecting it, and then cleaning the outside. Then I completely rebuilt the carb with a new needle valve, gaskets, high-speed jet removal and cleaning, and finally, blowing cleaner through all those tiny holes in the carb body.

Assemble, mount on the tractor and start: still surging.

Perhaps some tiny passageway is clogged and only needs high-speed cleaning? I increase the revolutions per minute of the engine to well beyond its regular running speed and then back off to normal. Nope. No change. I then increase rpm's again for several minutes and back off to no change in surging behavior.

Off comes the carb again and again, wholly apart, and I adjust the float setting on the needle valve and again blow out all passageways and again assemble and mount.

The engine starts fine again, but after a minute or less, it begins surging. This time, sitting on the tractor and leaning over the engine compartment, I again increase the engine rpm by forcing the throttle linkage. I look down into the carb throat and watch gasoline being sprayed into it.

I am now watching, feeling, listening, and trying to use some sense I cannot name to pinpoint the problem somehow. Down into the throat of that carb black hole, I stare, and then, some earthquake shaking, some planetary misalignment, as I somehow get pulled down into the black hole of mixtures.

At first, it is mathematics. Apples and oranges, what numbers represent and do not represent, and then I begin to see a mixture everywhere. Trees: the intake, the burn, the power and the exhaust. Just some soil, air, sun, and water in a mix of mathematics only chaos theory or fractals can describe. Then, deeper, at a more atomic level, mixtures of various atoms make elements and dance together as they flow down some 'black hole'.

We are in a 'black hole' where mixing occurs, flowing and mixing. All dances as it swirls around the throat of the beast.

Mixtures: of emotions and thoughts and concepts. 2 + 2 and colors mixing and love and hate mixing in proportions I can only guess at, and the precision or lack of it in the mixing amazes me, and down deeper I go into the black hole of the carb. Visible gasoline and invisible air are being pulled down and away, and I cannot stop myself from staring and being pulled in.

Surging: the surging is a mixture problem. Too many apples in the world: so I cut off the engine and eat one. Does not help.

Connections and swirling mixtures dance through the black hole, which pulls apart and combines in combinations never before seen and which can only exist in this space and time.

I think of mixed drinks and genetic mixtures. I am the product, the sum, the mixture, of thousands of years of mixing. What equation and what mathematics can define and predict the next element in the sequence?

As I said, it is all fading now, the trip and fall into the black hole of that carb mixing throat, but the after-glows remain, and I have learned something at some deep level I cannot convey in this mixture of words.

In the end, I had an air leak at one of the intake manifold mountings. Or so I want to believe because, to believe that it was really surging because there are one too many apples in the universe or hairs on some dog in China scares me, and yet, I know that these were the real reasons the engine surged and called me to look, listen, think, feel and ponder.

Mixtures: we and everything around us are mixtures, moving and remixing our way deeper and deeper into the cylinder of the universe.

All we are is the mix, burn, power, and exhaust.

"The Trial of Herman Schmitt"

The Arrest

3 September 2007, Monday.

Herman is half asleep in one corner of the day room when he hears his name being called and opening his eyes, sees two police officers standing in front of him. "Herman Schmitt?" one officer asks, looking down on Herman.

"Yes, I am Herman Schmitt," says Herman in a dazed voice, his mind beginning to churn through the possibilities of the police being there but finding nothing. "Herman Schmitt, you are under arrest by the authority granted by the United Nations to convene a Special Tribunal in the Case of Herman Schmitt participating in the Jewish Genocide starting in 1943."

"What? What is this? There must be some mistake. I am 88 years old and have lived here, in this place, for the past ten years. How could I have done anything to anyone? You have the wrong man," Herman pleads, but it is no good and the two policemen stand up Herman, handcuff him, and lead him out through the nursing home day room and then to their car. Herman shakes his head and mutters over and over, "I kill no one. I did not kill any Jews."

Although Herman has lived his whole life in Berlin, he has never been to the part of town the police are driving him through. He asks several times where the police are taking him, but he gets no response. After what seems to Herman to be an hour through heavy traffic, with Herman's arms and hands hurting the whole time from being behind his back, the car stops in front of an old, non-descript, post-WWII government building.

Once inside, Herman immediately has his handcuffs removed, handed a prisoner uniform, escorted to a small empty room, and told to put on the prison uniform.

After what seems like hours to Herman, a prison guard enters the room and escorts him into one wing of the building, which has rows of one-cot cells on either side of the central corridor. It is a dark, cold place of concrete, metal bars, pipes, and cinderblock, and as Herman walks along, he notices that all cells are empty.

Finally, the guard stops at the very last cell on the right, unlocks the door, and tells Herman to go in. Then the guard locks the door behind Herman and without saying another word, walks back down the corridor and out of the wing, leaving Herman completely alone.

Suddenly, Herman is aware of a great silence and looking around, finds his tiny windowless cell has a wet floor, a toilet but no toilet seat, a washbasin sink, a faucet dripping, and a cot with a blanket made into a roll with a pillow on top.

Overhead hangs a naked electric bulb and the head of a fire sprinkler system. Herman is in shock. From the light and cleanliness of a nursing home day room to a prison cell, he is not even sure what he has done.

"Genocide of Jews," the one police officer had said when he was arrested. "It cannot be; I was never a soldier and have not been in any trouble my entire life."

Tired from standing, Herman sits down on the cot and finds the mattress stinks of urine. "What a horrible place. What have I done?"

At 3 PM, Herman hears footsteps come down the corridor and a guard unlocks Herman's cell door and motions Herman out. "What is happening? Where are you taking me?" "You have a visitor." "Who is this visitor?" "Your defense attorney."

"Mr. Schmitt, I am Mr. Simple, your defense attorney and I would like to go over the charges brought against you."

"Defense attorney, I need no defense attorney. I have done nothing. I was a mechanical designer. I am given work, and I do it. That is all I know."

"Mr. Schmitt, is this your design?" Herman looks over a drawing on the table. "Yes, I design this. You see my name at the bottom. Yes, I design." "Well, correct me if I am wrong, but the one box at the bottom says "Zyklon B Gas Dispenser." Is that right?" "Yes, that is what I design for, but I never build; I just design."

"Mr. Schmitt, you freely admit that you designed this Zyklon B Gas Dispenser?" "Yes, of course." "Mr. Schmitt, the charges against you are very clear. It is being charged that you willingly designed what you knew would be a Zyklon B gas dispenser to be used at Nazi concentration camps to kill Jews."

"No, no, no, I was given a job, told to design, and I did. I know nothing about how it was to be used. Don't even know if the design was ever used. My company only did design work, never make anything."

"Yes, well, Mr. Schmitt, with your free admission that you did the design and the fact that Zyklon B was used by the Nazis to kill Jews, I am afraid there is little I can do."

"You do? I don't need you. I defend myself and my design."

"Mr. Schmitt, I highly recommend you not try to defend yourself. This is a very serious charge. Any charge that involves the Holocaust is very serious."

"Holocaust" "I have never been a soldier and have only done design work. At the time, I did not even know about camps; no one did. No, I am not guilty of killing Jews. I defend my design."

"Mr. Schmitt, it is your right to defend yourself, and if you want to do so, then please sign this document for me. It says you decline my services and will defend yourself."

"Yes, give me the document, I sign. I kill no Jews."

The Schmitt Article

Tuesday, 4 September 2007

The day after Herman's arrest, the charges against Herman are published in proceedings of the United Nations daily bulletin, but it is nothing more than a footnote. But Jack Luby, a reporter for 'The Journal,' who covers the United Nations, remembers something about the Israelis wanting to bring another German to the International Criminal Court for crimes against humanity. But since that initial posting, there has been nothing, but Luby knows such requests often took months, if not years, to process, but perhaps this Schmitt thing is that: the Israelis trying another German for the Holocaust.

Luby begins making phone calls to his contacts in the United Nations. Although it takes several calls to piece together a story, there is a story in what he hears; he knows it.

Herman Schmitt had apparently designed and overseen the installation of gas dispensing equipment at Nazi concentration camps. What is interesting to Luby is that Schmitt had not operated the equipment or been personally involved in any killings but rather that his design had been used, and according to the Israelis, he was complicit in the Holocaust. This expansion of criminal culpability seemed a stretch to Luby and could result in a serious new legal precedent, but the Israelis had shown before that they wanted every pound of flesh they could get when it came to the Holocaust.

And what seemed even more of note to Luby was that, the United Nations, after review of the charges against Mr. Schmitt, had decided, that the case against Schmitt did not meet the criteria of the International Criminal Court or ICC. But bowing to Israeli pressure, had authorized Israel to convene a Special Tribunal in The Haig just for Schmitt. The Tribunal was to use the Rome Statutes as used by the ICC, have three independent judges, and although authorized by the UN, Israel could not use UN facilities in the Hague and must provide the physical court and all security. The UN would provide Mr. Schmitt with a single defense attorney from their pool of attorneys at the ICC. The UN would also provide any and all translators required at Israeli expense. The trial was to begin on the 18th of September this year.

Luby's article, "A War Crimes Trial: Herman Schmitt," was in the next edition of the Journal and, although a small article, was on the front page.

Immediately picked up by various wire services, Herman's pending trial became news around the world. Sometimes, it is simply a small item in a newspaper, but other times, it is a larger piece recanting the horrors of the Holocaust. In Israel, Herman is front-page news. In the United States, Herman's arrest and pending trial even made broadcast news in various cities. There had not been a Holocaust trial in several years and any Holocaust trial, was to be promoted to remind all of Nazi atrocities.

Luby was stunned by all the attention the Schmitt article was getting and began to wonder. "What, if anything, the engineering community might have to say about a designer being charged as criminally culpable simply because he designed something that could be used to kill people or, more correctly, concentration camp Jews? Couldn't the charge lead to a new legal precedent?"

Luby began working the phones. In the United States, there are many professional organizations representing different segments of the engineering or scientific community and the first person willing to talk with Luby was, the legal counsel of the Institute of Electrical Engineers (IEE).

"Yes, we are aware of the Schmitt thing, but the details are a bit sketchy at this time. But it appears to us that the Israelis are moving into territory with no legal precedent. It is our understanding that Schmitt was not a soldier and was not in attendance at any concentration camp where his gas dispensing design was used."

A Phone Call

5 September 2007, Wednesday

Headquartered in New Jersey, the IEE was having its board meeting when a phone call from their lead legal counsel came in, and after much discussion, they were the first to act.

Although it would not be good publicity defending Schmitt in court, they decided they had little choice but to look into the matter, as their members worked for various defense contractors, both in the United States and abroad.

The lead counsel for the IEE agrees to have his staff gather more details about this Schmitt matter, contact other professional organizations, get their opinion, and then report on the actions, if any, the IEE should take.

Many organizations are aware of the Schmitt design issue but do not want the publicity of being a part of any defense. Instead, they are willing to be silent financial partners.

When the chief counsel for the IEE learns that Mr. Schmitt has rejected his UN appointed attorney, he speaks with the UN, and they agree that Mr. Schmitt needs representation no matter his wishes, and the UN would welcome the IEE providing a defense team.

The Defense Team

6 September 2007

On Thursday, the IEE chief counsel recommends that the board provide a 3-person defense team and a headquarters-based support staff to defend Mr. Schmitt. While other professional organizations are willing to help with cost sharing, they do not want their names in any way associated with Mr. Schmitt's defense.

After a limited discussion, the board agrees that the IEE must provide Mr. Schmitt with a defense.

The chief counsel then contacts the UN, formally declares their defense intentions, and requests copies of all documents.

With the trial to begin on the 17th, an appeal is made to delay the start of the Tribunal to allow proper defense preparation time, but the appeal is denied quickly.

From the start, the Israelis assumed no one would be defending Schmitt and that the court-appointed attorney would simply not put up much of a defense, and Schmitt would be found guilty, and the whole matter quickly over.

This request for delay by an actual defense team from the United States was totally unexpected and the Israelis, although confident in their prosecution case, were unwilling to have some group try to stretch out the case for weeks, if not months or even years. This, coupled with the fact that Israelis had already procured space to hold the court in The Hague was enough, for the UN to disallow a delay in the start of the trial. Once the trial started, the Tribunal judges could decide if a delay was warranted.

With so little time before trial, a defense team had to come from existing IEE's legal staff, and after reviewing the current caseload, Mr. Isaac Shapiro, himself a Jew, was asked to be lead counsel. Initially, he balked at the idea as he was currently the lead attorney in a liability case and did not like the idea of defending anyone associated with the Holocaust. But the head counsel insisted and outright told Shapiro, "A Jew had to lead the defense. Had to."

To help communicate with Mr. Schmitt, who only spoke German, Julies Jones was recruited even though he was an international trade lawyer with no criminal law experience. The 3rd attorney, the chief counsel selected, was a woman, Linda Hines. Hines was picked for the team as she had just finished a big case and her courtroom skills were excellent. She was especially cunning at cross-examination. When Shapiro was informed about Hines, he considered himself lucky. He would lead the team, but Hines would do all the talking in the courtroom.

Evidence and Research

7 September 2007

On Friday, Shapiro is handed all documents that had been requested from the UN and, with Hines and Jones in attendance, gives each a stack to review.

After an hour or so of review, it was clear that Mr. Schmitt had designed a "Zyklon B Gas Dispenser," and according to the prosecution, Mr. Schmitt knew the intended purpose of the dispenser was the mass killing of Jews at various Nazi labor and annihilation camps throughout Nazi-occupied Europe. But this evidence consisted only of a design drawing signed by Mr. Schmitt and then mounds of evidence as to the use of Zyklon B gas at the death camps. Evidence that Mr. Schmitt's design had ever been actually constructed or used is not in the UN-provided documents.

Shapiro immediately tasked his headquarters support team to thoroughly review Mr. Schmitt's design. Shapiro wanted to know anything and everything about it. Was it ever built? Could it have been built? Who would have built it, and when? Are there any pictures of the actual gas dispenser anywhere? No such images were in the documentation provided by the UN and find anything about who ordered or paid for the Schmitt design.

Although the use of Zyklon B gas by the Nazis had been well documented over the years, and what had been provided was indeed plenty of evidence to that fact, there was nothing in any of it about Mr. Schmitt's design. Shapiro needed to determine if there was a documented link between Schmitt's design and the use of gas at death camps.

Shapiro also asked the support staff to get background on 2 of the 3-member prosecution team. As the German on the team appeared to have no active role, he is of no interest. And he could do without it if he had to, but anything on the three assigned Tribunal judges.

The official language of the court will be English and German. The prosecution, defense, and the three judges all spoke English. German will be only for Mr. Schmitt. The UN will supply the

German-to-English translator and provide all the equipment needed. All court proceedings will be recorded...

The prosecution consisted of Mr. Isaak Metzmann, lead counsel and apparently the originator of the charges against Mr. Schmitt. Mr. Uri Portnoy, second chair and a criminal lawyer in Israel of some note, and finally, at the insistence of the Germans, a Mr. Karl Braun. Mr. Braun was to represent Germany to confirm that Germany supported any effort to seek out and prosecute those involved in the Holocaust. Mr. Jones spoke both German and English and would ensure all German translations of Mr. Schmitt and any other German-speaking witnesses were correct.

Designed for Camp Use?

8 September 2007, Saturday

Herman is still asleep when he hears his name and looks up to see a guard standing by him. "Herman, you must be some special engineer. The Americans have agreed to defend you." Herman is confused. He has already signed papers saying he will defend himself.

"Americans: I know no Americans, and I defend myself." "No, Herman, you cannot defend yourself that has been decided for you and if I were you, I would consider myself lucky that the Americans are willing to take your case. From what I hear, you ought to be hanged for what you did."

Shapiro, Hines, and Jones meet at noon and get a report from their support staff that the staff has not found anything new about Herman's design, but it has been quickly reviewed, and a document has been created explaining it in terms that Shapiro's team can understand. The background on the use of Zyklon B at the camps has also been expanded to provide some details on why, perhaps, Herman's design could have been intended for use at the camps. Finally, the support staff has compiled information about the prosecution team and the three judges.

Shapiro splits the documents and hands the judges' information to Hines, the prosecution to Jones, and he takes Herman's design and the use of Zyklon B at the death camps.

Shapiro starts with Herman's design first. Consisting of a large sealed tank, apparently on the tank top, the tank would accept any size sealed Zyklon B canister through a series of rubber seals. Then, using a lever on the outside of the tank, a long blade inside the drum would cut off the top of the sealed canister and, via a large magnet, pull the canister into a bin on the right side of the drum, while the Zyklon B pellets would drop to a plate in the bottom. Via a rubber-sealed hole on the left side of the drum, heated, moist air was to be pumped over the pellets, creating the gas that then was forced by the blower out another rubber-sealed opening near the bottom of the tank. The canisters could be taken out via a sealed drawer opening on one side.

The engineering review also included a section that pointed out that Herman's design called for a lot of natural rubber, which was in short supply in Germany in 1943.

As to intended use, the initial engineering review found that Herman's design would have been useful to the Germans for use at the death camps. At the time Zyklon B gas was being used, SS officers had to manually open a Zyklon B canister and either pour Zyklon B pellets into holes in the roof of the death houses or throw the whole open container into the hole. The larger, less air-tight death houses required many canisters to be opened and dumped. Although no SS officer had ever been injured during the dispensing of pellets, Zyklon B only really worked with warm, moist air, and thus, the death houses had to be heated before each use at considerable expense of fuel, which was also scarce by 1943. A device like Herman's dispenser would allow easy loading of the dispenser, not require multiple holes in the death house roof, and not require the death house to be heated. Once installed, the heated air through Herman's design would only take one SS Officer and someone to operate the blower.

However, it was also possible that Schmitt's design could have been used in some sort of mobile fumigation application. Zyklon B was a pesticide commonly used to fumigate ships, railroad cars, grain silos, and, in America, totally enclosed fruit trees.

At that time, to use as a pesticide, sealed canisters had to be taken into the area to be gassed, opened, pellets sprinkled around all over to include corners, and then the railroad car, whatever the enclosure, totally sealed for hours. Schmitt's design would have allowed Zyklon B gas to be pumped into an enclosed space and not require the manual sprinkle of the pellets.

Looking up from the Schmitt design review document, "Hines, what do we have on the judges?"

"Have not read it all yet, but to start with, it appears there is no evidence the Israelis influenced their selection. All three are senior judges in their home countries and well respected."

"Yes, yes, but that tells me nothing."

"Well, this might interest you. All three are very senior judges in countries with less than robust court systems, and any extended absence will quickly cause a case backlog. I take that to mean that all were told or at least believe the Tribunal will not be very long and would expect them to have an interest in speedy proceedings. And finally, all are known for their harsh sentencing."

"Anything about their impartiality: conviction, acquittal rates?"

"On only the chief judge, and he has only slightly convicted more than acquitted, but there is nothing in the documents as to the actual cases or even the number of cases he has presided over, so I am not sure his conviction rate means anything."

Shapiro looks at Jones, "Anything else, Linda?" "Not really. Think the biggest issue we are going to have is their desire to have a quick Tribunal and return home, which means there will be no delays."

"Yes, the whole matter is moving much too fast for my liking. The UN says, 'No delay,' and the judges need for it to be quick. I think the Israelis thought this was a done deal from day 1. I don't see it yet, but maybe they are right."

"Shapiro, the prosecution: the only thing I see that stands out about them is that Mr. Portnoy has political ambitions, and there are rumors that he wants to run for the Kismet. Background from support says that apparently, Mr. Portnoy's competition for the Kismet election leaned on some higher-up's and got Portnoy put on this case to get him out of the country. Support also says that Portnoy objected to being made a part of the prosecution but then when told, it would be a great publicity opportunity, willingly joined the prosecution. I would expect him to be their courtroom speaker."

Shapiro looks out the window. "Enough for today, leave all documents here, but I want everyone to have read them all by noon tomorrow. We will gather then again. Does anyone need anything more from support: any questions for them?" "No" "Tomorrow then."

"Oh, before we leave, anyone know where Herman is right now?"

"Jones, before tomorrow's meeting here, find out where Mr. Schmitt is and arrange to talk with him. Get his side of the story if you can." "I am not a criminal lawyer. Not sure I know what to be asking him." "Just hear him out, but make sure to ask him if he ever traveled to a camp while he was designing." "I will try."

The Witness

9 September 2007, Sunday

Herman is fetched from his cell and taken to a room. He is told there is a phone call coming in for him and to wait.

"Phone call: not reporters, is it? "No, it is someone on your defense team in America."

"America: a phone call from America!"

At 9 am, Jones places a call to the phone number he has been given, and Herman answers on the first ring.

"Mr. Schmitt?" "Yes, I am here."

"Mr. Schmitt, I am Julies Jones, a member of your defense team in America. Can you hear me?"

"I hear. Please, Mr. Jones, get me out of this terrible place. I did nothing wrong."

"Herman, may I call you that? Herman, we are working very hard on your case, but we need to hear your side of the story. Can you tell me why they think they arrested you?"

"I don't know. I am a designer that is all. I was never a soldier. The company I work for gives me a job to design, and I do; that's all I know."

"Herman, did your company build your design?" "No, the company I work for only does design work."

"Do you know who hired your company for the work?"

"No. Company designs for many chemical companies in Germany."

"Ok. Herman, did you ever visit a concentration camp?"

"Camp: I did not even know such places existed. I was a designer, nothing more."

"Herman, the prosecution says you knew the intended use of your design. Is that true?"

"No, kill, no one, I did not kill Jews. Never travel for work until after the war. I do nothing like they say. Design dispenser, yes, but nothing else. Get me out of here, Mr. Jones; I don't even have my own clothes!"

"Herman, I am sorry, but there is no way I or the team can get you out. However, I will look into having your clothes shipped to The Hague. It is our understanding that you will be moved to The

Hague tomorrow, and it will be much better for you. Do you have any questions for me?"

"When will you be there?" "Not sure Herman, but soon." "We have many questions for you and will see you as soon as we can when we get there."

"Ok, Mr. Jones. I am innocent. I kill no one." "Goodbye, Mr. Schmitt. Talk again soon."

When Shapiro arrives at the meeting room at the IEE headquarters, 2 documents from the UN are there. Upon opening, the prosecution has submitted two new pieces of evidence to the UN. One is a poor copy of an invoice from a company called Deutschland Mechanish to IG Farben, and the other is an announcement that the prosecution intends to present a witness that can place Herman at Auschwitz in 1943.

"New evidence now" He had understood from the beginning that Tribunal rules were different."

Hines and Jones come in, finding Shapiro staring out a window.

"Sir, are you alright?"

"Look on the table, the two new documents."

Jones picks up one and Hines the other. They read and then swap documents.

"Nice, huh, new evidence and a witness that says Schmitt was at Auschwitz in 1943. A witness: a Holocaust survivor witness!"

Jones and Hines say nothing.

Shapiro sits down and shoves the new documents out of the way. "So, everything we have now read? Jones, you talk to Schmitt?"

"Yes, a couple of hours ago. He claims he only designed the dispenser and did not know its intended use. He also claims he did not know about the camps at the time."

"You believe him?"

"I am not sure. As I said, I am not a criminal attorney." "Fine, fine, but what does your gut say?" "He is telling the truth. He admits he did the design, but then when he signed it, it was gone, and he never had anything to do with his design again. He also does not have his clothes from the nursing home. I am going to arrange for them to be shipped to the Hague."

"Get him a new suit or arrange to get him a new suit."

"A witness", Shapiro says, looking at Hines. "What do we do about a witness, Linda?" What can we do?"

"The announcement does not provide her name, I guess for safety or security reasons, so there is not much research we can do on her. Shapiro, I doubt there is much we can do other than somehow prove Herman never was at Auschwitz or any other camp."

"Prove something he did not do. Prove he was never at a camp. I will speak to support to see if they can research how Schmitt would have traveled in 1943 to Auschwitz or even if it was possible." " Any other ideas from you two?"

"Not about the witness and travel but this other document. I assume it is intended to show IG Farben was the one who ordered the design Schmitt did. Of course, IG Farben was into Zyklon B at the time, and it makes sense it might be them, but I don't remember any sort of work number or order number on Herman's signed design, so how can this invoice be for that? How do we know what it was for?"

Shapiro pulls out the design from a pile and spreads it out. "I don't see any work order or any kind of number on this copy. I will ask support to look into it. IG Farben." "An invoice to IG Farben, it says the amount is 600 Reichsmarks. How much did Schmitt make per week in 1943? I will have support look into it."

Hines leans back in her chair. "I think we ought to get to The Hague."

"Jones, did you tell Schmitt not to talk with anyone before we get there?" "No, should I have?"

Shapiro shakes his head from side to side. "You're right, Linda. We need to get to the Hague and meet Schmitt. He has to know something he is not telling. Let's give support a day to see what they can come up with on this new evidence, and we will think about heading to The Hague. Agreed?"

"Linda, I think we ought to submit. "Contesting of Evidence" documents on Schmitt's design and lack of any evidence it was ever actually fabricated or used as there are no images of it in any of the prosecution's evidence submissions. And with no work order number on Schmitt's drawings or the invoice, another contesting document about the invoice, and no clear link to Herman's design. Think you can get these two out the door tomorrow?"

"Of course, Shapiro, they will be headed to the UN tomorrow."

"The witness, what do you think, Linda?"

"The prosecution has submitted documents that prove she was at Auschwitz in 1943. I don't see much to challenge. Certainly, the man she saw could be anyone, but I don't think we ought to challenge her now. Maybe if we can prove Herman never traveled to Auschwitz, but I have my doubts, we will be able to prove that."

Ready?

10 September 2007

On Monday, Herman is taken from his cell, told to change back into his street clothes, handcuffed with his hands in front this time, and led out to a car and a trip to the airport. Herman is being moved to The Hague.

Herman does not like to fly and tells the two policemen who escort him so, but he gets only silence. On the plane, Herman, for the first time, actually feels like a criminal. He is handcuffed and seated between the 2 escorts, and more than once, someone walks the aisle of the plane and stares at Herman. Herman can tell by the looks he gets that everyone is wondering what an awful thing Herman has done.

When Herman and his escorts arrive in The Hague, 2 Israeli military are at the airport waiting, and they quickly sign various prisoner transfer forms and load Herman into a black, extra-large, American-made Suburban. If Herman felt like a criminal on the airplane, he now feels like someone being taken to an execution.

As a requirement for UN authorization of the Schmitt Tribunal, the Israelis must provide court facilities, and although unclear exactly how the prosecution team had managed it, the court was to be in a recently closed, grand old hotel that would serve as lodging for all and had several large ballrooms of which one would host the actual Tribunal. Security, provided by the Israelis, was to be tight, with guarded access to the hotel.

When the large Suburban pulls up into the covered entrance of the Tribunal's hotel, Herman looks out the window of the car and does not understand. Not sure what he had expected, he certainly did not expect this and is even more confused when he is led up the steps through the double glass doors and across an expansive lobby to what had obviously been the front desk of the hotel.

Room 1010: Herman is assigned room 1010 and, with handcuffs removed, is escorted to a double bank of elevators and up to an open room 1010, told to go in, the door closed, and he hears it lock from the outside.

Compared to the prison cell in Berlin, Herman's 'cell' here is a palace. In what must be his living room, there are couches, chairs, and floor-to-ceiling windows along the outer wall, and Herman has a separate bedroom and bath. Herman is not sure he has ever stayed in such an elegant hotel before and begins to feel a little better about his situation.

Sitting on the bed, the mattress is soft and does not smell, and Herman lies back and almost immediately falls asleep.

When Shapiro arrives at the New Jersey meeting room, he sits down, sips his coffee, and opens the documents that have been placed right in front of his chair. The first is labeled "Schmitt Design," and he opens it first.

Another engineer has been brought in to help perform a more detailed examination of Schmitt's gas dispenser, and both engineers agree that Herman's design would not work. Given a well-defined, well-known, sublimation rate of Zyklon B pellets, Schmitt's designed pellet chamber simply does not have enough surface area for any blower to pick up enough gas for any real use. Only if the sublimation chamber surface area was increased by at least 100 percent, if not closer to 200%, and pellets were continuously fed into the chamber, would there be any chance that enough air could be moved over the pellets to fumigate any enclosed space.

"It is a bad design. Herman's design is faulty. Even if someone had built the dispenser for use in the camps, it would not have worked! Would it be enough?"

Hines comes in, and Shapiro holds up the document. "Take a look at this!"

Hines sits down and begins to read: "Sublimation rate?"

"The rate at which a solid turns into gas without becoming a liquid first, old case," says Shapiro.

"Isaac, it won't work! Herman's design could not have ever been used by the Nazis! That is what I read. But is this going to be enough, Shapiro? We need about 5 or 10 engineers to agree and sign some document as evidence submitted to the Tribunal." "Agreed", says Shapiro. "You open this other document and wait for Jones while I go speak to the support folks."

Hines stands up and out loud: "Does not work. Cannot work!"

She is still standing when Jones comes in.

"Herman's design is faulty; it won't work!"

"What?" says Jones as Linda hands him the support document on Schmitt's design.

Jones reads and begins to laugh. "As designed, it will not meet any intended purpose. It is a dud!"

"Shapiro has seen it and gone to meet with the support staff. We need ten engineers to review, agree the design is faulty and all sign a document we can submit to the Tribunal."

"What Tribunal? This document should sink the whole case. There is no case. No one in their right mind would criminally convict someone for a design that is useless: maybe a breach of contract or something maybe, but only monetary, not criminal."

Shapiro returns smiling. "Support says they will get right on it. Apparently, Society of Industrial Engineers is willing to review and sign a document stating faulty design if they concur. But it might take until Wednesday to complete and sign such a document, and I don't think we can wait that long. We have to get to the Hague and Herman." "Linda, is there anything in the witness research document?"

"Research says they have narrowed down who the witness might be to 3 possibilities, all women, and of the 3, only 2 are well enough to travel."

"How did the prosecution find any witnesses that claim they saw Schmitt at Auschwitz?"

"Apparently, the Israeli government knows the name of every camp survivor, and they went through the names and associated camps and created a list and then interviewed survivors, showing them some pictures of Herman taken when he was first arrested until they found a witness or at least one woman who claims she saw Schmitt at the camp."

"She could not have been very old at that time. How can she be so sure that Herman is who she saw after all the years?"

"Support says all three possible witnesses were 12 or 13 years old in 1943, and all worked doing various duties around the camp. One of their jobs was to take sealed Zyklon B canisters that had been taken from a shed by other prisoners and stockpiled at the rear of the death house, up a ladder, and place several canisters around the holes in the roof of the death house. Apparently, during one of the times they were moving canisters to the roof, a man not wearing a uniform came to the camp, climbed the ladder, walked around the roof for a while, and then went down the ladder and left."

"And this witness says that man was Herman?"

"Yes."

"Linda, I don't know much, but my guess is Holocaust survivors are tough to cross-examine, "says Shapiro, the smile now gone from his face.

"I am going to have to really think about this one, Shapiro. You are right. Should we even cross-examine her? With Herman's design being faulty, isn't that enough if we can get a document proving it is a bad design?"

"Linda, I do not know. This is a Holocaust Tribunal involving Zyklon B. Who is to say what the judges might do? Right now, we don't have the document we need, and for all we know, the prosecution might pop out with some new evidence tomorrow, the day after, or even during the proceedings. No, we have to prepare for everything."

"If we get a signed, faulty design document, maybe you could present it to the lead prosecutor and suggest going forward with the Tribunal is not a good idea?"

"I am not sure how to handle the document we do not have. Perhaps present to Mr. Metzmann, perhaps simply enter into evidence before the Tribunal starts, or maybe wait until after the first day and submit it then. But now, we really must get to The Hague and Mr. Schmitt. When I talked to support earlier, they said that considering the flight time and time difference, we really must leave tonight at 10 or so to get into The Hague by 7 pm tomorrow. Ready?"

The Tribunal Hotel

11 September 2007, Tuesday

Only five days from the start of the Tribunal, Shapiro, Hines, and Jones arrive in The Hague a little after 7 pm local time and, after a short taxi ride, are outside the grand old hotel. At the door, an Israeli guard in military uniform meets them. "Defense Team, Shapiro"

The hotel lobby is immense but mostly empty. 2 long couches and a couple of padded chairs are arranged not far from the front desk. A mass of furniture that was obviously in the lobby is stacked along one wall but has been moved out of the way. Straight ahead, two banks of elevators, and to the left, a long, wide hallway with what appears to be a bar and several dining rooms.

Shapiro, Hines, and Jones take it all in. "Most unusual court I have ever been in," mutters Shapiro and turns to the front desk: "Shapiro and group for the defense."

"Yes sir, welcome. You are all set. All 3 of you will have rooms on the 10th floor: Mr. Shapiro, your key, Ms. Hines, Mr. Jones. Please note that no one has access to your rooms except you. Support staff must have someone present; thus, you must call when you wish to receive service of any kind. Your rooms are ready now." "Have any questions?"

Shapiro stands for a moment, "You have not asked for our credit cards?" "No sir, not needed. Israel is currently leasing the hotel and paying for everything. You will not be charged for hotel-provided service."

"Sorry, but I was not told about such an arrangement. Mr. Schmitt's defense team cannot be seen as taking favors from Israel; no, we must pay." "Sir, all services are being billed by name. I am sure we can produce a bill for all services you, Ms. Hines, and Mr. Jones use while here at the end of the Tribunal."

"Please confirm the separate billing with whoever is doing the billing. I need a document stating the arrangement." "Yes sir, I will attend to it. Do you need help with your baggage?" "No."

"Oh, if you can, can you tell me who is currently in the hotel?"

"Mr. Schmitt is on floor 10 and Mr. Metzmann and his team are on the 9th floor."

"The judges are not here yet?"

"No sir. I am told they will arrive on Sunday, the 16th."

"The room where the Tribunal is to be held"

"Just Down the hall, to the left of the elevators. The old Grand ballroom is being set up." "And if we need anything, someone will be at this desk to answer?" "Yes sir, day and night. Please note that our support staff is rather limited with so few guests, but we will make every effort to please any request as quickly as possible. The guards in the hotel go off duty at 11 pm when hotel access is barred for the night. Please do not exit the building after 11."

"I see security cameras." "Those have been turned off, sir." "Is there a Tribunal support office?" "Yes sir. We are using the utility room on this floor at the far end of the hallway, manned around the clock."

The guard at the elevator sees the group approach, opens an elevator door, and pushes the button for the 10th floor. "Meet in an hour, my room." Shapiro says, "Not long, as I know I need, we all need, some sleep."

Stepping out of the elevator, they are greeted by another military guard. "Shapiro, defense," and all quickly find their rooms.

Shapiro is given the largest room and finds that a large desk table has been placed in his "living room" equipped with multiple chairs, a telephone, pens, pencils, and paper, but no FAX machine and no waiting new documents from NJ or the UN.

He finds a small refrigerator but it is not stocked and could use a drink. He would have to look into getting a Fax machine and some water or even whiskey. After one quick look around his room, he heads down to the lobby to find the Tribunal support staff.

Hines and Jones find their rooms, and although not as large as they had expected, given the nature of the hotel, Hines immediately takes a shower while Jones calls his wife as promised upon arrival.

On the ground floor, Shapiro walks down the long hallway past ballroom after ballroom until he comes to the staff and cargo elevator on the right, the staff hotel entrance door, a kitchen door, one for laundry, and across from it, a metal door, marked "System Utilities." He tries the handle, and the door opens, and he steps inside.

"This place is huge!" At least four times the size of his own room, Shapiro begins looking about: the unfinished walls, the concrete ceiling covered with pipes and conduit, the uncarpeted concrete floor, and on every wall, huge metal boxes attached with giant levers on their sides and racks of racks of various control panels, some blinking their small indicator lights.

Along one wall is a small console and one chair, with three dark video displays. And out of place, not 5 feet from the door, is a long card table, hosting two sitting, suited men, smiling away at him.

"Sir, can we help you?"

"2, only 2", thinks Shapiro. "Bet the Israelis have a large staff somewhere."

"Good evening. I am Mr. Shapiro, lead defense counsel in the coming Tribunal. Is this the court support office?" The two men nod their heads. "I need a fax machine in my room. Also, can the refrigerator be stocked with water and perhaps some whiskey?"

"Yes, we can see to that. Someone will bring you a Fax machine from the old business center, and we will see the hotel support staff, what there is of it, will stock your refrigerator: anything else?"

"Please, lots of paper for the fax machine and a coffee maker that makes a full pot at a time." "Any particular brand of coffee" "No, just make sure there is plenty of coffee. Oh, and food? It was not clear in the information I received on Tribunal operation how food will be handled?"

"Food will be provided to your rooms, or if you would rather, the smaller dining room here can be used and staffed, and Mr. Metzmann has already ordered the bar reopened, open 24 hours a day and stocked."

"And a menu of food available"

"Sir, Mr. Metzmann insisted on two chefs, and you can order anything you wish, whatever you wish. Of course, some things like a country-specific dish will require a 1-day notice."

"Good. Can I call you if I need anything else?" "Yes, someone will man the telephone here 24 hours a day. Will that be all sir?"

Shapiro stands for a moment. "Can you produce typed documents or presentation materials I might need?"

"Sir, we cannot. We have been told it would be improper for a single office to support both the prosecution and the defense. I am sure you understand."

"Yes, well, thank you. I will call if I need something, and please make sure there is a lot of whisky in my room," and begins to turn away, "The Statues? Do I get a copy of the Tribunal statues? I did not see one in my room?"

"We do have a complete set of Statues but only one. If you call, we can arrange for your use in a room on this floor. Oh, and sir, since you are now here, the UN considers the Tribunal to have officially begun, and all document submissions, requests, etc., you might make are to be submitted to his office, sealed, to be presented to the judges when they arrive."

"I understand."

Shapiro leaves the doorway of the support staff office and heads to the bar. "Can I help you sir?" "Whiskey" "Yes sir, coming right up and a brand?" "No" "A bottle."

When Shapiro is at the elevator, the door opens, and out steps, a portly man with a smile and his hand stuck out, "Mr. Shapiro? I am Isaak Metzmann, the lead prosecutor. See, you have found the bar. You have everything you need?" Shapiro shakes Metzmann's hand.

"Well, yes and no. I understand I will have to have my own court materials created using an outside source, and I need to talk with you about this billing arrangement."

"Ah, yes, billing. I do understand your concern, and I apologize, but approval by the UN for the Tribunal was much faster coming than we anticipated, so there has been a rush with getting space, security, and such. Again, I apologize. I understand you want a document that states you were unaware of the billing arrangement and have agreed to pay an itemized bill at the end of the Tribunal?"

"Thank you, a document will be most helpful. A question, if I may? Why did the UN really turn down your use of the ICC?"

"The ICC was clear that they could only prosecute if the crime had been committed after 2002. I would have much preferred the ICC, but as you know, time is running out on prosecuting those that participated in the Holocaust."

"Well, nice to meet you, Mr. Metzmann, but I really must be going. I am meeting with the defense team in my room in a few minutes before getting some sleep. Nice to meet you outside of the courtroom."

"Yes, we will meet again soon." Metzmann turns and heads to the bar.

Whiskey and Sleep.

When Shapiro gets into his room, he opens the whiskey bottle, pours himself a large glass, and sits down at his desk. "Need to call

NJ tomorrow and check on the design review document," opening his huge briefcase and pulling out the file he has on Herman.

Married once, wife now deceased, one estranged son: never in the military and worked for Deutschland Mechanish for 20 years.

There is a knock at the door, and it is Hines and Jones.

Shapiro quickly relays what he has learned from the support office and tasks Jones with locating a documents and presentation service.

"Tomorrow, say 10 am, we meet here and talk about Mr. Schmitt before having him brought here?" Jones and Hines agree.

Another knock at the door, and it is one of the two men from the support office. There is a cart holding a fax machine and several reams of paper, but no coffee pot or stock for the refrigerator: "A good time, sir?" "Yes and can you hook the machine up?" "Yes sir."

Hines and Jones are talking, but Shapiro makes a loud, throat-clear sound, and talking stops.

The Fax machine is set on the desk and wired. Paper stacked under the desk.

"Thank you. Refrigerator and coffee pot tomorrow?" "Yes sir."

Shapiro hears the door latch, "No talking about the case with any hotel support staff present."

"Shapiro, what's to say our rooms aren't bugged?"

"I don't want to even think about that. It would be such a breach of conduct. No, I doubt Mr. Metzmann would risk such a thing. Anyone want some whiskey?"

"I just want to sleep," says Hines, rising to her feet.

Did Herman Know?

12 September 2007, Wednesday.

Shapiro is still asleep when he hears a loud knock: "Mr. Shapiro, are you in there, refrigerator stocking." "Hello?"

It is 9:30 am.

"Most sorry: slept late today." "Thanks for waking me up."

The refrigerator gets bottled water, some canned juices and 3 bottles of whiskey and a huge coffee maker are placed on the table housing the refrigerator.

"Sir, I found this outside your door," and Shapiro gets handed a document marked "Tribunal Submission: Mr. Schmitt to Testify".

The door latches and Shapiro, still wearing his robe and slippers, throws the document on his desk and begins to make a pot of coffee.

"Schmitt must testify." Well, that decision is made. From the beginning, he has gone back and forth over whether or not he should put Herman on the stand but was holding off making such a decision until he had had time to meet and question Mr. Schmitt.

Shapiro picks up the phone and calls NJ.

"Hello, Mr. Todd, speaking." "Todd, Shapiro." "Yes sir, how was your trip?" "Fine, very long, but we are here, and I have a fax machine now with the same phone number. What is the status of the design review signed document?"

"A document has been crafted and is now circulating among the engineers for signatures."

"They did all agree the design is faulty and would not work?"

"Yes sir."

"Fax a copy as soon as you can, no matter the time here, and have you arranged for the original to be sent to me via air mail?"

"Yes sir, but you will not get the original until the 14th, Friday, at the earliest."

"Friday: anything else?" "Research is still working on that invoice but still cannot find any additional invoices from Mechanish to Farben, nothing on the Schmitt design ever being built, and nothing on his possible travel to a camp." "Thank you, Bob."

"Perhaps a Fax copy later today."

Shapiro heads to his bedroom to get dressed when Hines and Jones knock on his door.

"Come in, just got off the phone with NJ. Help yourself to some coffee or what's in the refrigerator. I will be right back; I need to change. Oh, and check out the package on my desk. Metzmann is calling Herman to testify."

"Jones, it is time for Herman. Go get him."

Shapiro has changed and is at his desk while Hines is walking in circles around the room, thinking about Herman testifying, when there is a knock at the door. Hines goes and opens it. "Herman, meet Ms. Hines, Ms. Hines, meet Mr. Herman Schmitt," Jones says in German. In English: "Ok, to come in?" "Yes," calls out Shapiro, "let's meet Mr. Schmitt."

Shapiro stands up and is immediately shocked at how short and frail Herman is.

"Come in, come in. Have a seat right here. Good to finally meet you. I am Mr. Isaac Shapiro, lead defense counsel for this Tribunal, your Tribunal." Jones translates into German for Herman, but Herman does not say a word and sits down where instructed.

"Mr. Schmitt, may I call you Herman?" Jones translates and Herman nods. "Good, well Herman, we are here to see justice is done, and we feel that given what we know of the charges and the evidence, we think you are innocent and will work very hard to ensure that is the verdict of the Tribunal. But Herman, we must have your side of the story. First, have you talked with anyone since you were here, or have you called anyone? Have you spoken to your son? Has anyone from the prosecution or a reporter spoken with you?"

Herman waits for the translation, "No, not talk to son or anyone. I do talk sometimes to the girl who brings me breakfast every day. She speaks German. College student, work here just in the mornings. Thinks I must be important, to have such a big room and a guard outside my door."

Jones translates.

"So, you have never talked about the coming trial with anyone?"

"No."

"Now, Herman, why do you think the Israelis have charged you? According to them, you did some design work that dispenses gas. Can you tell us about your work, specifically this gas dispenser?"

Jones translates and Herman listens but does not speak. "Herman?" says Jones, "Please tell us about your work." Herman looks at the three and then out the window. "I am engineer. I was never a soldier. I did not kill anyone. I did not kill Jews. I am innocent." Jones translates and then, "But Herman, the design, your work, we have to know." "I was very young at the start of the war and, in 1941, graduated from mechanical engineering school. School is gone now, but I was hired by a small German company, now also gone, Deutschland Mechanish, to do various mechanical designs. Work came from large companies all over Germany. I was given the idea of what was required and told to come up with a design. And that is what I did: many projects over many years. I am not a soldier; I have never been a soldier and did what I was given to do." Jones translates.

"Herman, did you like your job? Everyone is nice there? What did you get paid a week?"

Jones translates and Herman has to think awhile.

"150 Reichsmarks per week, I think that is right. Yes, I like it there and worked there for 20 years. People come and go, but after a while, I am more senior, get more money, and better, bigger projects. Not so much to begin with."

Shapiro shuffles papers and then selects and opens one that becomes several rather large drawings and rotates them on the desktop until they are in front of Herman. "Herman, is this your signature at the bottom? Is this one of your designs?"

Herman picks up a corner and glances at it. "Yes, I do this. I design this: my signature. It has been so long ago, hard to remember. Not a difficult design, but it required a lot of natural rubber and rubber short in those days. All go to war."

"And the title of the design: it says 'Zyklon B Gas Dispenser,' is that correct?"

Herman leans back away from the table. "Yes, the design was for Zyklon B. The reason I say much rubber is required is because Zyklon B, a gas pesticide, is very harmful to breathe." "Yes, well, Herman, you admit you designed this Zyklon B gas dispenser unit, and you knew how it was to be used?" Shapiro raises his voice to emphasize, "Did you know how it was to be used?" Jones translates and Herman sits up straight.

"I know Zyklon B pesticide, so assume in some fumigation. I am aware that Zyklon B used to fumigate railroad cars, trucks, and ships, so I assume that. I was not told where it was to be used or even the company requesting the design. Just make the design safe for the user, and that is what I did. All I know."

"Herman, are you sure you did not know how your design was to be used? I mean, in the death camps to kill Jews?"

"No, no, no", Herman says, shaking his head. "I never knew about camps at the time. Who did? I was given a job and did it."

Shapiro looks at Jones and Hines, "Herman, did you build your design, or do you know if it was actually constructed?"

Herman's face changes for a moment, "No, you do not understand. I design, never build. The design, when complete, was taken by the boss, and I was given another design to do. My company, we only do design, not fabricate."

"Herman, I want to understand. You were given a job to design a Zyklon B gas dispenser that was safe for users, but you did not know how the design was to be used, and you, yourself, were not involved in the actual construction of your design? Did you ever have to go out and visit where your design was to be installed, ever?"

Herman looks annoyed, "No, I told you, I never build. I never have to go to any site to get any information needed to complete a design. I do not do that. I am only a junior engineer when I do this work. Design was simple, that is why given to me. Later, after many years and after the war, I worked with a team of engineers on larger, more complex design for chemical plants, but my portion did not require plant visits."

Shapiro looks at Hines and Jones, "Anything from you 2?"

Looking at the design, which is totally foreign to her, Jones says, "No, I don't but there must be more than just this document, design."

"Yes, lots of documents about the use of Zyklon at the concentration camps and even pictures of Zyklon canisters and German SS dropping canisters into holes in the roof of the gassing chamber. Plenty of evidence that Zyklon was used at the camps," says Shapiro, thumbing through a huge stack of paper and images.

"Herman, you say you did not know who ordered your design and its intended use."

Herman only nods in agreement.

"Herman, you ever heard of a company called IG Farben?

Herman only nods again.

"Did the company you worked for ever do work for IG Farben?"

"Yes, we did work for Farben, lots of work during the war but not so much after."

"Did you ever work on a job for Farben?"

"I not sure, I think, yes."

"Was the Zyklon B dispenser done for Farben?"

Herman is silent.

"Was the Zyklon B dispenser done for Farben?"

"Yes, the design was for Farben."

"The truth, Herman, did you know how your design was to be used?"

"No."

"Herman. When you were designing the dispenser, didn't you wonder where your design might be installed?" "Not even curious?"

"No, I only design."

"Herman, we need the truth. An engineer in the US says that because your design was for a stationary mount, you either knew or could have guessed that its intent was the camps. Did you know? Did you suspect?"

Herman is mute.

"Herman, if you knew, you must tell us. We have nothing in documents that say you knew, but if we present that you did not know about the intended use and then the prosecution has evidence that you did, it will be bad for everyone: the truth Herman."

"I knew. I was told to be used in the 'Jewish problem.' I did not know about camps at that time, but I knew Germans wanted all Jews gone. I did not want to think about it."

Shapiro writes down something and turns his chair away from Herman. "Jones, please take Mr. Schmitt back to his room. We are done with Mr. Schmitt for the day."

Jones stands up and motions for Herman to stand.

"Did you ever have to do a revision of your design? Is the design on Mr. Shapiro's desk the only time you did design on the dispenser?"

"No, no revision. Do and never see design again."

"Jones, please take Mr. Schmitt to his room and come right back, we need to visit the courtroom."

Shapiro and Hines sit in silence, trying to grasp how they will handle what they have just learned from Herman.

No evidence in any documentation they have proves that Herman knew his design was for the concentration camps or even any evidence that the work was done for IG Farben, other than the invoice with no work order number. However, in Shapiro's mind, a significant portion of Herman's defense is based on his not knowing the company that required the design or the intended use. If Shapiro used that as a core defense issue and Metzmann had documentation that proved Herman knew about IG Farben or the camps, then the case was lost. At a minimum, Shapiro could not start his presentation to the court that Herman knew nothing about use.

Hines was having the same thoughts.

Jones returns and Shapiro is up out of his chair; Hines follows, and they head down to find the courtroom for a view.

The Earpieces

In most trial cases, the layout of the court is usually not very significant, but, in this case, using a hotel called for at least a visit, an idea of what they might have to deal with: perhaps bad acoustics or limited light and the language issue.

Off the elevator, they turn towards the long hall that the desk clerk said would be the Tribunal room, and with another guard standing outside a double set of doors on the left. As they approach, the guard opens the door for them, follows them, and switches on all the lights.

"Grand Ballroom, indeed!" says Shapiro out loud, as the room is huge with multiple chandeliers and, along the right wall, full floor-to-ceiling windows. Stacked by the doors is a mass of what are round dining table and chairs, and deep inside on the rear wall is a long table with three folding chairs and a box with lights in front of the center chair. Above is a large electric clock. To the left side of the judge's 'bench' are two translator glass paneled boxes with wires strung along the front. To the right side of the bench a single chair, a witness chair, with a box and headpiece underneath.

On the left and right of the front table are two shorter tables, with the table on the left having four folding chairs and, on the right, only 3. On each table, again, a box in the middle with headpieces installed for translations.

Shapiro, Hines, and Jones walk towards their long table.

"It is stuffy in here," says Hines.

Jones picks up one of the headsets and tries it on. The earpieces fit well, and it is clear that a switch on the box on the table is for switching on and off the microphone portion of the four headsets provided. Jones flips a switch, but nothing happens.

"Shapiro, please inform the Tribunal support staff I must be allowed to test the translation support system. If possible, I would like the German-to-English translator to be in attendance when I test."

"You talk to the support staff and also mention we need some more air in here," Shapiro responds, sitting in the center folding chair. "Folding chairs is the best we can get? Jones, also ask the support staff about better chairs."

"Well, seen enough?"

"I think so," says Hines.

"Good, back to my room."

"I am going to the support office first. Will meet you in a bit," says Jones.

"Utility room at the end of the hall": Shapiro in a loud voice.

Beware

Shapiro and Hines step out on the 10th floor, and Hines stops at her room. "Give me a moment. I will be right there." Shapiro continues to his room further down the hall. When he gets there, no packages are waiting for him.

Shapiro goes to the whiskey, pours himself one, and just stands, sipping.

The phone rings. "Hello, Isaac Shapiro here."

"Ah Mr. Shapiro, it is Isaak Metzmann. How are you getting along now?" "Much better, thank you, the whiskey arrived." Metzmann laughs. "Mr. Shapiro, how about we all meet tonight for dinner?" Shapiro is taken aback. Not normal for the defense and prosecution to meet so informally, but Tribunal rules are different as he is learning.

"No, thank you. We have just gotten back from the Tribunal room and have some work to do. Dinner will be in our rooms or my room tonight: working."

"Oh, Mr. Shapiro, you must eat, and I would so like to get off on the right foot with you and your team. Are you sure you will not join me?"

Shapiro thinks about it. "Perhaps Ms. Hines could join you?"

"Yes, of course. I would like to have a drink with you, but Ms. Hines will be delightful. I have heard very good things about her. Say 6 o'clock outside the lobby elevator?" "Yes, she will be there. Thank you. We will have dinner soon, I promise."

"Tell Hines that she must beware of my Mr. Braun. He is German and has a reputation as a ladies' man!" "Of course, at 6 o'clock then, and thank you again."

Shapiro puts down the phone and hears Hines's knock.

"Ah, Linda, I just got a call from Mr. Metzmann. You are joining him, Mr. Portnoy, and Mr. Braun for dinner at 6. You were not here, or I would have asked you." "And why just me", Linda already knowing what is coming. "I initially told Metzmann that none of us could join him but then thought perhaps there is something to be gained by meeting all three, and I thought of you. Don't mean anything now, but being a woman and attractive and they all being men, well." "Shapiro, I could whack you for saying that! I have worked very hard to become a good lawyer, not a woman lawyer, but a good lawyer." "Linda, I am sorry, I apologize, but please do the dinner. Anything you can glean about any one of them might help us. Please."

Hines heads towards the whiskey but answers Jones's knock at the door.

"Tribunal support will try for better chairs and get some more air into the room. I am to test the German translator and the headpiece system tomorrow morning. I also want to line up the presentation service we need."

"Linda is meeting Metzmann and the group for dinner tonight!"

"And only her", Jones looking at Linda.

"I don't want to talk about it. I need a real drink. I'm going down to the bar before dinner."

"Jones, can you call up some food for us? We are working tonight."

Herman Swears

Braun is in the bar sipping away when he sees Ms. Hines in the mirror behind the bar come in and appear headed straight towards him.

"Mr. Braun, Linda Hines for the defense," sticking her hand out and Braun shaking it softly and quickly. With a big smile, eyes directly into hers, "How did you know it was me?" "Well, I understand Mr. Metzmann and Mr. Portnoy are a good bit older than you appear to be, so it leaves only you." "Well done, Ms. Hines, and if I may, you look very smart in the business suit. What would you like to drink?"

With the bar empty, the two begin sharing some about themselves, and after a while, Hines looks away and says to the empty bar more than to Braun, "I needed this."

"This trial: Schmitt? Why now? I mean, it has been 63 years, and he is an old man." Braun lifts his glass and takes a long drink, "Oh, the Tribunal, let's not talk of that. I am here because I was told to be. Germans are sorry: Holocaust and all that. Quite honestly, I don't know much about the case and don't care to. I am here to represent Germany and again declare that we are most sorry."

Hines picks up her wine and places the glass to her mouth, but she does not drink; instead, she moves it to one side. "OK, so can you at least tell me how Mr. Metzmann and Mr. Portnoy feel about their case? Are they confident? I understand the UN would not approve a trial at the ICC, so why go forward?"

Braun is listening, but his attention now is on Ms. Hines, 'Linda,' pretty face, perfect lipstick, and what seems to him through the business suit to have one hell of 'a good body.' "Oh, of course, they feel comfortable about a conviction, and although I should not be telling you this, but they want a harsh sentence or at least Mr. Portnoy does. It wasn't them, but the Israelis charged 2 German corporate types for knowingly making Zyklon B for the concentration camps, and old Herman is just a little further along that same path. Anyone who was involved in Zyklon B is fair game."

"I have not reviewed everything, but Herman swears he did not know how his design was to be used and was never told or even knew about the concentration camps."

"Oh, he did not know, he says, well that is surprising, isn't it? What else is he going to tell you that he hated all Jews and could not wait to install his Zyklon dispenser at Auschwitz, Dachau? I don't know much about the case, but I am sure you do not have the evidence Metzmann has."

Hines is about to ask, "What evidence?" when in walks Metzmann and Portnoy with Metzmann waving his hands, "Come on. I am starving."

An Hour's Silence

Thursday, 13 September 2007.

Shapiro is up early, hoping the Fax has been active overnight, but there is nothing.

He rereads the mechanical engineer's review of Herman's design and learns more than he ever wanted to know about how Zyklon B is normally used in fumigation and perhaps, why Herman had been tasked to design something new.

But Herman's design would not work, or so one engineer in the US has said. Shapiro needs a confirmation opinion of at least five experienced engineers and formalized for submission to the court.

At 9 am, Jones arrives and starts a pot of coffee. Shapiro stops reading but sees the death house in his mind. As a Jew, his family also lost relatives to the Nazis, and for a second, he feels dislike, disdain, and even revulsion for Herman.

Hines comes into the room and heads for the coffee.

"How was dinner Linda? Learn anything worth sharing?"

"Dinner: Nothing. Metzmann did most of the talking and eating and went on and on about the sites he wanted to see before returning to Israel. He is most definitely confident, and it is also clear that he does not think the trial will last long. He was surprised about us coming to Herman's defense, as he thought it would be a court-appointed defender and an easy win for them. But I did learn from the German Braun that Metzmann has some evidence against Herman they have not shared with us. I was about to ask what it might be, but then dinner."

"Braun, at dinner, said this", Shapiro taking a cup of coffee from Jones. "No, I went to the bar before dinner, and Braun was there, and we talked."

"Evidence we do not have. What the hell could it be? Perhaps they have some documents given to Herman in the way of specifications that said concentration camp on them. The US cannot find anything like that, but perhaps Metzmann has them."

The room falls silent. Jones sits down and opens one of the documents for review, followed by Hines.

For more than an hour, no one speaks.

No Choice

Since arriving in The Hague, Portnoy has been on the phone multiple times every day, working with his fledging campaign staff in Israel.

From the start, the news has not been good, with his campaign opponent taking every advantage of Portnoy's absence, and each day, Portnoy's anger about getting shoved out of Israel has grown and grown. As for Schmitt, he is simply guilty, and the sooner, the better.

So far, the opportunity for publicity, to get his name on the front page in Israel, has been limited. Even coverage of the Tribunal has slipped out of the news everywhere.

He has gone back and forth: lay low, and if Schmitt is acquitted, let Metzmann take all the blame or start talking, getting in the press, and taking all the credit for a conviction. Metzmann seems sure of a conviction, and Metzmann has already told him that Metzmann will do all the talking in front of the Tribunal.

It now seems clear to him: he has no choice. He has to risk it.

Finally!

Friday, 14 September 2007

At 2 am, Hines gets out of bed and dresses to return to her own room. Again, she has failed to get any information out of Braun.

As she finishes dressing, she quietly heads to the hotel room door when she notices Braun's briefcase by a small table, lamp, and chair. Looking back at Braun to be sure he is really asleep and not faking it, she lifts the briefcase off the floor, opens the door, and heads to her room, her heart pounding the whole time. If she gets caught with the briefcase, her career is over.

In the utility room, the elevator control console begins to blink as an elevator has been called to the 9th floor and is headed to the 10th. The lone on-call support sees the elevator call and makes a note of it. If video cameras were turned 'on,' he could easily check on who was using the guest's elevator at this time of night and between floors: "Quite strange."

Once back in her own room, Hines kicks off her shoes and opens the briefcase. "Careful now, need to put everything I get out exactly as it is now," pulling out a 1-inch stack of paper.

Slowly, she scans each page looking for anything she does not know about Herman or the charges against Herman but cannot find anything. Moving in her chair to be more comfortable, she notices her bedside clock reads 3 am: "Got to get this back." She's not gone through it all but cannot risk more tonight. "Maybe I will get another chance."

Out in the hallway and down the elevator, she lets herself in with Braun's key, places the briefcase back on the floor exactly where she found it, and then back out the door again, her heart pounding away.

Alert to elevator use now; the on-call support sees the guest elevator again being used, first with a call to the 10th floor headed for the 9th and minutes later, another call to the 9th floor headed to the 10th. Again, he makes a note of it to pass on to the hotel manager.

Back in her room, Hines undresses and gets into bed. "What could they have on Herman? Could Braun just be bluffing?"

Shapiro awakes to the FAX, humming away, sheet after sheet being pulled through. "Finally," but does not get up.

Wild Dogs Barking

At 9:50 am, Portnoy makes his way down to the lobby, happy to see through the hotel's double doors that the reporters are in mass. His slip to the woman who always brings him food had worked; the rumor of a press conference has worked.

Standing in front of the hotel's double doors, looking out, he adjusts his tie and brushes down his hair with his hand one last time, getting ready for the big show. Finally, lifting his head to diminish his double chin and pulling himself up as tall as he can be, he walks out the hotel's double doors onto the steps to the waiting crowd of newspaper reporters: "Time to make some news and friends back in Israel."

Outside the old hotel, close to 100 news reporters from all over the globe have assembled to scratch out any piece of news related to the Schmitt trial, and when they see Portnoy, they become like a pack of wild dogs barking.

Portnoy is prepared for this and raises his hands over his head, motioning them to back off and settle down. He approaches the microphone stand that he has arranged to have set up and speaks in a bold, clear voice, "I am Uri Portnoy speaking for the prosecution in the trial of Herman Schmitt. I will have some opening remarks, and then I will take a few questions." The reporters all crowd in close to hear, and the cameras all flash as Portnoy begins to get the type of media exposure he has only dreamed of back in Israel.

"Today is a new day for the people of the world and especially my Jewish brothers and sisters, as soon; we bring to trial a man who was, via his mind and talents, responsible for the death of thousands if not millions of Jews in Nazi concentration camps. As one of the 3-member team prosecuting Herman Schmitt for crimes against humanity, I am comfortable in saying that we have a strong case against Mr. Schmitt and are confident that the court will find him guilty. I cannot speak for the other members of the prosecution, but as for myself, I would like to see the court 'hang' a harsh sentence on Mr. Schmitt. Now, some in the media and elsewhere have said that no engineer or scientist has ever been prosecuted for crimes against humanity as it was their governments who used the results of their efforts, to which I respond, we are trying Mr. Schmitt for this one specific case and not all the engineering and scientific community. It is not my concern what position a court might or might not take in regards to other engineers involved in the design and development of technology whose express purpose is human death. Mr. Schmitt is a unique case and will be presented as such. The deaths of millions of Jews in German concentration camps cannot; must not; go unpunished. Yes, various Nazi government officials have already been tried and convicted of crimes against humanity, but this does not mean that all those involved in such crimes have been brought to justice. I am proud to be on the prosecution team and promise my Jewish countrymen I will not sleep until Mr. Schmitt is convicted and a lengthy, harsh sentence is hung on Mr. Schmitt."

"Mr. Portnoy!" "Mr. Portnoy!" comes a dozen or more voices from the crowd of reporters as Portnoy takes in his first breath after his opening remarks.

"Yes, you in the front," Portnoy says, pointing towards a TV camera more than the reporter beside it. "Israeli National News

Service," the reporter says in an almost screaming voice so he can be heard over the continuing yells for Portnoy's attention.

"Can you please tell me how long you expect the trial to last and what evidence you have that Mr. Schmitt is guilty of what he has been charged with?"

Portnoy steps back away from the microphone for a second to let a semi-silence take over the scene, with everyone waiting for his next words. "He is good," stepping back up to the microphone, again erect, head up.

"As to evidence, the prosecution has more than we need to convince the court that Mr. Schmitt knowingly and willingly designed the gas dispensing equipment for use at German concentration camps having such facilities. For example, because the Nazis were so thorough in their record keeping, we have actual design documents for the equipment signed at the bottom by Mr. Schmitt. As for how long the trial will last, I really cannot say, but I would imagine no more than one week, if that. This matter should be settled quickly, or that is the prosecution's view."

Again, at his anticipated spoken word, the gathered reporters explode into a yelling, hand-waving mob. Again, Portnoy goes to a TV camera, only this time, there is a tall, pretty blonde beside the cameraman holding the microphone.

"Mr. Portnoy, I am from the San Francisco Dispatch and would like to know your thoughts about Mr. Schmitt having an American defense team. Isn't it odd that with Israel and the United States being such close allies, the Americans should be involved in defending Mr. Schmitt?"

Again, Portnoy steps back from the microphone, only this time, he looks out over the heads in the crowd to the courtyard square and even beyond that to the small shops lining the street. For a moment, Portnoy wonders what exactly to say. He expected this question in advance and even had an answer prepared and practiced, but now, for some reason, he is not comfortable with it.

Maybe it is the fact that the reporter is a blonde woman or that he is now speaking to the United States and does not want to make too many enemies there, as he might need some political support from fellow Jews in the US one day.

Linda Has to Respond

Almost immediately after beginning his "press release," the telephones in the rooms of Metzmann and Shapiro ring, and a voice that neither recognizes tells them to turn on their television sets.

"Oh, my God," Metzmann says out loud once he flicks the channels and finds Portnoy speaking to the reporters. "What the hell is he doing? I am the lead counsel, and I did not say he could speak to reporters. Not a bad idea, but he should have asked."

Shapiro watches and listens as Portnoy goes on and on, responding to some reporter's question from the look of it. "Damn! I did not want to fight this in the media, but now that Portnoy has spoken, we have no choice but to present our side as he watches Portnoy strain his head in some odd way.

"Crap! I wanted to keep the whole thing low-key, but that is shot now. Fellows paying the bills are not going to like it, but that can't be helped. Well, can't be me and sure can't be Jones, so has to be Hines," and with that, Shapiro calls Hines's room and tells her what is going on, and tomorrow at this time, he expects her to be out front speaking to those very same reporters telling them why Herman is not guilty of anything. Hines does not argue, but when she hangs up the phone, she wishes she had never gotten involved.

In an hour, he will call the US again to see if his staff there has made any progress on learning more about IG Farben or the actual production of Herman's faulty design.

Thumbing through the Fax document, he begins to sort out what he should do: immediately submit it to the court, talk to Metzmann about it, or wait until Hines presents the defense's opening remarks, the first day of the Tribunal?

In New York, Jack Luby has been reading what drips and drabs he can find after the initial pop of Herman's trial, but there is not much. He hasn't even called any of his UN contacts in a week.

But when Portnoy's public statement hits the wire services, Luby begins catching up.

He places a call. "Ah, yeah, that. I heard. What do you want now?"

"I can't seem to find anything about the press being allowed in the courtroom. Know anything?"

"Let me look; hold on."

Jack has never been to The Hague. Jack has not been anywhere on the Journal's 'time'.

"Ok, I gather that no press is allowed in the courtroom when the court is in session. Something about the Israelis wanting or rather demanding, they are the only source for the media."

"What?" says Jack, "A story like this and no reporters to give the unbiased view?"

"Tell that to the Israelis. I got to go."

Up one flight of stairs and into his boss's office, "You know about the Schmitt thing, right, remember? Well, I have just learned there are to be no reporters inside the courtroom. Israelis want to control the narrative. Is it just me, or do you also think we should be there covering the design aspect? You know I am willing to go. Now, only if you agree, you could place a few calls to your friends and maybe get the UN to allow a couple of special reporters to be in the courtroom: for transparency, unbiased."

Luby's boss has listened to it all. He says nothing but picks up his phone.

Luby begins to think of The Hague.

A Favor

Saturday, 15 September 2007

"Good morning. I am Linda Hines, and I am here to speak for Mr. Schmitt's defense team. As you all know by now, Mr. Isaac Shapiro is the lead counsel, Mr. Julies Jones is our German translator, and I will also be representing Herman in court. I would like to begin by saying that Herman is well and that all our efforts are to show that Herman is completely innocent of what the prosecution has said about him. Herman Schmitt was and is simply a mechanical engineer. He was not a soldier during the war, did not work at a concentration camp, and was never a member of the Nazi party. He is retired now, but the prosecution thinks he should pay for some design he did 60 years or so ago, and although Mr. Schmitt does not deny he designed a Zyklon B gas dispenser, he was never at a concentration camp and certainly never operated his design at a camp."

"Trying to criminally prosecute an engineer for a design that anyone may have used at any time for any purpose could result in a new, dangerous legal precedent. There has never been a case like this, and Mr. Schmitt's defense team is convinced designers cannot be held criminally accountable for their work."

"If Herman is convicted simply on his design, then what is to stop Japan from forming a Tribunal of all atomic bomb scientists? What was the total, 50,000, 100,000 killed at Hiroshima and Nagasaki? Designers of weapons they themselves never used?"

"Of course, the concentration camps were horrible, and millions died, but to hang this atrocity on Herman's head, well."

Pausing and putting on her best serious face, "Herman looks forward to his day in court," raising her hand and waving, she turns and makes her way back into the grand old hotel, ignoring the shouts of questions, profanity, and the constant blast of a flash camera.

In his room, Shapiro watched Hines on television and was happy with it overall. "Perhaps a little too stinging toward the prosecution", but other than that, a good start, and he will tell Hines that.

Shapiro turns off the television as the phone begins to ring, but he ignores it, and once it stops ringing, the ring of the next call and the one after that and the one after that until he simply lifts the receiver off the hook and lays it on the table.

At 11, Shapiro picks up the phone, looks up Metzmann's phone number, and dials it.

"Hello, this is Mr. Metzmann." "Mr. Metzmann, it's Shapiro."

"Good morning. It was quite a press conference your Hines gave."

"Yes, well, after Mr. Portnoy's release, I seemed to have no choice but to respond."

"Mr. Shapiro, I must tell you, the press conference was not my idea. Portnoy did not even ask me about it; he just did it on his own."

"Mr. Metzmann, I have a favor to ask."

"Favor"

"Mr. Schmitt has been in custody for almost two weeks now, and I would like to take him outside tomorrow for a walk. Maybe have some lunch out. I was unsure if I should ask one of the judges, but I thought you might be able to help me?"

"I see no problem: you responsible for him?"

"Yes, of course."

"No work for you and Hines tomorrow?"

"Of course, we could read over everything again, but it is time to take a break. Quite honestly, I am unsure if a walk outside is not more for me than Mr. Schmitt. You know, clear the head."

"I understand. Everything has moved so fast since the UN approved our request. Of course, take Mr. Schmitt out for the day. Might be the last time he sees the sun for a long time."

Shapiro pauses. "So, you can arrange for me to take Mr. Schmitt out for the day?"

"Yes, consider it done. I will inform the support office, the guards, and so on. I suggest you use the hotel staff entrance. Reporters like to hang out in the front."

"Well, thank you, Mr. Metzmann."

At noon, Hines and Jones join Shapiro.

"Anything I should know about?" Shapiro asks from behind his desk.

Both shake their heads.

"Well, I have been thinking, and I think you two should have tomorrow off. With the Tribunal Monday, we are as prepared as we are going to be."

"You sure, Shapiro?" says Jones. "Don't need to talk with Herman one last time? Not even to tell him his design is flawed?"

"Actually, I am going to take Herman out for a walk and lunch tomorrow. Think some time away from this place would do us both good, and Metzmann is arranging it now."

"Don't need me to translate for you?"

"Well, do you mind going now and telling Herman about tomorrow? Tomorrow, I think we can make it on our own."

"Sure, I can do that. What time tomorrow?"

"Let's say 9 or so. That will give you most of the day. And Linda, it should be obvious by now, and I should have said something earlier, but you will do the talking for the defense at the Tribunal."

"You sure Isaac, I have no problem in a courtroom and have to say, I am not surprised, but still, you sure?"

"Yes, Linda, I am sure. As you both know or should know, I am a Jew, and defending Schmitt is one thing, but talking to the Tribunal is another. I just don't want to do it."

"I understand, Isaac. Be glad to do it. Opening statement thoughts?"

"Linda, up to you, you know the case or lack of one. Whatever you come up with will be fine, I am sure."

"Ok, Isaac. I will prepare."

"Good. Say we meet here on Monday, around 10. The Tribunal does not start until 1, so we can go over everything one last time. I am hoping we get something from NJ today or tomorrow, but they have been pretty quiet for days. Just don't think there is much more they can get for us."

Hines and Jones rise from their chairs.

"I will go speak to Herman. Sure, he is ready for some air."

No sooner than Shapiro hears the door click shut, the telephone rings. "Yes, Mr. Shapiro, speaking."

"Sir, a rather large package has been delivered here for you. Shall I send it up?"

"Yes, please, I will be waiting."

The signed original engineers report: "finally."

Flash Of Anxiety

When Linda is back in her room, Braun comes to mind.

"Karl, Linda. I am free the rest of the evening and all day tomorrow. Want to do something?"

"Of course: when are you coming down?"

"Karl, I said I was free tonight and all of tomorrow."

"When you coming down?"

"Give me 10 minutes. I assume it's your room and not the bar?"

"I can't wait."

Linda begins to rise out of her chair when a sudden flash of anxiety hits her: she is going to get caught. Karl might not be an attorney, but if anyone were to learn about their late-night activities, it would be the end of her career, and only God knows what would happen to Schmitt or Shapiro.

"Karl?" "Yes."

"I can't make it. I like you; I really do, but if anyone were to find out about us, it would be the end of my career."

"We don't talk about the case. There is nothing to worry about."

"Karl, the fact we meet outside the courtroom is enough to sink us both, and you know that!"

"OK, but I think you are making too much of us just having fun."

"I am sorry, Karl, I really am."

Linda hears the line click dead.

With Karl now gone from the immediate future, Linda is at a loss as to what to do with herself.

Work: always work. She kicks off her shoes, calls the support staff office, and tells them to send up a salad and a bottle of wine.

She will reread every last scrap of paper she has on the case. Maybe she can find something they have missed, or perhaps a question will form that has not been asked of Herman or the state-side support staff.

As to her defense opening remarks, she has decided to simply repeat what she told the reporters outside. There is no need for anything more in the opening.

The Back Entrance

Sunday, 16 September 2007

Isaac is up early on the phone with the states, but support has nothing new to offer. As attentive to documenting almost every detail as the Nazis were during the war, support can find little about travel during 1943. Everything is military with nothing on citizen travel.

Isaac sits sipping coffee, trying to think what he is missing. "What else should he have research looking for?"

"Ok, if there is limited civilian travel documentation, what about IG Farben personnel? They might have fallen under military travel. We know that the commandant of Auschwitz in 1943 met with industrialists several times in an attempt to improve the extermination rate. Perhaps an IG Farben executive of some kind traveled to Auschwitz and nothing more, on the invoice paid by Farben to Deutschland Mechanish?"

"No. Have found some accounting of Farben, but it is incomplete with entire years missing, presumably destroyed to eliminate evidence of the role in the death camps."

"Ok, keep digging, and thanks."

Shapiro hangs up the phone but picks it up again and calls Jones.

"Hope I didn't wake you, but I have rethought taking Hermann out today and think you should come along. Think I might want to ask Hermann some more questions. You make any plans for the day?"

"No, Isaac. I have already talked with my wife and kids and was just going to go out walking like you. Be glad to join you."

"Thanks, Julies. Can you fetch Hermann around 10 or so?"

"Will do and meet in the lobby?"

"No, come here. We are going out the back entrance to avoid the reporters."

New Evidence

"So, he will do it? Good, good, and the money? No way to trace it back to me? Good, just what I needed. Get him here no later than tomorrow evening. Yes, I have everything ready at this end. Thanks. Is polling looking any better? Only 4%? And that bastard, what is he doing? Yes, of course, he would say that, wouldn't he? Well, keep me informed."

Portnoy puts down the phone and picks up his prepared witness document. He reads it one more time and then heads down to the Tribunal support staff to submit his new evidence.

A co-worker of Schmitt's has agreed to testify that he clearly remembers Schmitt being absent from work for a week in 1943. Although it does not prove Schmitt traveled to Auschwitz, it does provide the possibility that he could have, and with the eyewitness testimony already in Tribunal evidence, this ought to be all he needs to get Tribunal floor time as he is going to demand from Metzmann that Portnoy question the co-worker when he testifies.

Submitted to the support staff, Portnoy heads out the front of the hotel and is greeted by a rather small crowd of reporters.

"Another chance to make some headlines," and moves through the hotel doors out to the waiting crowd.

So Nice To Be Out

Isaac is ready when the knock comes, and he opens the door to find Jones and Herman.

"I have explained to Hermann that we all are going out today, and he is really thankful you arranged it, aren't you Herman?"

Herman listens as Jones repeats in German.

"Yes, Mr. Shapiro, thank you very much. It has been so long I get to walk about, free."

"Herman, is there anything you would especially like to do when we go out? Something you need?"

Jones translates.

"I would like to visit a bookstore. I need books to read."

"Will do, and maybe some lunch, perhaps?" Shapiro looks around his room and motions all out the door.

Metzmann, as promised, has cleared with security, Schmitt leaving the Tribunal hotel, and a guard escorts them to the employee entrance at the rear of the hotel. Opening the door, Isaac is a little anxious as they might face a crowd of reporters, but there are none, and the guard points in the direction away from the front of the hotel towards a park and several shop-lined streets to visit.

For several minutes, all take in the air, the sun, the clear blue sky and simply walk.

"Herman, what was Berlin like during the war? I mean, early in the war when you first started at Mechanish?"

Jones translates, and Herman, with a smile on his face, the likes of which Shapiro has not seen before, says, "At first, it was good. Everyone had work, money, and food that did not cost much, but as the war went on, Berlin was full of soldiers, and everything went for the war. Things got hard to get, even food."

"Herman, did you ever see Hitler? I mean, attend a rally or ever hear him speak?"

"I never attended any rally and never saw him in person, but when I start work, the first thing I was told I had to buy with my pay was a radio. There were very cheap radios for everyone in Germany at the time, and it was important we listen to every Hitler broadcast speech. Sometimes, talk about speech at work, but not so much. Oh, bookstore, can I stop here?"

Jones translates and Shapiro agrees. "Tell Herman I will pay for four books if he can find four that he would like to have."

The bookstore is small but does have a German section, and Herman begins to browse.

"Shapiro, you believe Herman that he did not attend a Hitler rally?"

"Yes, I do. Think Herman is an engineer and only an engineer. Think he lives and breathes engineering and would have little use for politics. We know he was never a party member, and from what I know, the radio thing was common at the time. Almost forced to buy them and listen to the Fuhrer. Anything you think I should ask him?"

"He says he never traveled during 1943 and even seldom after that, but there is a witness, Shapiro. Perhaps some more questions about his traveling or if his co-workers traveled?"

"I did request support to look into the possibility that someone from IG Farben might have visited Auschwitz, and that is who the witness saw there and not Hermann."

"I understand that there was an IG Farben forced labor camp at Auschwitz, and it is highly possible one of their people is who the witness saw and claims it was Herman."

"Could be, I will talk to Linda. It's going to be tough to cross-examine the camp survivors. Oh, I see Herman has his books."

"All set, Herman?"

"Yes, thank you. 4 fine books on chemical manufacturing. I have seen these but never owned them. Thank you."

"Sorry, you did not have some books earlier. Did you have a lot of books at home?"

"Yes many, all engineering."

"Herman, did any of your co-workers have to travel as part of their design work?"

"Some, I think, and maybe one away for a long time, but mostly, we don't have to see where our designs are used: most for chemical plants."

"Did your company do a lot of work for IG Farben?"

"Yes, but also work for many others. Even toaster designed in our shop: funny toaster."

"Herman, did the military ever visit your shop?"

"Not during the war, but when Russians come, they search for people with special skills like those who machine metal. Nobody was taken from a shop by Russians."

"And after the war and the Russians, how was life then?"

"Very bad: no food and electricity out all the time. Even water only now and again."

"Well, Herman, ready to head for some lunch?"

"Please, so nice to be out."

The Only Way

When Shapiro, Jones, and Herman return to the Tribunal hotel, the taller of the two support staff men sees Shapiro and waves at him to come to their office.

"From the Tribunal": handing Shapiro, Portnoy's new 'evidence' submission.

"What's this?" scanning the pages of the document.

"Herman, this says that a coworker of yours in 1943 remembers you being gone from work for a week! Is that true?"

Jones translates, but Herman looks puzzled at first.

"I never gone from work. Every day, I work unless I get sick. Oh, I remember being out for maybe 2 or 3 days one time, but I don't remember when. Guess it could be in 43, I'm not sure."

"Sick? Did you see a doctor?"

"No. Just bad cold and I stay home to protect my coworkers."

"Well co-worker's name is Gruber, Hans Gruber. You know him?"

"I do not remember any Gruber. Many engineers; they come and go, and I never know their names or work with them. I sure I never work with a Gruber."

"Sure, Herman" "Mr. Gruber is swearing under oath that he knew you and that you were not at work for a week in 1943, the same time you did the Zyklon B dispenser design."

"I do not know Gruber, and I am never away from work except when sick and never for a week. I did not kill anyone."

"Ok, Herman, we will look into it, but try remembering when you were sick or not at work: anything."

Jones translates and then switches to English. "Shapiro, we have not talked about it much, but why haven't you introduced our signed engineer's report about Herman's design? You haven't even put it into a Tribunal submission yet."

"I know. I roll it over and over in my head as to when and keep coming up with hold, hold, hold. Not sure why."

"Jones, I am going to tell Herman what our engineers have to say about his design."

"Sure that's a good idea?"

"I am just not sure how he is going to react, but better now, than during the Tribunal."

"Ok. Hope he takes it well," and begins speaking German to Herman, alerting him that Mr. Shapiro has something important he needs to share with Herman."

Herman nods.

"Perhaps in my room would be best," and all three get into the elevator and head to Shapiro's room.

Once inside, Herman and Jones sit on the couch, and Isaac sits down at his desk facing them. He picks up the signed engineer's report and opens it.

"Linda?"

"Yes, I am here, Shapiro."

"I know I said you could take Sunday off, but there has been a new submission to the Tribunal, and I think it is time to tell Herman about the engineer's report and think you ought to be here."

"Be right there."

"Linda will be joining us. Does Herman need anything?"

Jones asks Herman, but Herman has to look up from one of the books he is reading to simply shake his head, 'No.'

Shapiro reads over the co-worker's testimony again and again: "A witness but no hard proof."

There is a knock at the door, and Jones lets Linda in.

"Linda, take a look at this before we begin," and hands over to Linda the new witness document about Herman being gone for a week.

"What does Herman say about this?"

"Says, only ever missed a day or two of work, because he was sick but never a week. He also says he does not know a Gruber."

"A witness, but nothing supporting he ever even worked with Schmitt?"

"Yes."

"I'll prepare a contest evidence document and submit it later today. A witness with no supporting documentation that this Gruber, ever worked with Herman or even the same company as Herman! What is Metzmann thinking?"

"As I said, with this new submission to the court, I think it is time to tell Herman that his design does not work or, rather, would not work if ever turned into a dispenser: better here, now, that in court."

"Herman, we had ten engineers in the United States look at your gas dispenser design. I wanted to understand how it was supposed to work and wanted them to explain it to me. Herman, when they looked over your design, ten different, experienced engineers have now agreed that it is faulty and could not have worked as designed."

Jones translates, and Shapiro sees Herman tense up, his body physically tense up until, "No, they wrong, my design it works. I make no mistake. I am sure of it. What they say is wrong with my design, what?"

"As I understand it, not enough surface area on Zyklon B pellets plate for enough sublimation to produce any real quantity of gas, even with a giant blower of heated, moist air."

"No, they're wrong. I use the sublimation rate from IG Farben. They provided it. 'No', they wrong, my design work."

"Herman, ten professional engineers in America, all well respected there, agree your design, as you drafted it, simply would not work. Perhaps made 3 or 4 times larger with some sort of continuous pellet feed, but no, it would not work, and more importantly, Herman, I have to tell the Tribunal Judges that your design does not and could not work."

Herman stands up and looks like he is ready to fight. Yelling now, "You do not tell anyone about my design and your engineers, they wrong. I know my work and do not make a mistake. No, you do not submit to judges, I forbid."

"Herman, I understand, I really do, but I have to submit this document. Although not proof your design was ever implemented, some credibility that if it had been fabricated as you designed it, could never have been used at any camp."

"No, you not submit. I would rather be 'guilty' than have my design slandered. I make no mistake. I am very proud of all my designs, but I never kill anyone."

"Herman, do you want to die in prison?"

"No submit, I forbid."

"Jones, package this and take it down to the support office, please."

Jones looks at Herman, "Herman, the only way for you ever to be able to walk around free," and is on his way to the door.

Opening Statement

Monday, 17 September 2007

Herman gets up from the chair, by one of the large windows in his living room, and picks up the suit Jones has brought him. He meant to try it on yesterday but just could not muster the strength: all the talk of his design not working!

Taking the suit out of the bag, when Herman puts it on, he finds it is 2 sizes too big on him. "I will look pathetic wearing this!" The very idea Shapiro had, when he ordered the suit.

With the Tribunal to begin at 1 pm, both the defense and prosecution teams meet in the lead counsel's room for a quick review. Over in Metzmann's room, he sits munching an iced pastry from a huge cart filled with such treats, but neither Uri nor Karl is partaking, only drinking coffee and shuffling papers on the large table before them all.

"This American engineers' report, I don't like it. Why did none of our engineers ever look at design viability?"

"Portnoy"

"Oh, can't blame me. Remember, I joined well after you filed the charges."

"Well, this report is going to hurt us."

"So what if the design was faulty; he designed a dispenser to kill Jews. That should be enough. It is intent, not actual implementation. We never said Schmitt actually built the damn thing."

"Still don't like it and this new witness of yours. Where is the supporting documentation to prove he actually worked with Schmitt?"

"I haven't got it yet, but not to worry: very credible witness."

"Uri, I have been thinking, and since you made it clear, you are the one to be questioning your co-worker witness, I think perhaps you should just do all the talking during the Tribunal."

Portnoy is delighted. "Of course, I can handle the Tribunal. Be glad to. Of course, you must pass on your wisdom on matters as the trial goes along."

"Yes, yes, of course, I will offer my advice, but it just seems right that you be the one representing Israel."

"Don't take this the wrong way, but I have already prepared our opening statement," says Portnoy with a smile.

"Of course, you have," Metzmann mutters.

Hereby Closed

At 20 minutes to 1, Herman hears a knock at his door and then, "Hello, Herman. Are you ready?"

"This suit, it is wrong. Look at me; I am swallowed by it. Please, is there another I could wear?"

"I am sorry Herman, right now, there is only one suit, but I will speak to Isaac; perhaps he can get you a better one soon."

Outside the courtroom, Shapiro and Hines are waiting, "Well, Herman, it begins," says Shapiro. "Now Herman, to be clear, you are not to speak unless spoken to, and because of the language differences, what you hear might not be clear, but do not say anything. Jones will help you understand any translation as needed. Is that clear, Herman?"

"This suit, it is way too big on me. Please, another suit," Herman says, looking towards the doors of the courtroom.

As is the custom, Herman and his defense are the first to enter the make-do courtroom and slowly move to the large table on the left in the immense old ballroom.

The German translator is in his booth, and along the back wall near the double doors, another table with headphones and three chairs have appeared.

At 5 minutes to 1, the rear doors open, and some commotion is heard as everyone in the room turns their head towards the back and sees Metzmann, Portnoy, and Braun enter the room, and just outside the doors, a crowd of cameras and reporters. "What? Reporters?" thinks Shapiro. "No reporters or cameras allowed. Isn't that what he was told?", but then the door closes behind the prosecution team, and Shapiro sighs and turns to his papers.

Metzmann and his team split, with Portnoy and Braun moving to the far right while Metzmann moves towards the defense table.

"So, here we are," says Metzmann as Shapiro rises to his feet, shaking the hand thrust his way.

"Ah, 'yes', we are. We have a strange arrangement here, don't you think?"

"Well, 'yes' it is actually," Metzmann says as he looks about quickly, "But it will do, and Mr. Schmitt?", now looking straight down at Herman.

Shapiro lets go of Metzmann's hand. "Mr. Schmitt is ready for this all to be over and knows he will be found innocent."

"Well, that is for the court to decide, and I must be honest with you Mr. Shapiro, our evidence is overwhelming." With that, Metzmann turns and proceeds to the prosecution table and the metal chair he finds most uncomfortable, for his large frame. "Perhaps a pillow from his room?"

It is now quiet, all wearing their headsets, papers laid out in front, as the large clock moves to exactly 1 pm.

The doors in the rear of the room open, and the earphone portion of their headsets come alive with "Rise" in German and English, and in walks, in single file, the three judges, each dressed in the court robes of their respective country.

As both the prosecution and the defense watch, the three slowly walk towards their judging table in the front; Shapiro guesses the head judge has to be the first of the three and the tallest by at least 6 inches. All have their hands clasped across their front.

When the three reach the front table, the tallest and first to enter, takes the middle seat, clearly indicating he is the chief judge.

Once all are standing behind their chairs, the chief judge unclasps his hands, places his headset on, and then waits for the judge on either side to do the same. Then, a light is lit in front of him. "I am the chief judge of these proceedings. Beside me are the two other judges and we 3 will decide the outcome of these proceedings?"

"Understanding that many languages could be spoken and translated, our names, those who stand before you, are unimportant. You will address us as 'Your Honors.' Because translations are required, please, when told to do so, speak slowly. Now I must ask, have all heard and understood me? If so, simply nod your head." All nod.

The chief judge picks up a glass of water and, after taking a sip, "Reporters. I have been instructed to allow 3 reporters to observe and report. One is from America, one from Germany, and an Israeli. I understand all parties were told there would be no reporters, but those who authorized this Tribunal have decided that transparency has become important due to the nature of the case. Although not what I would prefer, I have made it clear that I will tolerate no proceedings distractions from the three, and if one violates, they all will be ejected and not allowed to return."

"Now, please instruct the three reporters to come in and be seated."

Luby steps inside the courtroom and pauses. Not sure what he expected, but not this, and, "Folding metal chairs?" Following Luby is the German reporter named Litz, and finally, Mr. Acarmeli.

Luby looks around, and the only table and chairs not occupied are right inside the door. With Luby in the lead, the three move to the table, chairs, and headphones.

The chief looks and picks up a document. "Mr. Herman Schmitt." The Chief looks at the defense table and right at Herman. "Mr. Schmitt, I want to assure you that the three judges here have no bias in this matter. We will hear and see evidence, and using the guidance given to us and agreed to by all parties, we will make an impartial decision. I am sure you are aware, or should be aware, that a guilty verdict requires all three of us to agree. This should both comfort you and suggest to you that if found guilty, our sentencing could be harsh."

"Now, as chief justice, I declare the Tribunal in the case of 'crimes against humanity by Mr. Herman Schmitt' is officially open."

The chief removes his headset and sits down. All is quiet.

A minute or two passes in silence, and then the chief places his headset on and standing, turns on his microphone.

"Evidence. Court submissions and truth: we three judges before you are from different countries with different criminal laws and different criminal justice systems, but in our countries and every country of the world with criminal laws and courts, any charges of criminal behavior must be evident by 'truths,' not supposition or inference.

Yes, in this case, there are known truths: Mr. Schmitt designed a Zyklon B gas dispenser; Zyklon B gas was used by Nazi Germany to kill millions in concentration camps; the German company known as IG Farben supplied Zyklon B to those who ran the death camps and finally, Mr. Schmitt's employer in 1943, did work for IG Farben. These are truths we accept."

The chief turns and looks directly at the prosecution table. "Yes, truths, but never have we three seen a case where the links between truths are totally missing. Yes, you have supplied dozens of concentration camp photos of gas being used but not one single image of Schmitt's design in any form of practicality, much less actually used at a death camp. The prosecution claims Mr. Schmitt's design was ordered by and paid for by IG Farben, a supplier of Zyklon B. The evidence provided of this is by way of an invoice to IG Farben from Mr. Schmitt's employer in 1943, but neither Mr. Schmitt's design nor the invoice carries any work order number. This invoice could be for anything and is thus not evidence connecting Mr. Schmitt's design to IG Farben. Furthermore, if the submitted invoice was for Mr. Schmitt's work, there is no evidence Mr. Schmitt knew IG Farben's intended use."

The chief pauses and looks about the ballroom.

"A criminal charge of 'crimes against humanity' for designing a device, could be used to kill millions? Is a designer responsible for deaths his device might be designed to cause? This is not the question in this case. This case is specific to Mr. Schmitt's design."

"Finally, one last truth: Mr. Schmitt's design would not or could not work if actually fabricated in steel and rubber. This Tribunal accepts the American Engineer's report as truth."

The chief turns to his left and then to his right, and all three justices are standing.

"It is the finding of this Tribunal that, Mr. Schmitt is not guilty of 'crimes against humanity' due to the lack of evidence connecting the 'truths' of this case. A report will be filed with the UN and the ICC detailing the gross lack of evidence in this case. Mr. Schmitt, you are free to go, and the Tribunal apologizes for your arrest and incarceration. This Tribunal is hereby closed."

The Truths

In every earpiece, "Please stand," and the judges once again form a line and make their way out the door at the rear of the ballroom.

"Please do not leave. You will be told when you may exit."

Everyone in the ballroom is stunned except for Herman, who keeps asking in German, "What is going on? I don't understand."

Shapiro and Hines have been staring at each other from the moment the chief justice began to dissect truth from conjecture. To them, it had been obvious that a criminal charge should never have been brought against Herman, but considering the horrors of the Holocaust, it had always been possible that three unknown judges would be willing to make connections where none existed.

"Ever, have this happened to you, Shapiro?"

"Linda, never before and doubt will happen ever again." "My highest respect for the judges and their seeing the lack of evidence." "Never know, could have gone a different way."

"Ms. Jones, Ms. Jones. My name is Jack Luby, and I am a reporter for the Journal. I am the one who got your organization to defend Mr. Schmitt."

"I don't talk with reporters."

"Ms. Jones, I have become aware of some information about Mr. Braun's behavior before the Tribunal and would rather not have to include it in my article."

"OK, meet me in the bar, say, an hour?"

"My design it works. I tell you; your engineers are wrong."

"Herman, forget about all this. You are free. You can go home now!"

"Newspapers: my design, not work, going to be in newspapers?"

"I don't know, Herman. Maybe"

Metzmann, Portnoy and Braun are sitting at the prosecution table and have not said a word since they were pummeled by the chief justice

"So rushed, if we had more time and they had given us more money, we could have made all the connections. This is not my fault."

"Well, it isn't my fault. You are the one who brought the charges and told me it would be an easy case." Portnoy, well aware that his chances of a Kismet seat are now gone.

"Gentlemen, Acarmeli from Israel News. We need to talk. I am not sure how to put the best light on what has just happened: any Ideas?"

Metzmann and Portnoy look at each other. Neither has a clue how to 'spin' the acquittal for Israeli media consumption.

"Damn Americans. If they had not decided to defend Schmitt, we would be looking at a conviction now," Portnoy utters.

"You may leave now," is announced over earpieces.

His Design

In the United States, the news of Mr. Schmitt's acquittal did not get a lot of press, nothing like when the charges against him were first brought.

Luby's article played well in the engineering community, but beyond that, it was not picked up or referenced by many other news outlets.

Shapiro, Hines, and Jones returned to New Jersey after a couple of days of seeing the sites of The Hague together. At headquarters, Shapiro was tasked to create a final report on the trial and the issue of possible future criminal culpability of scientists and engineers designing, creating, with the intent of human death.

Metzmann and Portnoy returned to Israel a week after the acquittal, but by then, the news of the acquittal had come and gone, and they faced only a few reporters from minor publications.

As for Herman, once again, on any sunny afternoon, he could be found asleep in a chair in the day room of his nursing care facility. And when asked about the Tribunal, he would only say, "His design works."

The Final Report

When tasked with creating a final report for the IEE, at first, the report wrote itself due to the specifics of Herman's case. But the core issue, that had been the reason the IEE had provided a defense for Mr. Schmitt, had not been resolved and needed to be addressed and possible action items created or suggested.

Are scientists and engineers criminally culpable for the deaths that result from their "given a task and simply doing it?"

It was clear to Shapiro that the minds of scientists and engineers had resulted in many achievements that benefitted all mankind, but also, the minds of scientists and engineers had been instrumental in the creation of devices or procedures whose only purpose was human death. Sometimes, as in the nuclear bomb or biological warfare, mass human death, if not the possible end of the human species on the earth.

Certainly, the position of the IEE and other professional organizations would always be that scientists and engineers could not be held accountable for their efforts when the use of designs, discoveries, was the responsibility of country governments. But Shapiro could also see that if those same scientists and engineers had refused to participate in the creation of anything, with the intended purpose of human death, perhaps mankind might be spared mass death of its own making.

Actions: but what actions could or should be taken to keep mankind from destroying itself via the minds of scientists and engineers?

Scientists and engineers were like Mr. Schmitt. Given a challenge, they used their minds to discover, design, no matter the consequences. The challenge might always be, just too much to resist.

Shapiro wrestled with issues which all, seemed too large to be dealt with, in any meaningful way. "It is always the 'Department of Defense', never the 'Department of War'." And there seems to be no answer yet, if man's intelligence is enough of an evolutionary advantage, to ensure the long-term survival of the species.

In the end, Shapiro recommended to the IEE that the IEE and other professional organizations fund an effort to introduce in all institutions of higher learning, required courses in ethics. The idea was to: introduce ethics and consequences, as parameters to be considered, in any intellectual challenge or design.

Shapiro doubted that such courses would ever be enough to stop what appeared to him, to be the ultimate demise of the human race at its own hands, but perhaps, given time, some awareness might begin and take root.

Shapiro finished the report and submitted it to the IEE.

When the IEE made the report public, it was immediately condemned by various governments around the world. Countries must have ways of defending themselves, and scientists and engineers were required to accomplish that end. But over time, around the world, ethics began to be included in course requirements in various university disciplines.

In the end, the fate of mankind rests in the hands of those with minds capable of being given very difficult tasks and solving them.

The challenge might always be just too much temptation, and mankind's fate is sealed.

Ron Stultz

The challenge might always be just too much temptation, and mankind's fate is sealed.

Musing: "The Bolt Box"

I was told once that you could tell if a farmer had a chance of being successful long-term by looking at the size of his junk pile. The larger the junk pile, the better the chance the farmer would survive and be successful. As a junk pile could be a source of no-cost parts if ever needed, and money was and is always an issue for a farmer.

Perhaps this is why I started my bolt box (junk pile) initially, many, many years ago: to be a successful "farmer." But as the bolt box has grown and supplied me with plenty of "no-cost" parts, the contents of the box have become more a box of memories.

In the garage, in a box that measures 2 feet by 3 feet by 3 feet, marked "Property of the US Postal Service," is where I keep all my left-over parts from years of living.

A glance in the box reveals: 10-penny nails; lag bolts; curtain rod hooks; molly bolts; cotter pins; hitch pens; metal screws of every size and length; hex nuts; flat washers; pieces of a door lock; cabinet handles and hollow wall fasteners.

Taking a 10-penny nail to stir the contents, which is at least 3 inches deep, I uncover bolts left over from one of the 4 baby cribs we had, and I can easily remember assembling the first one for our first child; washers from our first lawn mower; pieces from a lamp which once resided by my bed; training wheel bolts from my oldest daughter's first bicycle; odd-shaped hangers from one or more of the kid's hamster and mice cages, which were with us for years and years.

Wire brads; flat head, pan head, Phillips head screws; screen door screen clips; toilet seat bolts; set screws, lag bolt shields; electrical wire guides and staples and floor coasters for furniture. The special seat bolt from one of the kids' old bicycles, and I can still remember trying to teach them how to ride and how I would run along behind them, holding the seat ever so lightly, providing balance now and then; wooden plugs to fit into the hope chest, which was my wife's mother's and which needed repair before it could take up its honored place in our bedroom and left-over brick lag bolts from when I built the deck sun screen for our first house.

Picture frame hangers; a small paintbrush; screen door hooks; wing nuts and pennies, and cigarette butts from my pockets when I emptied them after some project.

Electrical outlet protectors, which kept little fingers away from danger when they all began to crawl and explore; wire staples from the basement electrical rewire; a brass lanyard tie down from the window shades we made and installed to keep the windows from freezing solid in cold winters; plastic washers from the metal shed I bought against the good advice of my father who said, that everything inside would rust and it did; finger door pulls from closet doors and angle brackets used to reinforce one or more of the many desks or pieces of furniture I built for one or more of the kids over the years.

Just pieces of metal, wood or plastic in funny shapes and some with shapes that I will never need again but cannot throw out, knowing as soon as I do, I will need it for something just broken.

Over the years, I do not know how many times the bolt box has saved me from discarding something or how much money or time it has saved me from going out to look for and buy one bolt or screw. Still, it has been a lot, and now, sometimes, in a rush to complete some project, I am half tempted to forget the box and just go procure what I specifically need. But I always catch myself and root through the box anyway, all times finding what I need or a suitable substitute.

A small can of plumber's grease; 5-inch-long bolts, which held on a carburetor; screw eyes; toggle bolts; rubber bumpers to be placed under small appliances; garden hose connectors; hose nipples; thumb screws; rubber, steel and lead shaft bushings; thumbtacks; decorative brass nuts; push pins; plastic electrical wire connectors; strips of metal with holes in them from what I can no longer remember; deck wood screws; brick nails; concrete nails and finishing nails.

Thousands of pieces of metal, which started as rock, pulled from the earth in South America or Africa. and shipped to America and then melted and shaped and sharpened.

Automotive bolts, which held on a trim piece to the Triumph Spitfire I bought just before my father's death, in some effort to be immediate in responding to my needs before it was too late. Tiny flat head screws, which I could only remove with a jeweler's screwdriver, mirror brackets left over from installing a mirror in one of my daughter's first college dorm room and leftover bolts from the same daughter's college loft bed.

They are not a very colorful lot, the hunks of metal, plastic, and wood that inhabit my bolt box. Mostly gray or dull metal, and hard to distinguish one from the other. I wonder if a day will come when my eyes will not allow me to search the bolt box. At least the flat washers shine and stand out from the crowd.

One wonders why only one special tree holding screws from our first Christmas tree stand, which broke the year we bought our first 16-foot-tall tree; nuts, which only fit small electrical toggle switches, which I must admit to having a love affair with when I was younger and stick-on rubber bumpers from some long-broken door stop but the rubber is still good and never know when I may need it.

Just leftovers from countless projects or disassembles, which I cannot part with as if each were a photograph or had a life and I am not the one to let it die. And I take some strange pleasure now, in using a bolt from a tricycle, 20 years gone, to repair something now being used by that same tricycle rider who now drives cars: some reincarnation of iron ore, some integration of time, where the past melts, with the present.

And looking into the box one more time, I wonder where all the blood went that I lost handling all those pieces of metal. Why is each not covered with spots of my blood as I nicked myself with some tool, rushing to complete some repair or assembly?

Perhaps in the future, some archeologist will find my bolt box, and after trying to classify all the various items he has found, he will discover the traces of blood and be able to DNA me back into existence, at least on some computer screen.

Screws in their original plastic tub container; nuts and bolts in small freezer bags; Venetian blind rod pieces still wrapped snugly in their shrink-wrap package; old pens and pencils; lock washers and small door hinges.

Metal and memories. Metric and curses. Hands and eyes.

Once, I read a book about a famous engineer who actually had sorted out his bolt box into small glass jars, with each jar only holding one type of shaped metal. But I cannot imagine myself ever doing that.

Three inches of metal and memory fragments and a stir with a 10-penny nail is all I need to get lost for a moment, and forget what I am looking for.

Just bits and pieces in various shapes and sizes, like my memories or the yellow tattered photographs stored in albums under beds, except this album is kept in the garage.

"The Good Night"

The sun has just set below the opposite shore's tree line as he begins to wade into the lake, naked, his eyes fixed on the floating dock, positioned in the middle. The water is cold, but he quickly makes his way out to where the water is waist-deep and then launches himself forward, beginning to swim.

As he strokes, arm over arm, he struggles to make any headway at all and thinks to himself that it is the cancer, but he knows it is simply old age. "Bummer getting old: nothing works like it once did," raising another arm and throwing it forward into the water, finally finding a rhythm with his feet kick.

About halfway to the dock, the cold water makes the calf muscle of his right leg cramp and the pain forces him to immediately turn over onto his back and begin to massage it. Now just floating with his ears below the water line, the sky above begins to take on a lovely night-time blue hue.

Once he is sure the leg cramp is gone completely, he swims again towards the dock.

Finally, he reaches the dock, finds the wooden ladder attached to one side, and lifts himself up on the floating barge. At first, he simply stands and celebrates his achievement, surveying everything around him.

The forest around the shore is completely dark now, but he can make out where the lake ends and the forest begins, and although faint, he can hear whippoorwills calling all around him. "So quiet, so peaceful here", sitting down on the rough-cut boards of the dock and then laying down on his back, spread eagle, looking up at the night's sky.

"So nice here, the lake, the quiet, so peaceful. I sure have loved it here, this place, this living." Oh, they say the chemotherapy has been or will be successful, but he knows in his gut that he is going to die soon. The thought makes him sad. "Should have done more; should have given more; should have lived more. Well, I got what I got and did what I could. Hope God saw it, saw what I tried to do."

As the air begins to cool, he begins to feel cold, but it is a good kind of cold. "Good to feel things, like the time he took a shower in the rain. Like the time he hid naked under a waterfall." "Always, so insulated: air-conditioned in the summer; heated in the winter; clothed; covered; insulated", but not now. Out in the middle of the lake, he lays naked, beginning to shiver from the cold.

He thinks of his wife and children and what a shock it will be to them, but the thought of a lengthy illness and then them having to watch him deteriorate slowly into death, well, this is better, he is sure.

Finally, the moon rises above the shoreline forest, and he knows it is time. Sitting up, he shuffles over to the dock ladder and, finding the chain and lock, begins to pull up the boat anchor he placed there earlier in the day. "Nice big heavy boat anchor, maybe 30 pounds," and struggles to bring it to the surface and then lift it up onto the dock. Then, without any thoughts or feelings at all, he wraps the loose end of the chain around one of his legs tightly, clips on the lock, and snaps it shut. It has always been this way with him: get presented with a problem and find a way to solve it, no matter what it takes. And this is so much more of a man's way to go out than in some hospital bed, the ceiling, his last glimpse of this life. He knows he will struggle and fight, as it should be.

He has wondered about others in his situation: the man on death row being led to the lethal injection room, the woman headed into open heart surgery with little chance of surviving, and others with their end in clear sight. What did they think and feel? Were they afraid, out of their minds: with fear, remorse, regret, anger? He feels none of these. Living has been such a treat, a miracle, and he is so grateful for it.

Again, his wife and children come to mind, and he is overwhelmed with sadness for a moment, but only a moment. Then, looking up at the full moon now shining brightly over him and the lake, he shoves the boat anchor over the side of the dock and is immediately jerked into the water.

He knew he would but could not help it. He holds his breath as he descends below the lake surface, the weight of the boat anchor obeying the laws of gravity, headed for the bottom some 50 feet below. As he descends, he looks upward and sees the moonlight begin to fade and darkness surrounding him. Then, when his lungs can stand it no longer, he exhales, and with that first gulp of the lake, "Thank you." one last time.

"John Wayne at 30 Paces"

Verbatim from a Dream

With sentence handed down,

the crowd gathered in the street.

The pistol, primed and loaded,

thrown at Ron's feet.

Without hesitation,

without a thought or care,

barrel moved to his head

trigger pulled

but did not move a hair.

"No" the crowd shouted,

not what we came to see.

So, John Wayne at this finest

marched out into the street.

A shootout at 30 paces

he had decided it would be.

With rifles picked and loaded

words between John and me.

"Sorry son to take you down

But way it got to be."

The crowd gathered round again.

Lined both sides of the street.

Blood thirsty bunch just had to have

what they had come to see.

John, slow to position,

raised and fired.

But Ron never moved.

He knew it time to expire.

Blasted to the ground,

with blue sky above

and the smell of dirt below,

Ron uttered his last

and let this mortal coil go.

"Didn't mean nothing"

Some heard him say

and that

with "John Wayne at 30 Paces"

is what is on his tombstone. Today!

Musing: "I Still Look for Her in Crowds"

As the years begin to pile up, now and again, I begin to think of all those people I have met or known ever so slightly.

The Italian co-worker, who rebuilt antique cars, only married women with their first names beginning with the letter "M" (at least 3 while I worked with him) and once designed automotive engine heads for Detroit. The beautiful, divorced, or separated (never knew which) secretary who had awful taste in picking male lovers and who had some dark secret in her past I never learned.

Eddie and Joey, and our 4 long days hiking the Appalachian Trail, when I was only 14. The social worker, who worked with abused children every day and who, only ate baked potatoes as if anything other than a potato would be decadent.

Faces and names, but I wonder where they are now and how they are. And why did I not take the time and more of an interest in them to get closer to them when we shared the same spaces?

Perhaps I was born shy or withdrawn, or perhaps I was born with some secret and was afraid that "they" would find out. I wish now, I had taken more time and smiled more.

Oh, I can talk with just about everyone. I learned a long time ago that everyone likes to talk about themselves, so I have become a good interviewer. At parties, I can meet strangers and question them and get them to talk for hours about themselves, and then on the way home, they realize, or so I often fantasize, they have no clue who that person was they were talking to. And I take some pleasure in being "invisible." And I wonder if, in my own way, I did and do become close to others, although not in a way I seem satisfied with today.

The minister, the physicist, and the afternoons I spent being the middle man between these two co-workers and the philosophical worlds we explored.

And as I think of all those people, men and women, I wonder now what I am feeling? We were all in motion, moving through our lives and careers, and perhaps we knew at the time that there was no time for closer ties.

The captain in the army who loved art and could hold an egg in his hand, marvel at its shape, and then pile randomly selected rocks on top of each other in a way that was as perfect in form or integration as that egg.

And if I have known or met a lot of people in my life's travels or so I think, every time I go to a concert or am in a large group or crowd, I marvel at how few people I have actually met, much less gotten to know.

There are many interesting lives and stories, and I wish I could speak with them all and ask them all questions and learn about their lives, yet I would never allow them to know me.

Perhaps I have nothing to tell and know it. Perhaps, if I questioned or interviewed myself, I would not find very much to be interested in.

The son of a successful and famous Dallas psychiatrist who considered himself a failure, because his father did: he was only an engineer. The cocktail waitress, who raised 300 guinea pigs and who at 30, had just registered for veterinarian school. The retired old man from Wyoming who was riding around the country on a motorcycle, seeing sites he had always wanted to see and who had a smile, I think you can only get it when you feel completely free of bonds and requirements.

Why am I sad? Am I sad? Or is it some other feeling I am experiencing that is new and cannot yet stick an established label on? What do I think I have missed?

The uncle: a master carpenter. My father: a reincarnated American Indian only happy out in the forest. The computer professor from Egypt, and the afternoons I spent, talking about his homeland and how his father had been a rug merchant and who could focus his PHD mind to a laser point.

Souls in the same orbit or life motion: but only for a little while. And I wonder if I did actually meet them or, rather, they were simply in some dream I had.

The genius laser specialist who had an affair with the tall, dumb blonde secretary and who later moved to Vermont to raise chickens. My alcoholic grandfather, who at 65, could still out work anyone I have ever met and who could talk politics as well as any television show talking head.

I cannot help but think of herds of animals or all those birds sitting on a telephone wire. For a brief moment, we were there on that wire, running in the herd from the beasts, sharing the same watering hole, and yet, some aspect of their soul invaded me and will not let me go. Perhaps it is nothing more than the spiritual desire for a tighter unit, for a closer integration?

Once, long ago, under the influence of psychoactive drugs, I thought I could hear the thoughts of others, and they could hear mine, and it was terrible. There was no room to hide, no way to lie, and although I had thought that this would be union, heaven, I found it not to be so or not in the manner I seem to be trying to define now. Or perhaps this is a union: a union so tight that it keeps folks from entering heaven?

The Middle Eastern mechanic I stumbled on one day that helped me diagnose a car engine problem, and although I went to see him several times thereafter, he never charged me a cent and was always helpful and smiling. The girl I met when I was 14 on a trip, who would not let me sleep for days because I had fallen in love with her instantly but was too shy to tell her so.

Perhaps I am not sad at all but rather feeling a new form of happiness because as I think about all the folks I have known, I detect feelings of joy to have met all these souls and, at least for a little while, shared the same time and space.

They say, "Birds of a feather flock together," and so I wonder if all the folks I have met were like me in feather. Was or is it Karma? Am I "programmed" to only meet certain people? People who have something to teach, challenge, or test me?

The fellow army officer who could only talk with you if his face was a foot or less from your face and who knew, at age 26, more about auto mechanics, cameras, and photography than I will ever know. The retired house mover who became a house mover because, as a child, he was watching a house being moved and the moving foreman handed a rope to him and had him pull an entire house. The Washington Post reporter who moved to Nashville: to write a rock opera. The Navy Academy graduate, who once flew fighter planes, made video documentaries for the Public Broadcasting Service and is now an alcoholic and crack cocaine user, with some unknown demon on his back.

And I think of clouds or a stand of trees on a bluff overlooking a stream and wonder how different all the folks I have met are from clouds or that stand of trees. The flow of life through each is the same somehow, and yes, I am happy to have met them and known something about their lives. I wonder what, if anything, I brought to them?

I used to think that one of the roles I was to have or play in this life was, "example." I have always thought of myself as honest and moral, with the God-given gift of sorting the wheat from the chaff, and now, I wonder if anyone actually perceived this and learned from it.

So many souls: with amazing stories and lives. How lucky I have been to have met them all. And thinking about it now, perhaps my feelings of sadness come from some feeling that perhaps they gave me more than I ever gave them. Could this be so?

The brother, who, as a child, fished in mud holes created in our front yard after a hard rain and who always caught fish, at least in his mind. The lady who, without a college degree and no husband, raised three daughters and herself to be the head of a 10-million-dollar business, only to lose it because, to her, style was everything.

And I wonder what has evoked this look to the past? Some scheduled time to review and adjust for the future? Some feelings of remorse about my standoffishness? And I still wonder why I could not have gotten closer to all these people.

One line of thought about heaven says, that in heaven, one gives up his or her identity to merge with all other spirits, and this then is the grand union, the feeling of closeness that cannot be obtained here in this plane of existence, this earth, space and time. And perhaps I believe that and long for the union.

Another thought in physics is that everything we know of or see or can touch, exists as energy in some semi-stable state and that everything is connected to everything else by the pull and push of forces we cannot see or understand, and perhaps this, too I believe or even know, deep inside my mind's gut, and I want to cross some boundary and touch and be touched more deeply than in the past.

The Middle Ages scholar who lives around the corner that keeps herself busy to stave off depression. The mild-mannered author of children's books who also developed devices to navigate on the stars.

Souls in orbits or on some vector and for a little while, me and them, in parallel tracks and able to communicate, to report to each other what we have seen and heard and learned and then move away from each other in our new and different trajectories.

A friend, who at 19, was told she could never have any children of her own, later married a man with three children and now has four grandchildren and a big, giving smile. The teacher who looked at me, saw me, and asked me questions to which he did not know the answer. The gentle giant of a manager I once had, who I found out only years after parting orbit with him, drowned trying to save a little boy from a raging ocean. Just souls rubbing together for a little while and then gone.

Years ago, when a newly discovered comet came to visit our solar system, I got the idea for a special party and invited all the people I had ever met, but no one came. I want to say it was the theme of the party that kept them away, but thinking about it now, our orbits were just too different, too far apart.

I do not know if there is a heaven or a hell, but if there is a heaven and I make it there, I sure hope I get to see all those faces and smiles and lives again, if not just for a little while. Until then, I will continue to look for "her" in crowds.

"The End Game"

The Mission

He is at the ladder, about to climb, when he hears the hydraulics begin to lift 'the cargo.' "Wonder who will be in first?" stepping up on the ladder, climbing for the cockpit.

He wins, but only by a couple of seconds, and he hears and feels the cargo bay door close and latch.

The route pilot is already on board, helmet on, running various diagnostic tests. "Captain," he says and gets a "Major" in reply. He sits down in the co-pilot seat.

The Major puts on his helmet, connects all hoses and cables, and then, using his eyes, finds the mission icon on the visor of his helmet, and his right eye 'clicks' it.

Begin retina scan.

Scan complete.

This is an end game 3 mission. The total flight time is 17 hours to the destination. Route pilot will fly the first 14-hour leg. The end game pilot will sleep during this period. Cargo is a cluster of low-yield neutron bombs set for air burst at 2000 feet. Cargo must be dropped from 70,000 feet at end game destination to allow cluster bombs to fall to their preprogrammed GPS coordinates.

"End game 3?", the Major, shaking his head in disbelief. He has never been on an end game 3 mission and doesn't like the idea. Cluster neutron bombs: "Killing people but not the buildings, Killing."

"Captain, how soon do we leave?"

"I have been told we must be airborne at the hour."

"And are we ready?"

"I have the mission, and all systems have been checked. Yes sir, ready."

"Let's get to the runway."

The route pilot starts one engine, and then the other and both pilots watch engine performance displays.

Using his eyes, the Major toggles several system self-test icons displayed in his helmet visor, with all indicating 'no faults found.'

"Looks good to me", the Major says looking over the Captain.

"I agree."

The Captain pushes the throttles, the engines spin up, and the bird begins to move.

The Major continues to check the instrument panel and confirm both engines and all support systems are in normal ranges.

"Captain: your portion of the mission?"

"14 hours, sir."

"Ever been on one of these?"

"No sir."

"Longest: sustained flight?"

"10 hours."

"Use the pill?"

"No sir."

"Tested with the pill?"

"Yes sir: mental acuity degradation only 5 % at hour 14."

"Ok, good. Clear on your part of the mission?"

"Yes sir. I fly for 14 hours while you sleep, and then I wake you up with the injection. You take command, and I retire to sleep for the end game and the first portion of the return trip. Cruise is 70,000 feet."

"That's it."

"Anything in maintenance records I should be aware of?"

"No sir. The entire plane was sent through full maintenance for this mission. All systems have been tested several times using the latest up and down links. Bird is good to go."

"Anything from command?"

"No sir."

The Autopilot

On the hour, they are cleared to take off, and the route pilot takes the bird down the runway and is up and climbing.

The Major has never met his route pilot, but his takeoff is perfect. Having switched the display on his helmet to route pilot health, he watches heart rate and respiration, and neither has varied at all during takeoff.

The bird rapidly climbs towards cruise altitude, and various systems move to "route."

The Major watches his route pilot clean up various systems after their takeoff and climb and sets the autopilot.

"All good sir."

"Great takeoff, Captain."

"Thanks, sir."

"Captain, curious: total flight hours?"

"6000, sir, with 4000 on type."

"Ever have equipment or bird malfunctions?"

"Several. Lost hydraulics during a landing; GPS went 4 hours out from touchdown and had to old-school it, and another time, had to shut down an engine 6 hours into a 10-hour mission."

The Major turns to the Captain and sticks out his gloved hand.

"Sir, the end game?"

"Yes, what about it?"

"After I completed all flight training and had maybe 3000 hours, I was sent through a battery of tests. Various people interviewed me, asking questions about this and that, and I had no idea why. But then I got official notice that I was and will always be a 'routing pilot.' I never really thought about it; I mean, I knew there were 'routing pilots' and 'end game' pilots, but why was I not selected to be an 'end game' pilot?"

The Major is quiet, looking away.

"Captain, can't answer that. I went through the same tests as you or similar and then some additional ones after that first battery, and I do not know why I was designated 'end game.'"

"Sir, have you flown any 'end game' missions before?"

"Yes, twice, but 'end game' canceled 3 hours before destination."

"And this time?"

"Don't know, Captain, never know. I train and practice like we all do and do the missions given to me."

A warning light begins to flash in the center console, and then a computer voice is heard in the earpieces of their smart helmets.

Radar scan detected. Long range, low angle, suspected origin determined but not confirmed.

"Ever flown this route, Captain?"

"Yes sir, well, part of it. Normal for a scan about here. Detection by RDAL, but never lasts long."

The Major uses his eye movement to shut down the displays inside his helmet.

At 70,000 feet, moving at almost two times the speed of sound, the blackness outside is not black at all but filled with the light of millions of stars, seemingly fixed all around him. Always amazes him, and he feels a sense of awe. "As close to the stars as he will ever get," he thinks.

"Sir, RDAL is no longer reporting scanning."

Not A War But...

In each of the capitol's four negotiation rooms, there is a large 6-digit digital display, always showing 17:00:00, glowing red.

In meeting room 3, both delegations enter and are seated; both have a full view of the digital display.

Negotiations have been ongoing for two weeks, and although some progress had been made, the president has grown tired of all the resistance and has decided it was time for the 'end game.'

"This is unacceptable," the chief negotiator says, defiant. "We have already given you everything we can. You must leave us something."

"Sir, I warned you early on that our president has only so much patience, and today, if we do not come to an agreement, I am authorized to start the end game.

"What is this end game?"

"Think of it as a sort of encouragement to agree to our terms."

"Encouragement" "I do not understand."

"If we do not reach an agreement today, our country will take action on your country 17 hours after that countdown display is started," pointing to the counter on the wall.

"Action?" "What action?" "War?"

"War" "No" "Not war." "Your country does not have the technical means to engage us in war. No, not war but persuasion. We have many different persuaders to choose from, but as an example, let's say you do not agree to our terms as they stand now; the first end game could well be we destroy the electrical infrastructure of one of your country's major cities. Not the capitol, of course, as after the first end game, you will get another chance to agree to our terms, or there will be a second end game. Finally, and I hope we never come to that, a 3rd and final end game."

"I know of no country that has suffered any sort of major event of which you speak of!"

"Yes, well, the president has been very close to executing the 1st end game several times, but an agreement was made, and the end game was cancelled."

"Your president would take action against us? I do not believe such a thing is possible. It would be all over the news. The world would object! No, this is not possible, what you say!"

"Sir, our country can and will take action, and the world will learn nothing of it, or the second end game will have a much shorter window for us to reach an agreement. We would much prefer you to agree to our terms today."

"Your country would not dare!"

"Now my patience is growing thin. Do you agree to our terms as they are defined, or must your country endure the first end game or perhaps even the second before agreeing? We so desire you freely sign the agreement."

"Freely, willingly, agree? You threaten my country but want me to agree to your terms freely? No, I will never agree under some threat."

"To be clear then, sir, are you saying the negotiations for today are over? You will not sign the agreement as defined today?"

"I will not sign today or, next week, or next year! We must have some rights as to future mining in our country."

"Sir, we have made your country a very robust offer in terms of money and our expertise in certain technology domains you stated you wanted, and you have done nothing but continue to demand a share of future mining rights. From the beginning, we made it clear we must control it all. Of course, you will provide workers, and we will pay a premium wage, but all mining and ore export decisions will be with us. All that said, with your unwillingness to sign our agreement today, now, you leave me no choice but to end these negotiations and start end game 1."

"Your country would never!"

A button is pushed and the countdown display begins ticking off seconds.

"As you can see, you now have less than 17 hours to reconsider your position and agree to our terms, or when that counter reaches 00:00:00, the first end game will begin. Between now and the time that is remaining, if we receive an electronically signed agreement, the end game will be canceled. These negotiations are officially closed for the day."

The Muffled Sounds

For over an hour, the Major sits with the Captain in the cockpit, just listening to the sound of the engines roaring away and looking up at the stars overhead. The Major finds great peace here and always has.

When artificial intelligence came along, it was thought that soon there would no longer be the need for human pilots, and perhaps one day that might be true, but no matter how much money was thrown at the problem, AI just was not up to the task of performing complex flight missions and the Major was glad.

He understands that he might not make it to retirement age because of AI, but as long as he can fly, he will.

"Sir ought to start setting up for the injection."

"Yes, of course, but a little more star watching first."

"Yes sir, but not too long."

The Major moves his eyes to switch back on the helmet visor system display, looks at the estimated travel time, and checks comms for any notices from command.

"Yes, ok. Give me a minute," and reaches into his flight bag and pulls out the sleep sedation gas injector, sealed in its case, his name stenciled on it.

He hands the injector to the Captain.

"Make sure it is right."

The Captain looks it over and scans the bar code on the side.

"Confirmed; this sleep package was designed specifically for you, sir."

"Ok, let's do it, and the Major begins the seat incline maneuver.

His seat begins to move backward away from the cockpit instrument panel, and his backrest begins to incline, his feet rising.

Fully prone now, the Major feels the seat latches click closed and is lock in place.

"Ready, Sir?"

"Just do it."

The Captain opens the injector package, holds it in his left hand, and pulls out the tube in the Major's flight suit that accepts the injector.

"All set?"

"Yes sir."

"See you in a bit then, Captain."

"No dreams, Major," pressing the injector trigger, releasing the sedation gas into the Major's air supply.

The Major instantly feels the sedation; he undresses, opens the bed covers, and gets in. Positioning himself as far down into the bed as possible, he rolls over on his left side, puts a pillow into a roll, places his head on the roll, tucks the rest of the pillow against his body, and then pulls the bed covers over his head. With arms and legs in the initial positions, it only takes a few breaths before he begins micro-movements to get every last pressure point or muscle contraction out of his body, and listening to the sound of the engines, now muffled by the bed covers, sleeps.

A New 360

The Captain watches the Major's health display on and off for over an hour, just to be sure. Early on, there were a few problems with injector sleep, but those have been corrected. Still, it's the route pilot's responsibility to get the end game pilot to designated coordinates.

For another hour, the Captain sits simply watching all instrument displays for any sign of trouble, but all is running normally.

The Captain switches out autopilot and engages the AI assistant pilot. Still in the testing phase and not in every mission aircraft at this point, the Captain is curious and has been authorized to engage and monitor the system.

"AI, produce an audible status report every hour of flight."

Understood. Current report: all systems are fully operational. Of note, fuel consumption is greater than planned. At this point, consumption should not impact a completed mission, but it is possible that additional analysis could result in a change of return destination.

"AI, how much is fuel consumption off?"

5% more than expected

"AI, no known cause?"

Not at this point. No malfunctions found in any system, and the engine's fuel management is within boundaries for this altitude.

"AI, thanks. Anything else?"

On the last 360 scan, two unknowns were tracked for a very short period and then disappeared.

"AI, unknowns? What is your definition of an unknown?"

An unknown is anything that returns a scan pulse and creates a track for at least 60 seconds.

"AI, how long track?"

3 minutes.

"AI, 3 minutes and then gone?"

Yes. Do you wish for a new 360 scan now?

"AI, yes."

Scan complete. Null.

The Captain does not know what to think. Never heard of a multi-bird mission, although it certainly could be, but confident that in stealth mode, no country has the capability to detect or intercept the mission.

"AI, do a full 360 scan every 15 minutes and report if unknowns are found again."

Understood.

The Captain puts his head back into his seat and closes his eyes. "Route Pilot. Hours and hours of nothing happening and he is in control of nothing happening."

The Captain leans forward, reaches into his flight bag, and pulls out his PDA.

He has started reading a new book at home and has decided to bring it along. He begins to read. He will let the AI Assistant do all the watching and be there if needed.

'Execute'

During all previous injection sleeps, the Major simply went to sleep, and then almost immediately, he was awake again, but hours had passed. Absolutely no sense of time passage with the injection.

"Baba, Baba, Dad! Dad!"

Some pinprick to the mind. Some splash of water onto a sponge. Deep in a dark cave, something.

For a second, the light is blinding, and then he is in his own backyard with his son and wife, knowing he is in a dream. He can feel he is asleep but can also see that he is in a dream.

The mission, the end game: Cluster neutron bombs. If the 'execute' command comes, he must drop the cargo, killing people, children, and sons like his own son.

"Dad, time to start the grill!" shakes him back to his yard. "What if this mission is execute?"

"Dad, wake up. Where are you? Time to light the grill!"

He is dazed and confused. He is asleep; he knows it, can feel it, and knows he is streaming across the sky to the end game, but here he is, in his backyard.

He finally moves and goes to the grill, but it is all in slow motion. The image of the ground, children at play and then, intense flashes. He feels, for the first time, intense horror.

And then the memory of the test: end game pilot final test. Taken to a room and finding his mother, told to shoot her in the head. He does not think; he simply does what he is told. A terrible test, as the gun was not loaded and his mother was sworn to secrecy, under penalty of a memory override.

His son is beside him, "You want the stuff? Grill hot enough?"

"Yes, I think so."

He looks up at the sky and then all around. So real, but it has to be a dream.

"End game: if he does not drop the cargo at 'execute,' it will be the end for him and his family. He has never been anything but a pilot and knows if he does not follow the execute order, he will never fly again. How would he provide for his family?"

Wake The Pilot

Detection of 2 unknowns at the far end of the scan distance. Track not established.

The Captain looks up from his book and engages the display on his helmet.

"AI, focus scan only in the region of unknowns and increase the power of scan to the maximum."

Max scan power might be intercepted and vectored.

"AI, I authorize," beginning to be annoyed by the, know-it-all, AI Assist.

Note that fuel consumption continues to be above normal. If the end game pilot route is not canceled, an authorized landing destination is unknown at this time.

"AI, estimated flight time after end game flight leg?"

6 hours.

"AI, no authorized airfields within 6 hours of the end game?"

Only commercial.

"AI, possible for landing on water in 6 hours of end game?"

You are not authorized this information.

"AI, time to end of my route?"

58 minutes

"AI, policies, if any, on waking the end game pilot early?"

Route pilot discretion.

"Log entry: Situation requires immediate wake of end game pilot. Wake injection now."

Contacting Command

The Major's eyes open, and he is back in the cockpit.

The Captain commands the Major's seat to return to flight status, and the seat begins to move.

As his seat locks into flight mode, "Like always, just went to sleep. Time for me to take over?"

"Sir, I had to wake you a little early. We have one real problem and maybe another."

"Real problem?" the Major engaging his visor display of all engine performance data.

"We are consuming too much fuel. According to the AI assistant, we have enough for you to complete the end game, but if you fly the end game, we will only have 6 hours of flight time after that, and there is no authorized runway in the 6-hour range."

"And nothing from any system as to the problem with fuel?"

"No sir, all in acceptable ranges and no faults found."

The Major thinks for a minute. "The Cargo."

"Captain, think cargo weight is the problem. We left fully loaded with fuel?"

"Yes sir."

"Don't understand. In prep for the mission, cargo weight had to be factored into route planning fuel consumption."

"Ah, sir, the other thing. 360 scans have picked up two unknowns at the far end of our scan range. There is limited length tracking, but they have appeared in 2 scans, hours apart. Don't know what to make of it."

"2 unknowns. Assume the system thinks they are two different aircraft?"

"Unknown is anything returning a pulse. System unable to identify."

"Makes no sense. As far as I know, there have never been multiple end game missions at the same time."

"Reason, I woke you a little early."

"No authorized runways in the post end game 6-hour range?"

"Only commercial."

"Water landing?

"I not authorized that information."

The Major moves his eyes, brings up his portion of the end game flight, and confirms that there is only 6 hours of fuel post end game.

"AI, is water landing possible, post end game?"

No potential water landing site in the 6-hour window.

The Major switches the visor display to comms but finds nothing in the queue.

"How much longer to my command?"

"50 minutes or so."

The Major tries to think of what to do but comes up empty. Reducing speed is not an option, as he must be at the end game destination point exactly 17 hours after mission start. With only 6 hours of fuel after the end game, he knows of no policy or procedure defined as what to do.

"Might have to break stealth."

"Sir, is that advisable?"

"No, but it appears to be the end game or us, and I am not sure what command would pick, but they must make a decision as I am not going to."

"Outgoing comms even work from this distance?"

"Hope so but unknown."

The Major is silent for several minutes.

"Ok, we get to the end of your route and then contact command."

Two unknowns tracking at the far end of the scan range. Steady parallel track, below at 60,000 feet.

The Major and Captain exchange glances.

"Who the hell could they be? Has to be two more end game birds, but why? Maybe end games are always multiple birds, and I just never knew, but it seems odd."

"AI, unknowns changing track for intercept?"

No change in the scanned track. Time to end game does allow for potential intercept.

"Captain, are we carrying any air-to-air?"

"No sir, all rails are empty."

"Ok, no weapons, two birds following, fuel problem. I'm contacting command."

Abort?

In the capitol, the digital clock has counted down to 3:00:00, and there is still no signed electronic agreement.

In the president's office, an identical counter is also counting away, and the president is getting angrier by the minute.

"Damn fools. Who do they think they are dealing with? I could make their country 8000 degrees if I wanted to. They must know that. Damn fools." He lifts the secure phone and calls his lead negotiator on the mining agreement.

"Anything?"

"No sir, not even a request for additional negotiations."

"You were very clear with them about our ability to persuade?"

"Yes sir, they have been told."

"And end game missions are on schedule?"

"As far as we know. Out of our scan range and in stealth mode, so no contact, but nothing to say they are not on schedule."

"Did we multi-bird this one?"

"Yes sir, we did, as you instructed."

"Call their lead negotiator and tell him I want the signed agreement now. If he refuses, tell him we are going to end game his country, 1, 2 and 3."

"Sir, please, I advise against that. An end game 3, the consequences!"

"Yes, I know, but I think it is time we demonstrate to the world we mean business. We need that ore, and perhaps it is time to reveal some of our persuasion methods."

"Sir, a cluster neutron weapon has never been used. If we use it, other countries will race to develop one."

"We have our defenses for that."

"Sir, please reconsider. Yes, we have very limited adversaries at this time, but such an action could brew up one hell of a storm."

"Yes, well, you're right. Only end game 1, but get them to sign! If they try anything, like even trying to shoot down our birds, I want end game 3. Is that clear?"

"Yes, sir, but again, I have to advise against it."

"Noted: I will make decision on 'execute' or 'abort' at destination."

Null

The Major uses a console to create a very short but concise situation message to command. He reads it over and over, editing it to try to get it as short as possible and yet convey his quandary. Finally, he thinks he has it.

The Captain has been watching, and when the Major pauses, "You got it?"

"Think so. Could be trouble for us both, but I take full responsibility," and the Major eye clicks 'send.' "Now we wait."

"Sir, we are almost at the end of my mission leg. Should I do the sleep or hang with you until we hear?"

"Have thought about that and think it best you do the sleep. If I need you, I will wake you whenever. That OK with you?"

"Yes sir. Could use some sleep, and wakeup drowse is minimal."

The Captain lifts up his flight bag, pulls out the injector pouch, hands it to the Major, and begins the seat maneuver, and before he is fully back, prone, he is asleep.

The Major switches routing to the end game, and the bird begins to make a very sharp bank to the left.

360 scan now tracking turn in position of 2 unknowns, to parallel track. Distance is closing.

"AI, focus scan on the 2 unknowns, track and continue updates to me each minute."

Focus scan. No transponder ID squawking.

"AI, anything from engine pattern recognition?"

No engine pattern detected.

"AI, stealth?"

Further analysis required. 78% probability of identical birds of this configuration.

"3 end game birds? Doesn't make sense unless destination has some air defense that might reach."

"AI, detection of any form of ground scanning?"

Null.

The Countdown Clock

At command, a young lieutenant sees a message come in on the end game channel and is startled. No message has ever come in on that channel. He has sent out messages but never received them. He calls over the colonel.

"Sir, a message is in the queue from an end game mission."

The colonel taps his headset and, after a moment, begins talking rapidly.

"Open the message and read it out loud." The lieutenant obeys.

"Yes, you heard. Well, make it quick."

The received message is immediately relayed from one office to another, moving further and further of the chain of command until the mission phone rings in the president's office.

"End game 3 mission short of fuel? How did that happen? Enough fuel for end game destination leg?"

"Yes sir, but if end game mission leg is flown, no post end game authorized landing runway within the remaining fuel prediction estimate."

The countdown clock in the president's office displays 2:03:59.

Against My Country?

The chief negotiator sees an incoming video call, puts the headset on, and taps 'accept.'

It is the mining country president.

"We will not be bullied. You hear? We will not sign the agreement and have put our defenses on alert. I am warning you now that any entry into our air space not squawking a transponder ID will be shot down. Do you understand?"

"Sir, please, take a moment. You do not want to engage in any form of hostile action against our persuaders. Please, I advise you. Do not sign the agreement, as that is your decision, but take no hostile action. Doing so and its consequences are not something I have any say over. Please, no action."

"You tell me I must sign, or else, and now you tell me not to resist this action against my country?"

"Sir, are you willing to start a war over the dropping of some leaflets for your people to read? You are well aware of our military capabilities, and any action you take would not be in the best interest of your country. I urge you to sign the agreement in place."

"Leaflets? My people said you might take out our electricity or worse."

"Sir, as I told your chief negotiator, we have many types of persuaders in our arsenal, and yes, electrical infrastructure is one, but so too we have food, medicine, leaflets, and some very powerful weapons. Please sign the agreement. Time is running out."

"My country will defend itself," and the video conference is over.

Launch Defender

"Sir, I'm getting an odd reading on the wide-band scanner receiver. Now and again, it appears to be some sort of scanner sweep but not one of ours as frequency is wrong."

"Anything on our scanner?"

"No sir."

"You run equipment tests?"

"Yes sir, and both scanner and receiver are fully functional."

"How long have you been seeing scanner sweeps?"

"On and off for several minutes now, and sir, it appears the signal is getting stronger as if approaching."

"And nothing on our scanner?"

"No sir and I am now getting the same scan frequency but in the form of echo's off two objects."

"I am going to radio command. You keep watching."

The lieutenant of Battery B, high altitude defense, radios his captain.

"Receiver detecting scan sweeps, but nothing on our scanner?"

"Correct Sir."

"Lieutenant, I have just received an alert message that we might soon be under attack from a high-altitude aircraft or missile, and now you are the second battery in my mining district command to call in such a report."

"Stealth aircraft, sir?

"Would explain nothing on our scanner, but why would the enemy use a high-power scan and risk our detection? Makes no sense."

"I don't like it, sir."

"Neither do I. Your battery? You ever get a full store of missiles?"

"No sir. Only the 3 already on the rails."

"Keep me posted, and if your receiver's main sweep signal continues to get stronger, you are cleared to launch when your defenders are in range."

"Yes sir."

When the lieutenant returns to the converted shipping container, the scanner operator is standing at the console.

"It's a stealth aircraft. Actually, 3 and closing on us!"

"What? Our scanner is showing 3 aircraft?"

"No sir, only wideband receiver, but the source of the scan is moving, and now and again, I see reflections off 2 other aircraft. We can't see them with our scanner, but one of their aircraft is scanning at a very high power and illuminating the 2 other aircraft."

"None squawking IDs?"

"No sir."

"With just the receiver, can you tell me how far out they are from us?"

"Well, not exactly, sir, but based on continued signal strength, they are not more than 50 miles out, if that."

"Can you tell the altitude of objects from the scan receiver?"

"Not directly, sir, but based on scan sweep signal strength and angle, all are at or near 60 to 70,000 feet."

"Is the launcher prepped?"

"Yes sir."

"Any of the 3 within missile range?"

"2 of the 3."

"Can we use our receiver to guide our defenders?"

"Yes sir. I have to override the defender built-in scanner and replace it with ground control, but it is possible."

"Do it and launch one defender."

"Yes sir."

Backyard, Son and Wife

Command message being received.

The Major eye clicks comms.

Situation with the end game has worsened. Surface-to-air missiles are probable. Your mission must continue, and if no other message follows, you are to execute end game.

The Major shakes his head. "Missiles, running out of fuel, and 2 unknowns closing."

"AI, time to end game destination?"

14 minutes.

"AI, any information about destination?"

Classified.

"AI, fuel status?"

Current estimate, with normal time over end game destination, is 5 hours of flying time.

"AI, still no authorized runway in flight time remaining?"

Null.

Warning: multiple ground-based scans detected. None tracking.

The Major has practiced for every possible system failure and even ditching in the sea, but never where there is no authorized landing site available.

"Put it down or crash it?"

"Putting it down, only God knows where, could give tech to folks who would eat it up, or 5 hours might get him into friendly territory."

The Major clicks cargo control monitoring and wonders if he should wake up the Captain.

With no weapons, if a missile is sent his way, his only hope is chaff and a steep climb.

"Who has missiles that can reach 70,000 feet? He doesn't know of any country other than his own. Another intelligence blunder and damn things are everywhere?"

The cargo passes self-test and will automatically arm when the end game destination is reached. At the destination, command has 5 minutes to cancel the mission, or according to his last orders, the cargo is to be dropped.

"It is some sort of test. They are just testing me. Will I shoot my mother? How many times do I have to prove myself?"

His backyard, son, and wife come to mind, and he suddenly wonders if there is a pilot like him, just over his yard, the end game destination of his mission.

Health warning. End game pilot heart rate increasing, blood pressure rising. Command automatically being notified.

Time to end game destination is now 1 minute.

Warning, scanning ground-based missile launch.

Missile tracking 1 of 2 unknowns.

Unknown 1 beginning climb.

Missile has destroyed unknown 1.

Warning, scanning 2 ground-based missiles launched.

One is tracking 2nd unknown, and one is tracking this airframe.

Time to impact. 90 seconds.

The Major pushes the engine throttles to the max, manually lifts the engine pulse mode override switch cover, flips the switch to 'armed,' commands chaff release, and then presses and holds the engine pulse mode button on his control stick and holds it.

Immediately, the Major is pushed hard back into his seat, and he watches the altitude indicator as he climbs through 74,000 feet on his way to 80,000.

Missile closing on unknown 2.

Missile exploded at the end of fuel.

Unknown 2 hit and falling.

No pilots ejected.

Unknown 2 disintegrating.

Missile tracking this airframe has expended all fuel.

Missile has exploded.

This vehicle has sustained no damage.

The Major pushes the control stick forward, let's go of the pulse engine mode button, and levels out at 78,000.

"AI, missile threat assessment."

No additional missiles launched. Probability of the missile being capable of reaching this altitude: Null.

Destination reached. End Game.

End game pilot health alert.

Blood pressure continues to rise, and heart rate becoming extremely elevated.

"Oh, shut up," the Major, watching the cargo arm itself.

Scan is still set for maximum power. Continue?

With two unknowns now gone, the Major eye clicks the scanner icon and reduces power back to normal.

"5 minutes. Can he stay aloft for 5 minutes and maybe get an 'abort' message?"

"Dad, Baba, don't do it. Don't drop the cargo. Please."

Command comms message incoming.

"Execute!"

The Major is stunned. "Can't be!"

"AI, if I don't drop cargo, what happens?"

Violation.

"AI, what happens? Does the cargo disarm itself?"

Once armed, only command can disarm.

"AI, cargo set for 2000 feet air burst?"

Correct.

"AI, can the altitude of air burst be changed by end game pilot?"

Low end of cargo air burst is 2000, and fixed. Pilot discretion on increasing the detonation altitude.

"AI, the highest altitude of air burst?"

No upper limit.

"AI, the operational ceiling of this airframe to include cargo weight?"

110,000 feet. Warning! Altitudes above 90,000 feet require pulse injection of both engines. Not recommended. Possible airframe fracture.

"AI, safe to eject sleeping route pilot at current altitude?"

Not recommended.

"AI, Can it be done?"

If additional pilot constraints are in place and the oxygen generator in the seat is activated before ejection.

"AI, if I eject the route pilot, with the cockpit ejection panel removed from the cockpit, can I continue to fly the airplane?"

Not recommended.

"AI, can I survive route pilot ejection?"

Yes.

"AI, and fly plane?"

Ambient air temperature at altitude is fatal after 3 minutes.

"AI, time to climb to max altitude from current?"

3 minutes.

Command message in queue.

The major opens the message, knowing what it will say.

End game cargo activated but not deployed. Problem?

The Major thinks about a response.

Stand Down

Based on the size of falling debris fields, the Battery B lieutenant has watched his scanner track his 3 launched defenders and is convinced 2 of the 3 aircraft have been destroyed.

"Captain, we have destroyed 2 of 3 stealth aircraft."

"Yes, I am getting reports from all batteries in the district, but apparently one aircraft climbed above the range of our defenders."

"Yes sir, and sir, the wide band scanner receiver is no longer receiving any scan sweep, and our scanner is still not picking up the lone stealth aircraft. We do not know and have no way of knowing where the third stealth is or could be."

"Lieutenant, good job, and stand down. I can't get you a missile restock at this time."

"Understood."

The captain radios the colonel of the situation, who then calls the capitol.

Divulge

"End games 1 and 2 are gone? Destroyed? They destroyed our birds?"

"What? What do you mean end game 3 cargo has not been dropped? Thought I gave very specific instructions that if any action was taken against our persuaders, we would execute end game 3. Can we command cargo drop remotely?"

"No, Mr. President. The doctrine requires man-in-loop for actual cargo drop."

"Ok, so what can we do? Can we trigger the cargo remotely?"

"No sir. We can only deactivate the cargo remotely. Current thought is that the end game pilot will drop the cargo as instructed. If he does not and the cargo is not disarmed by you, it will detonate at programmed altitude, which, in this case, is 2000 feet. Meaning that the end game pilot cannot try to land the plane as the cargo will explode."

"So, all we can do is disarm the cargo?"

"Yes sir, that is our only option as the situation exists at this moment."

"No way to shoot him down? If we disarm, he could land anywhere and get a handsome reward for the cargo."

"He would not do that, sir."

"What the hell do you know what he will do? He hasn't dropped the cargo as instructed by his president!"

"Sir, we have no assets in the region with the capability to reach aircraft at altitude."

"Our friends in the region?"

"No sir."

"So, what is the Major going to do?"

"Sir, at this point, we simply do not know. This situation has never happened before, and this is the first time end game 3 has been invoked. Should I have the cargo disarmed?"

"No, not yet. We have time, correct?"

"We are not tracking the aircraft, but since the pilot has not dropped cargo, assume he will either circle end game destination and perhaps, eventually, drop the cargo or try to start the return route."

"And sir, our chief negotiator on the mining agreement has been made aware of the current situation and is suggesting he contact their chief negotiator and divulge that the one remaining persuader's cargo is a cluster neutron device large enough to blanket their mining district. His thoughts are that with the cargo hanging over their heads, above the altitude of their defenders, it might be enough to get a signed agreement."

OK, we'll wait, but I want you to get anybody who is anybody to come up with a good solution to your problem."

1 Minute

With the AI assistant engaged and set to simply circle the end game destination, the Major leans back into his seat.

"I'm not dropping cargo. We are not at war. I am not killing innocents," and he begins to mull over his options. None seem very good, but perhaps setting the cargo to air burst at 80,000 feet while he is at a max of 110,000, he will have time to get the plane and the Captain a safe distance away and land at any runway within the remaining fuel range. Some risk of engine pulse burn at max altitude, but he has to only climb up, drop cargo, drop down, and pulse jet away.

"AI, lethality radius in miles of cluster cargo."

No cluster data available.

Single, low yield 1KT, 2000 feet altitude air burst: 1 mile.

"AI, projected number of neutron bombs required to lethally blanket 5 square miles of ground?"

9 to 12.

"AI, the time it will take for cargo to drop from 110.000 feet until air bursts at 60,000 feet?"

1 minute.

"AI, from airdrop coordinates, using engine pulse mode at 90,000 feet, distance airframe away from detonation?"

22 miles.

"AI, is 22 miles safe distance from all radiation forms of detonation?"

Altitude will diminish ionization radiation.

"AI, safe distance?"

80% probability radiation survivable.

The Major looks over at the sleeping Captain.

"Might be wrong, but if what I am about to do goes bad, I think sleeping into it is best for you. You can't help me now, and if we do survive this, it will be clear you had no part in it."

AI Cannot Be Used

"Yes. What have you got?"

"Mr. President, we have moved a satellite over the end game destination and are now tracking the end game 3 aircraft. It continues to circle the end game 3 destination."

"And?"

"Sir, of the package: the pilots, the plane, and the cargo, the cargo is the most important. It cannot get into foreign hands, friend or foe. To ensure that, we cannot risk disarming the cargo. We suggest that the end game pilot be instructed to set the cargo air burst to 70,000 feet, climb to the aircraft limit of 110,000, drop cargo, and pulse inject away. The aircraft and pilots may or may not get far enough away to not be destroyed, but it is the only real option. If aircraft and pilots survive cargo detonation, we can deal with that problem at that time. Also, from a query to our intelligence community, there might be an abandoned runway within the post end game fuel range. Runway is a little short for the aircraft type, but in stealth mode, the pilot could at least land, and we would control the ground situation."

"Only option?"

"Yes sir, we agree the only option as end game pilot apparently is not going to drop cargo as instructed."

"Ok, do it. Where is our AI pilot program?"

"Unless doctrine changes, AI cannot be used to drop cargo."

Drops Down

The Major eye clicks cargo settings and moves air burst detonation to 60,000 feet. "Might be a little low, but gives him more time to get away from detonation radiation."

Cargo accepts new air burst settings.

The Major flips up the pulse jet override switch cover and toggles the engine pulse switch to 'arm,' takes a deep breath, presses the pulse jet button on his stick, and pulls the stick back hard.

The bird enters a steep upward climb, and the Major is again pushed back into his seat.

82,000 feet, 94,000 feet, 104,000 feet.

Warning: The maximum ceiling for the aircraft type is exceeded. Possible airframe fracture. Reduce altitude.

At 110,000 feet, the Major eye clicks the cargo drop icon and immediately pushes the stick forward to drop the plane altitude but keeps the pulse jets burning.

Warning: aircraft altitude is above the safe limit. Reduce airframe altitude to below 90,000 feet. Warning: airframe speed above the recommended maximum, reduce airspeed.

"AI, time to air burst?"

45 seconds.

The Major continues to hold the pulse jet button and levels out at 90,000 feet.

Warning! Airspeed at the current altitude is not recommended. Reduce airspeed or altitude.

"AI, the distance from cargo airdrop?"

18 miles.

Warning: airspeed exceeding airframe limit. Frame fracture possible. Reduce airspeed now.

"Just a little longer."

Airburst detected.

"AI, distance from air burst?"

24 miles.

Warning: Radiation detected.

"AI, radiation detected lethality?"

Neutron radiation only nominally high: not lethal. Ionization null.

The pulse jet button is released and disarmed, and the Major drops down to 80,000 feet.

Congratulations

"Sir, end game 3 cargo has detonated at 60,000 feet and end game three aircraft has survived and has started the return route."

"Results of cargo detonation?"

"No ground casualties, and sir, we have just received a signed mining agreement. Apparently, their inability to defend and their detection of cargo detonation was enough. We have agreement."

"Good, very good: curious. Did the end game 3 pilot receive our instructions about high-altitude detonation?"

"No sir. The message had not been sent at the time of detonation as waiting on getting details on the intelligence agency runway, thinking runway information would help persuade the pilot of our post end game intent."

"Our intent?"

"Action to be taken against him and the route pilot. End game pilot did not follow orders as instructed."

"Ok, work on getting him down, but do not arrest him. I want to see him as soon as he can return here."

"Yes sir, and congratulations on getting the mining agreement."

Dismissed

The door to the president's office opens, and the Major enters, approaches the president's desk, stops, and stands at military attention.

"Sir, you wanted to see me."

"Ah, yes, Major. It is my understanding that your routing pilot was not involved in the mission's end game."

"That is correct, sir. He was asleep as defined by mission instructions."

"Major, you disobeyed my orders to drop the cargo, and I want to know why. You're an end game pilot. I thought you were chosen for the role because you obeyed orders."

The Major is silent.

"Major, I asked you a question."

"Sir, I have a wife and a son. Over the end game destination, knowing what the cargo was and the death it would bring below, all I could see was my son and many other fathers' sons on the ground, dead."

"Didn't you shoot your mother?"

"Yes sir."

"So having a wife and son was the reason you did not drop the cargo?"

"I just could not kill innocents, sir. We are not at war."

"You know I could have you jailed for life?"

"Yes sir."

"Major, you may or may not know, but the purpose of the end game mission was achieved when you detonated the cargo without causing harm on the ground, and after much consideration, your procedure of a high-altitude burst has now been defined as protocol for all cluster cargo."

"Major, I should jail you, but I'm not. It is my decision that you be demoted to route pilot status. You OK with that?"

"Sir, being a pilot is what I am, have ever been. It would be an honor to fly for you as a route pilot. Thank you for your consideration."

"Major, you are dismissed."

"Yes sir."

The Major does a quick, clean, precise military about-face and starts towards the door.

"Oh, Major! I'm curious. How did you know your bird would not tear itself to pieces with pulse jets going at max altitude?"

Doing a military about-face, "I didn't, sir. Have flown the type many times and has never failed me even when I had to push it to the limit."

"And Major, had it torn itself to pieces?"

"I would have tried to land whatever was left of the airframe. I have a wife and son, sir."

Musing: "Carnival Hootchy Coochie"

In the 1950s, my mother's parents lived on a large farm out in the country. I lived on a city street in a small town, a good hour car ride from them. But we visited them often, and in August of each year, my grandparents and my family would always go to the 'local' county fair.

On a large tract of land, owned by whom I never knew, the fair consisted of many livestock show buildings, a grandstand with a large oval dirt track with an infield, and lots of open fields that hosted car parking and various carnival rides and side shows.

Can't say about all fairs, but the August fair I visited for many years, had judged livestock of all kinds, including pigs, cows, sheep, and various farm fowl of all types and sizes. Also judged, with ribbons awarded, were jarred vegetables, jams, pies, cakes, farm crops from corn and fruits to wheat and other grains, handicrafts from cross stitch to quilts, baskets, and even a painting or 2.

Each year, entertainment was available for the price of grandstand admission, and it could be some current country music artist or band, horse racing, and now again, a car demolition derby or stock car race.

Over the years, I saw various country music artists just starting out who later became famous.

But for me, the fair was the midway, where various carnival rides, games of chance, foods of all types, and side shows created an 'avenue', stretching for perhaps a hundred yards.

I tasted cotton candy for the first time at that fair and once spent a quarter to go inside a sideshow tent that promised a sword swallower, a bearded fat lady, a two-headed calf, and other bizarre people or animals from around the world. It turned out to be nothing but walls and walls of pictures.

And 'yes' there was a picture of a very, very, large bearded fat lady and a two-headed calf but also a woman pushing around their enormous boobs in a wheelbarrow and some dark-skinned native from some far-off land with a huge bone stuck through his nose.

Three rings for a dime with one ring over the neck of any one of the dozens of soda pop bottles set up, tightly packed, on a table, would get you your choice of a piece of what was to become known as "carnival glass."

I did often try the baseball throw to knock over stacked wooden milk bottles but never got all 3 with one shot. Pretty sure the prize for getting all 3 was not carnival glass but a stuffed animal.

With the old folks sitting on benches along the outside of the grandstand, I would wander up and down the midway over and over again and rode my first Ferris wheel at the fair.

At the far end of the midway, some 50 yards or so out in the field by itself was an enormous, fully enclosed tent. For many years, I never saw any activity outside the tent and simply thought it was some sort of housing for those who worked the carnival rides.

One year, some country music artist of note was to perform at dusk and my grandparents and my parents had decided they would pay the price to see the show in the grandstand. I told them I was not interested and would simply walk the midway until their show was over.

I sat on a bench outside the grandstand for a long time and then, the midway lights came on, and the avenue was bathed in all sorts of colors, and it took on a special kind of look that beckoned me to walk end-to-end, once again.

This time, when I reached the far end of the midway, that huge tent off in the field was now bathed in light, and a crowd was gathering around it. "What was going on at that big tent?"

Once past the last of the midway booths and tents, the large tent gave off so much light that it was an easy walk.

As I approached the tent, some man was talking loudly to a crowd of only men and on a stage along one side of the tent, I had never noticed before, were some 3 or 4 women dressed in very suggestive, flimsy clothes, dancing or shimming while the carnival barker suggested that for a mere $5 tent admission, one could witness these beautiful, exotic creatures dance and strip off all their clothes. "Yes, these beautiful, young, Hootchy Coochie girls will become naked before your very eyes for a mere $5."

Don't remember how old I was, but I had never seen anything like this before in my life. At that time, my knowledge of naked women was nothing more than bra or panties advertisements in some catalog used in the outhouse or bare-chested Africans in a National Geographic magazine I had seen a time or two. No, this was something else.

Over and over: "Only 5 US dollars. You fellows haven't never seen anything like what is inside this tent. Now, come on, it's time for the show to start. Who is going to join the ladies inside?" And with that, the dancing ladies stopped moving, wrapped a shawl around them and disappeared off the stage and into the tent.

I stood a while and watched maybe 8 or 9 men pay the barker, lift the flap, and enter the tent. When no one else stepped forward, the barker shut off the stage floor lights and disappeared inside the tent as well.

With those that had not paid and gone inside, I returned to the midway and roamed again, thinking about what I had just seen.

"Did my dad know of this tent? Had he ever been inside? My Uncles?"

I returned to the benches outside the grandstand and simply sat and watched the crowd begin to thin out. But it was not long until I noticed the lights at that big tent were full bright again, and I could see a crowd gathering: another show.

As I never had $5, I never went inside the tent for a show, but after this first encounter, in subsequent years, I would always find myself outside watching the free stage show anytime I was at the fair at dark.

Then life moved on, and I have not been to a county fair in many, many years, but now and again, in August, I remember and wonder.

If the ladies inside the tent were the same ladies doing the free shows outside?

Who were these ladies that danced and supposedly stripped at county fairs? I don't see how they could have been local recruits, but does that mean they traveled around the country with others and that big tent?

Runaway and join the Hootchy Coochie show? "Runaway and join the circus," 'Yes,' as a boy, I heard that, but did little girls get told a different version?

Actually, strip naked? I know now there are laws about public nudity, but I have no idea, what if any, laws were in effect at the time of the Hootchy shows.

Never saw a policeman, ever, all the years I attended the same fair. Did the police ever raid the big tent? Make arrests or simply watch the show for free?

How did one become a Hootchy Coochie woman? Suspect not something posted in "Want Ads" and never saw a flyer for "carnival stripper wanted" stapled to a telephone pole.

Did a boyfriend or husband working the fair, manning a carnival ride or game of chance, get his wife or girlfriend into the trade?

Did women actually show up at a fair and ask if they could be a dancer on that stage?

Although all the "ladies" on the teasing stage were white, I wonder if, in other parts of the country, there were indeed black Hootchy Coochie girls.

If the tent got paid $5 per head, what did a Hootchy Coochie woman get paid per show or night or per fair? Inside, did women get tips from attendees or perform special acts for an additional fee?

Don't remember any of the free stage show women having specific performer names like 'Wild Cherry' or 'Princess Lay-me', but perhaps they did, and I just don't remember. For all I know, one or more of these stage women could have gone on to be a porno star, a famous stripper, an actress of note or even a politician. There must be some history book written on this subject somewhere.

Seems to me all the women were rather thin or, else, 'curvy,' as it is called now, and actually quite attractive, which bodes the question if they actually worked at their craft and ran miles or lifted weights or worked out in-between shows? Or did they simply sleep and eat and then do shows?

Wonder if they ever went down into the local towns, looked around, and shopped or had their hair done?

With me being so young and naïve at the time, perhaps these women on the stage and inside the tent were drug users?

And I wonder if there is some woman, somewhere, still living, that once was a carnival fair, Hootchy Coochie woman?

When I was in the Army, stationed in South Korea, prostitutes outnumbered soldiers 2 to 1, and I was aware that there were 'homes,' places, where old prostitutes retired. Never heard about a Hootchy Coochie retirement home, but what if there is or was?

Wonder if county fairs in certain parts of the country still have that big tent out beyond the midway where men gather when it gets dark?

Finally, the term "hoochie coochie" comes from the French word 'hochequeue' which means "to shake a tail."

"The Record"

Once more, she made her way over to where the numbers and the records were posted, and once more, she stood in silence, looking up at that one number. That one 'time,' she knew she had to beat.

She had tried three times and missed three times, and now her last chance was coming soon, and again, she looked up and stared.

Finally, she was called for her event, the event, and as she walked away from the record board, all she could see in her mind was that 'time,' those precious seconds.

She broke the record that day and after her parents and friends had packed up and headed home, she walked to the record board, stared at it one more time, and thought: "Now my name will be up there."

Over the next several years, she broke three other records, but the feeling she got from breaking them never equaled the feeling she got the day she broke her first record. Then, she entered high school, competing each year and even through college. She was good but never broke another record of any kind, and then, after three children and a divorce, she had stopped competing altogether.

It was a shock when she received the call of her father's death. They had not seen much of each other over the past several years, with her living now on the West Coast, but he had always seemed to be there, to be there for her, and on the long plane ride, she could think of nothing else but him.

After the funeral and the wake, she and her mother sat for a long time in the home kitchen that evening talking, and then finally, her mother headed off to bed and she was left alone with her thoughts.

At first, she only remembered the trips her dad had made to her home and the time he had crashed the car but not been hurt, and then, for some reason, she began to think how he had been her greatest and best supporter when she competed. Always encouraging and critiquing to make her better. He had beamed with pride and joy the day she broke her first record. "That first record," she thought. "Wonder if it still stands? Wonder if my name is still up there on the board?"

At first, she was tempted to go to her mother's room and ask her but thought better of it. "No," she thought, and feeling like a walk might do her some good, she grabbed her coat and hat and headed out the door. She would see for herself.

It was cold out and light snow was beginning to fall as she left the house and headed down the street. "It isn't far, or at least it used not to be," pulling the coat collar up around her neck.

As she walked, she remembered that day, now so long ago, and how she had not felt good but somehow had managed, to her surprise, to break the record and how all her friends had cheered and congratulated her. A smile came over her face for the first time in many days.

As she turned the final corner, she suddenly remembered the fence, the gate, the lock. "How would she get in? Maybe she would be able to see the record board through the fence?"

When she reached the fence, the gate was locked with a long chain, but the lock had been put on the chain in such a way that when she pushed the gates apart, she thought she could just slip between, and with some squeezing and pulling, she made it inside.

Everything appeared to be the same as she remembered it and quickly crunched her way through the new-fallen snow to where the record board hung. "Dam", it was too dark to see, and fumbling in her pockets, found her car key chain and its small flashlight. "Would her name still be there?"

Her eyes went directly to the event and age, and there, instead of her name, was another name, a name she did not recognize or know. Somehow, she had known in the back of her mind that chances were not good that she still held the record, but then again, she hoped she would still be up there. "D. Shorter." "I wonder who 'D. Shorter' is and if she knew how hard it had been for her to break the record and then it occurred to her. She could not remember the name of the record holder she had beaten and then realized that she had never looked at the name, only the 'time,' only those seconds to be beaten."

After another moment, her vision came back, and she looked around the record board, and there, in an event she had never liked but had competed in at her father's urging, was her name. She still held one record after all the years.

The next morning, she was up early looking in the telephone books for Mr. Shorter. After a few rings, a man answered. "Yes, he was Mr. Shorter and yes, his daughter Doris did swim."

When Doris got on the phone, she talked with Doris for a long time.

"The Crow"

He had not expected her. He had not expected anything. He had learned never to expect.

He was just there lazily watching when he caught a glimpse of a bright-shiny out of the corner of one eye. Turning and cocking his head to get a better view and inspect, he almost took flight at the blazing, intense eyes and wide happy smile that he saw.

He had not seen a bright-shiny like this one in a long time and at once, he was attracted and wanted to own and, at the same time, frightened and wanted to fly or jump or move. But he did not jump or fly but instead simply looked away, hoping to find something else of interest, but his eyes quickly were drawn back to the bright-shiny and once again; he was so blinded by the light she gave off he almost took to flight. "Why was he so frightened of this bright-shiny and yet, why could he not leave?"

Thoughts: he did not like thoughts, and his heart lifted him up and out over the river and under the bridge and then straight into the setting sun, and he soared and sailed until slowly, the bright-shiny faded from his mind, and he felt strong enough to circle back.

With his mind free of her, he folded his wings from flight and then, without even looking, knew the bright-shiny was no longer there, and suddenly, he missed her.

"Where was the bright-shiny?" How crazy it was for him to want to get away and then be terrified that he might never see the bright-shiny again. He stretched out his neck, narrowed his eyes, and looked all about for her.

She was gone a long time, and all the while, the old crow, the ancient wind sailor, searched the horizon over and over, hoping for a glimpse of the bright-shiny, and when he did see her, she was still far off, and he felt safe watching her from his distance.

When she finally came to where he was, he hid from view to watch her undetected. But as he watched, he suddenly thought to himself, "She was aware of him and perhaps even watching him," and he bolted and again sailed high up, and her hair, flowing down her back, stuck with him and moved in his mind as he twisted one wing and then the other and banked and turned and fell steeply down.

But the flight and the wind could not erase her from his mind, and he knew he would have to get closer to this bright-shiny.

Without thinking another thought, he spread his wings to slow his descent and sat down beside her. He could not help himself, and he hated himself for it. "Foolish old crow, he could never own her."

When she turned to him and her bright eyes and smile came full force on him, his heart leaped, for now, he was bathed in her light and could feel the heat of the bright-shiny eyes, and suddenly it was as if he had climbed too high into the sun and had become blind and disoriented. Only after hearing enough of her sounds did he remember where he was and slowly regain his vision and balance.

Some shiny's were all empty inside, and his interest in these never lasted long, but he was not disappointed with this one, for she was genuine and clean and clear as the view of a mountain lake from high above, and her sounds flowed over and about him like the wind when he was in flight.

As her sounds poured over him, he watched her watch him in his mind's eye, and he could see that she saw him for the old crow that he was and nothing more. Somehow knowing, "nothing more", helped him calm himself, and slowly, he began to regain control of himself, and after a while, he simply turned and leaped away.

He was content for a long time after leaving her, and then the wind shifted, the bright-shiny began to move away, and he found himself following her even though he knew he could not expect more from her.

She came and went in his mind that evening many times, and he took flights of fancy now and then with her.

His imagination lifted him across the tree tops and in and out of gentle conscious touching's he thought they shared, and his heart would leap, and he would disdain it and move about agitated, and still her light kept the night bright until finally he watched her go out of sight and all the longings in the world could not make him follow her or she come back to him.

The old crow sits now high above and again watches lazily, and sometimes, without warning, his heart remembers her and thoughts of her lift him up like an updraft from the earth on a summer's day.

"Foolish old crow," and yet he wishes he could see the bright-shiny again and make her his.

"The Memory That Never Was"

Ever have a memory that is so vivid, so real, and yet you know that it never happened, could not have happened?

I suspect psychologists would say what I call a memory is really a fantasy, and they are probably right. But this fantasy has been around so long, that it has gotten all tangled up with my real memories and has made itself a home there. In the end, it seems to me, that it does not make any difference if it is a memory or fantasy; I like it either way.

I do wonder though, if, over time, our minds fill up with memories that we think are real but, in actuality, are just long-lived fantasies? Nevertheless, what follows below is one of my favorite "memories."

***

I am a baseball pitcher in the minor league farm system of the New York Yankees and have been so for three years. I am not a bad pitcher, and I do continue to improve, but I am not the best pitcher in the Yankee's system either, or so I think. Thus, I was stunned, when my team manager called me just after the farm league season ended, and told me that the Yankees had called me up to join the team in New York.

I knew the Yankees were in the World Series against the Atlanta Braves or would be so in a few days, but why call me up to join the team? "Kid," said my manager, "I have no idea why they want you. They did say they think they are short one relief pitcher with Winger injured and I guess they just chose you. Now, don't get your hopes up, as there is no way in hell you will ever pitch in the series. You will probably only be up there for the series and then right back here with me!"

When I hung up the phone, I was in total shock. I was going to be in the World Series with the New York Yankees, and if they won the series, even if I never pitched one ball, I would still get a World Series ring, just like all the other team players.

I telephoned everyone I knew, even some I hardly knew, telling them the news. Then, I crammed a few things in a small bag and headed to the airport and New York.

The next day, I got to Yankee Stadium an hour before I was told to report. I was nervous and just wanted to look around before the other players came in for practice. Walking out onto the field, I could not believe how huge the stadium was on the inside, and I thought of all the incredible players who had played inside this park over the years. It was simply a dream I was having; it had to be. And then, I heard my name being called and when I turned, there walking towards me was "Fish," as he was called by everyone, Carlton, the manager of the Yankees.

"You the new kid, the pitcher I sent for?" looking down at the perfectly maintained infield grass. "Yes sir, and I want to thank you for giving me this opportunity, I." but he interrupted. "Kid, I doubt you will throw one pitch during the series, but I just could not go into the series short one relief pitcher. Besides, you will give all our catchers some practice, and they need it. Go inside now and someone will get you a uniform and a locker, and then get back out here. Practice starts in half an hour." And with that, Fish turned around and headed to the dugout.

***

That first practice with the team was pretty uncomfortable. It seemed like no one wanted to talk with me, and I found it hard to even get a catcher to throw to, to loosen the arm. My guess was they were all resentful of me being on the team now, at the end of the regular season and the playoffs, and potentially getting a World Series Championship ring, just like them. Guess they felt I had not worked for it, and in a way, they were right, but it was not them riding a crowded old bus from ball field to ball field and eating crappy food and paying for it yourself.

Baseball farm leagues are a "slave labor" system, but some of these players had never been there and did not know what it was like. Anyway, I did manage to get some pitches thrown and, overall, felt happy with the first day of practice.

The second day was similar to the first, but some of the players actually began to talk to me, and by late afternoon, I became known as "The Kid," and that was fine with me.

Finally, the World Series started with the first two games in New York, to be followed by three games in Atlanta, and then a return to New York for the final two games, if needed.

From the dugout, I watched the New York Yankees just slaughter the Atlanta Braves in games 1 and 2, with our starting pitchers making it deep into the game before getting relieved. "I would never play", I told myself, relaxed and just could not believe my luck on being there. "The series is going to be over in another 2 games as the Yankee hitters were too strong and the relief pitching too deep."

But after the series moved to Atlanta, as good as we had been in New York; we were as bad in Atlanta. Atlanta easily won the next 2 games, and Fish threw pitcher after pitcher at the Braves, hoping to take at least one win back with the team to New York, but it did not turn out that way.

The third game in Atlanta was close, and we held our own for most of the way, but in the 9th, our relief pitcher threw a wild pitch, and Atlanta scored the winning run.

3 games Atlanta, 2 games Yankees, and back to New York.

***

Game 6 was a pitching duel with both teams going through relief pitcher after pitcher, but in the 8th inning, we managed a rally and eventually won the game, tying the series 3 games apiece. The World Series was going to a final, deciding 7th game.

When I got to the stadium for the 7th game, the locker room was so quiet it scared me. Had the team's confidence been shaken, or were they concentrating on what must be done? No one said a word, and it was a quiet walk out to the dugout. The warm-up was spooky, with not nearly a word being spoken, even among the usually talkative infield players.

Finally, the game began, and we started out great with 4 runs in the first inning, but then it stayed that way until the 7th when Atlanta staged their own rally and came up with 3 runs, so with 2 innings to go, we led by a single run.

At the bottom of the 7th, we managed to get one man on base, but that was it, and going into the 8th inning, the score remained Yankees 4, the Atlanta Braves 3.

After the Braves rally in the 7th, Fish yanked the starting pitcher and put in Ruddock, one of our best relief pitchers who had not thrown since game 2. For a while, he looked sharp and struck out the first 2 batters of the 8th inning easily and quickly, but then a hit, a walk, and Ruddock was in trouble. Luckily for us, the next batter hit into an infield out and the inning ended with no additional runs for the Braves.

Our at-bat in the 8th yielded nothing, as the Braves had switched pitchers and we could not connect to anything.

***

9th inning of the World Series, 4 to 3 Yankees. Just one more inning, just 3 more outs, and the Yankees would win the Series.

When the 9th started, Ruddock was again on the mound, but he did not look good from the start. He 'walked' the first batter, putting the tying run on base, and then gave up a single to deep left field. He got the next 2 batters on pop flies for 'outs', but he obviously was struggling with control.

As I watched Ruddock standing nervously on the pitcher's mound, all of a sudden, my view was blocked, and when I looked up, Fish was standing in front of me. I stood up. "Kid," Fish began. "I know this is a hell of a time to be sending you in, but Ruddock just doesn't have his stuff right now and we are fresh out of relief. I have watched you in practice and you can do this. All I am asking for is just one 'out'. Just one lousy 'out', kid." And with that, he turned towards the dugout stairs, and I followed him up the stairs and out onto the field.

As he walked out on the field, he called "Time" and proceeded with me in tow to the pitcher's mound. All this time, I had been focusing on the game so much that I had not really been listening to the crowd, but now there seemed to be this giant question of noise coming from everywhere. "What was Fish doing? Who is that kid? What is he doing putting in a kid now? Is he crazy?"

When we got to the mound, Ruddock looked relieved as he really had been struggling, and he knew it. He took off his cap and mopped his brow. Fish began, "Look, you know and I know you just don't have it today, so thanks for the great effort, but I just have to replace you." Ruddock did not argue with Fish to stay in the game like some pitchers do and handing me the ball, he simply said, "Good luck, kid." Then Ruddock and Fish walked to the dugout, and I was left alone. Alone on the pitcher's mound in the middle of Yankee Stadium, 7th and deciding game of the World Series, 4 to 3 Yankees, the tying and winning runs on base, 2 'outs', 9th inning, and sweat dripping out of every pore on my body. My heart pounding away, I just knew everyone in that stadium could hear it. "Calm yourself. Calm yourself," I thought, but it did not seem to help very much. Finger the ball over and over, look out at centerfield, and breathe.

Not ready to face home plate yet, I finger the ball in my hand, wipe my forehead, try to dry my hands on my pants. Finally, I turn towards home plate and there, in the on-deck batter's circle, is the Brave's best hitter. With only 1 'out' to go, they had nothing to lose using the pinch hitter rule, and so they had. Oh God, his bat looked monstrous as he swung it over and over, and then, stepping up to the plate, he swung his bat in a half swing pointing directly at me. "Watch out, kid, I am going to send one to you!"

I throw a few pitches to loosen up the arm, and then the umpire calls out, "Play Ball," and I again turn away from home plate. "Ok, I can do this," I say to myself. "I can do this." I turn and look for the sign from the catcher, McGill.

It's low and outside. He wants me to throw the first pitch low and outside. I guess he does not trust me very much as he does not want me to give the batter anything he could hit with any power, and he might even swing at the low and away pitch and miss. I calm myself, put one foot on the pitcher's mound rubber, wind up, and throw.

Low and away it is, but too low and too away, and the umpire calls out, "Ball 1." Immediately, McGill calls "time" and comes walking out to the pitcher's mound. "Kid," he says to me, "Kid, did you ever play any sandlot baseball? You know, just a bunch of kids playing the game for fun. Did you kid? Well, this here is just like that. Just think of playing for fun, the games, and you will be okay. Now, when I go back there, you throw exactly what I tell you to. You can do this, kid." And with that, he turned and walked back to home plate.

"Sandlot. All the fun games on Saturday." As sweat poured down my face and my heart pounded, it sure did not feel like "sandlot or fun" but then I remembered the time I had struck out the loud mouth of the neighborhood. Don't think he ever forgot it and was not all that loud of the mouth ever again. "Sandlot. Fun. Sandlot."

I check the bases to see if anyone is thinking about running on the pitch, but they are hugging their bases. Once again, I look at home plate and the sign from McGill is right across the plate and high. "No, it can't be," and I wag off the pitch with my head. Again, McGill flashes me the sign for right across the plate and high. I look towards Fish in the dugout but read nothing.

I wind up and after I see the batter swing ever so hard, the ball finds its home in McGill's catcher's mitt with a loud thud. "Strike 1," calls the umpire and the batter begins to swing his bat more furiously now, over and over and again, then half swings and points it at me.

Runners are holding on bases and McGill signals a curve ball, low and away. I take my time and the sandlot loud mouth comes to mind. "Sandlot. Fun." I bring the ball forward, and this time, I can see the batter ready. He is going to smash this one out of the park, but at the last moment, the ball curves just like it is supposed to and again smashes into McGill's catcher's mitt. "Strike 2!" yells the umpire.

The crowd, which had been subdued, is now on their feet and screaming. "One more out! One more Out!"

"Sandlot, Sandlot", I keep repeating to myself and remember all the games, all the fun, all the lost balls, and deciding who would be on which team and how it really did not matter.

McGill gets back down into this stance and signals another low and away, while the batter continues to swing and swing his mighty bat.

The last pitch must have scared McGill, and maybe, just maybe, I will hit the corner of the plate low and away and still give the batter nothing to really hit. I compose, draw the ball and glove to my chest, and reach way back and throw it with all I have. Again, it's too low and away, and the batter never even thinks about trying for it. "Ball 2," calls the umpire.

McGill stands upright and shakes out the kinks in his knees and legs, giving me some time. Then, he is back down in his stance and signals for a sinker. "A sinker? What if it hangs over the plate? What if the ball does not sink at the last moment like it is supposed to, and this guy blasts the ball out of the park?" I shake my head, "No!" but McGill again shows me the sign for a sinker.

I check the bases, but the runners are holding. I wind up and let it go. It looks good, and then, just over the plate, it falls like a rock, and the ump yells, "Ball 3!" "Oh God, could this get any worse?"

It is now Yankees 4 to 3 over the Atlanta Braves in the 7th game of the World Series, 9th inning, 2 out, 2 men on base, 3 balls, and 2 strikes, and here I am, a farm league team pitcher alone on the mound.

"Sandlot, sandlot", like some mantra, over and over again. "A tipped ball into the jungle of sticker bushes behind home plate and the ensuring search for our only ball."

I wipe my pitching hand on my pants and mop the sweat from my eyes. "I can do this", I say to myself. "I can do this."

Then I once more, face the Braves batter and check McGill for the sign. Low and away, he signals. "What? I have already thrown 2 of those, and neither has been on the edge of the plate for a strike. What?" Again, I shake my head to wave off what he wants me to throw, but again, he flashes me low and away. And then, for some reason, I will never be sure why, I begin to focus on the eyes of the batter instead of home plate. His eyes seem to burn like glowing coals, and for a moment, I think I can see myself through them.

"One potato, 2 potato, 3 potato, 4." I put my foot on the pitcher's mound rubber and draw back my arm.

I never heard the umpires call, but I saw the dust fly out of McGill's mitt when the ball hit, and then the crowd going crazy loud, and the whole team running out onto the field and surrounding me.

It had been low and away but had just nipped the outside of the home plate and the batter was left standing there as the umpire had called, "Strike 3."

Like nothing I have ever experienced before or since, the celebration parties lasted for two days, and through it all, there was no resentment about "The Kid" getting a ring.

Finally, on the 3rd day after the end of the series, it came time for everyone to clean out their lockers and head home for the winter. As I packed my bag, Fish approached me and said, "Kid, you did well, you really did, but 3 strikes don't make a player in this league and I have to send you back down. Maybe next year, kid, maybe next year."

***

So, I returned home just flying high, but when spring training started for my farm league team, I told them I could not play anymore. Nothing would ever be as good as my moments in the big leagues, and I have never regretted my decision.

See what I mean by a memory? It felt real, didn't it? Not one of yours, I know, but you must have some sort of similar long-lived memory, or is it a fantasy?

Memories: memories are funny things.

Ron Stultz

Musing: "El Cortez Never Slept Here, I'll Bet"

El Cortez Motel, Serra Vista Arizona

Heat pipe clock,

ticking, popping, hissing.

The heat seems like an extra.

I am not unfamiliar with this place,

this cave from the wind and sun.

A bed for tossed sleep.

Two doors,

One for exit,

One for sewer.

Not ugly.

Not pretty.

Barren.

And I am here now,

and I am everywhere I have ever been

or will be.

It comes when I need it?

Does it talk of home?

Home with paint,

color and warmth.

But is the skin the difference,

or is it the shape, the texture

of the living?

The smile I can see

and not have to look into the mirror

to get?

Inside.

Inside the body.

Inside the mind,

there is the deepest longing

for love.

Am I a man in want

of companionship?

A TV mate?

An after 5 ear?

How many dimensions do we live in?

How many separate lives?

How many joined?

See-through curtains,

and a yellow walk light

outside to welcome.

Mail slot in a wooden door.

Could this place be?

Has it been someone's home?

Solitude and heat pipes.

Faint mumbling through the walls.

Neighbors perhaps?

Two pillows for one man.

A bed badly slept in and unmade.

Lusting for sex,

cats scream outside and fight.

Solitude and lust.

Are they the days of night love?

Is love something to fill a vacancy?

There are always vacancies here.

Without a clock,

there is no time inside.

The sun comes early,

up over the window sill,

across the chrome faucet

and into the room.

"Sunlight will renew your pride",

but the voice is mine.

Books on a countertop.

A stone collected adds some charm,

but no, Marvin Gardens is this.

No stop on the quest for the 7 Cities of Gold,

Cortez never slept here.

A sore lip.

Visibly, a fever in my mind.

Longing for home,

I know this is a part of my life,

I should not condemn.

I see wanting and needing are two separate things.

Wanting love?

Wanting to touch you?

Wanting to love you?

Filling voids

or needing?

Needs, what are they?

To drink so as not to thirst

or to drink so as not to perish?

To love and be loved

to fill

or only to make whole?

Clothes thrown in floor corners.

Shoes stepped out of still tied.

A carpet the color of dust and dirt.

A blue fringed bedspread.

Non-fitted sheets.

Light switches that control nothing and

a doorbell on number 12.

I get weary of being here.

Maybe sleep will release?

Transport.

Dreams that do not have me

inside these white walls.

No food odors.

No cooking grease.

Somehow, it all fits together, this room and me.

I am glad I have seen it.

Do not hate it,

but have heard its silent,

low-ceiling echo.

It's one thing,

and makes no attempt to be more.

I wonder if it loves me

or even notices I am here?

Do I fill its holes, voids?

Its needs?

Love and the future.

Looking out for more

or at least

a steady supply.

Needing a familiar face to reassure

that the world has not moved on

and left me here,

behind.

One sitting chair occupied,

pushed up against an empty dresser,

beside the wall box heater,

next to a pile of dirties,

feet shoed,

pushing the blue fringe.

I am here,

legs crossed.

"Entertainment for Men",

a desktop.

Writing on soldier's form.

Eyes to the paper.

Eyes through the glass window,

out.

No time has gone by since I started to write.

The heat is "On."

The heat is "Off."

I must decide what to do,

but the room provides no answer

and does not care.

I am only extra furniture.

How many days?

How many nights more?

Heat pipe clock,

Ticking, popping, hissing.

The heat seems like an extra.

"The Hunt"

The forest is still

and the cold

sits on the land.

I stand frozen, becoming a tree

or some bush,

at least a part of,

and not a visitor.

Quietly, the forest comes alive

with twig drops and birds,

leaf rustles

and my own breathing.

I am here watching and waiting.

Will the stag show himself?

Will I see or hear him first?

The dawn becomes day around me

Now sounds from the tree tops

and the hunter is deadly still.

Beyond sight and hearing now,

I fade into this little world.

Another sense grows inside me.

One without time as a backbone

for "waiting" has no meaning here.

The day grows bright.

The wind begins to build

and the silent forest becomes

a river of wind waves and rustle.

Ants move about my feet,

birds overhead.

I cough suddenly, unexpectedly,

and the explosion rocks the nearby.

How far was it heard?

I sense a sudden tenseness in the leaves.

They all know I am here,

in their world.

"What motivation?"

The gun barrel scatters light.

"No need to ask,"

"I mean no harm."

"Is it true?"

Does this place know violent death?

A twisted, burnt tree,

Lightning perhaps?

A squirrel snatched by a hawk?

Slow decay and rebirth.

A leaf sails to the ground from high above.

The cold settles into my bones.

My hands are stiff.

I want to move.

My eyes sweep the world,

all I can see.

What about behind me?

I have no fear here.

What danger for me?

Listening and looking;

my head, my neck

makes a sound as I survey.

My thoughts drift.

I do not sense my prey.

I think about the moment.

If it comes, will I shoot?

Why can't the sound of the stag's death

be silent?

I dread the explosion, the blast,

that will shatter this peace.

Will he see me first and sense who I am;

Death come to wait for him?

Drifting thoughts see ancient times.

I am a hunter six days out

having to have meat for my lodge.

I've tracked this one,

this one God has assigned to me.

I cannot have another.
And if another comes
I will not kill.

Worlds of petty concern bubble
away.
Here, everything is open.
Slow, steady life.
death.

I hear sounds.
Another hunter nearby
and noisy.

I watch for game fleeing his path
but none come my way.

"Game" a funny word to use
for flesh and bones,
breath.

I envision a roadway down the ridge
that stretches before me.
A highway for game on the move.

But no 'highway' exists here.

No "stops" and "go."

I question my spot.

Am I in the right place?

Morning moves to noon, and I envision the stag's movements.

He is coming now slowly, cautiously

down off the mountaintop to his destiny.

This is his world,

and he senses out the forest

ahead of him.

Does he smell the city on me?

Does he feel or hear my breathing?

Does my weapon give off some explosion echo,

I cannot hear?

I see warriors and war games.

Battles fought over and for,

with no lasting results.

Trees sway in the breeze.

The wind has shifted.

Will the bull elephant get my scent?

Charge?

Native and equipment bearers trek through.

A lost safari.

A tiger lurks nearby,

deep in the rushes.

I am his prey.

I think of snakes and check the ground around me.

No. I am safe.

Old words come to mind.

Old names.

Names of hunters and warriors.

Visions of the celebration of the kill.

Women and children singing praises.

The skins will make new boots.

The bones, new hair ornaments.

The littlest boy longs to join me in my hunts.

I have much to teach him.

My hands ache now.

The fingers slow to move.

Some sort of handicap

to make the odds more even?

I am thirsty,

but there is no water.

The stag will eat select leaves

and be quenched.

I do not have the evolution for it.

Out through the eyes,

everything remains the same,

yet changes.

I feel my soul shrink

and expand.

I begin to know this place.

I begin to not think anymore,

just be.

Being and moving slightly in the wind.

Am I blending now?

Am I here?

I see his horns first,

twigs that move out of step

with the wind.

His head

down to the ground

and up,

pulling the air through his nostrils.

He hasn't seen me.

I am here, waiting.

He senses no danger.

I have let that slip away

from me.

He's taken my roadway,

the path I would have taken.

Slowly, he moves,

ever so slowly.

I see him all now.

I see nothing else.

I cannot hear him.

I am stiff.

I must begin to move,

to align myself to strike.

Down off the ridge he comes,

towards me.

He looks at me,

but I am only a bush.

I do not move.

Hides of many,

salted down,

hanging in the shed.

The knife all honed

and waiting.

Visions of blood,

bloody hands,

and he, laying there.

I take another drink

and smile.

They all listen to the story again.

We count the stag's horned points.

The tribe is happy.

We have meat.

The Great Spirit has directed life,

new life into our warriors.

Supermarket meat,

all neat and clean,

wrapped.

No blood showing.

My arms have slowly risen,

the grip tightening.

Bits of metal all homed in their beds,

waiting for my order to strike.

He moves quicker now.

Has he sensed my movement,

as I first sensed his?

The wind gusts, and I move with it.

Almost to my shoulder.

Bowstring tight.

The warrior whispers

to the feathered limb,

"Strike with my hand."

Hours spent making the head

sharp and deadly.

Full moon in the morning sky

and vampires and werewolves out somewhere

searching for their prey.

Why do I feel different from them?

What contest or battle

or struggle is this?

He comes out of the flats

and up the ridge.

Moving away from me,

I have the eye to the sight.

She was cautious

when we first saw her,

that first hunt.

He looked over at me

from behind his tree.

"Wait."

Maybe the stag will follow.

I was ready then,

for him,

my father.

I would have pulled the hammer,

exploded the silence,

seen her shock

and fall.

I couldn't miss then.

The target range skills honed

as sharp as the knife

he had given me.

It would have been only another target.

Bull's-eye center.

But she is not ours.

Only a stag will do

for the boy hunter.

The tribe has its rituals.

The blood from the first must be drawn

from the horned beast.

There is no other way

for a boy to become a man.

He has stopped now.

What does he sense?

He sees me, I know it.

I see his concentration.

His head extends up his neck.

His neck draws tight.

The hammer is back

my fingers grip tighter.

I see him down my barrel

just at the bottom of the "V."

I will see the lead leave the metal arm.

Quickly it will travel the distance between us

and strike.

I will see his surprise.

Surprise, shock.

I will be true of aim

of purpose.

He falls.

Heads on a wall.

Moose head.

The deer head.

A wild boar,

tusks and all.

We stare at each other,

and my heart pounds.

He has come to my death stand

and is waiting.

Does he say one last prayer?

Does he think of crisp dawns

he has known?

Does he jump about in his mind,

young and fresh horned?

The world is in the bottom of a "V."

I have a direction,

an aim,

a very set path.

Only one act more to perform.

His lungs expel clouds of moisture.

He stands watching me.

Only seconds have gone by.

How long will he wait?

How long will God hold him here?

I think of the warm car,

the conversation,

The expectations.

The children at school

and their bloodless lessons.

Is it really his time?

Am I to bring him his death?

Thrust it upon him?

My father.

His soul invades me.

His vision is mine.

I feel the differences.

This old hunter has been here,

at this moment,

many times before.

He would not hesitate.

Just let out one breath

and the world is one finger

and eye.

The stag turns away,

and I am shocked by it.

But I feel myself relax.

No, I will not be death

today.

The tribe must pack and move.

They must have meat.

The old ones speak of the great-horned ones

beyond the high mountain.

It will be better there.

The tiger moves away,

tracking a small pig.

The kids go to recess.

A leaf falls.

The battlefield is silent once again.

The stag moves on down my ridge.

He does not think of me,

our meeting,

or why.

I finally blink

and the world comes back.

The weapon is coming down to my side.

Why am I here,

if not to slay the dragon,

to save the tribe,

post the trophy on the wall?

My hands find my pockets

and I fumble with loose change.

I don't see or hear.

If he comes back.

If he fights me.

If he laughs at me.

But he will not do any of these.

Do I pretend

or do I sit down?

Is it over or

do I watch for new movement?

My heart has slowed now

and I feel a twinge of hunger.

I can taste his flesh

and it would have been good.

The old man looks at the boy.

He must be a warrior,

a hunter.

Why can he not kill?

The boy offers no explanation.

Was he not taught how to hunt,

stalk, as was his father?

The boy stands ashamed.

He will do it next time,

he must.

He is confused,

abandoned.

His father is disgraced.

A proud and wise man,

he will not push the boy.

They do not speak

as they prepare the arrows.

Each arrowhead sharpened

on the horns of a previous kill.

There is a crashing,

a deer running,

coming fast.

I jump up and spin towards the sound.

I am so stiff.

There he is,

running head high,

stabbing the air with his nose.

The shot rings out

and my father hears it.

Smiles on the tribe tonight.

The boy has come to manhood

in a twinkle of an eye.

The stag lays at my feet.

Too sudden for either of us,

to understand the moment.

He is dead and somehow,

I feel very little.

I've taken his life

and yet the trees do not bend

and weep.

All seems as it should be.

The boy climbs a rock peak

this night and,

looks deep into the sky.

The stars shine down on him

and he thinks of other times.

He has become a man, a warrior.

It wasn't hard.

But he feels a loss,

as if the forest knows him now

and will never trust him again.

He is sad to have lost that

but the horns are his.

89 cents a pound, packaged.

Flesh and bone,

blood and guts.

The children clap as dinner is served.

The tiger has caught a pig

and sets gorged on the fresh kill.

Scavengers gather and wait.

They will have their turn.

The tusks lay in the dirt.

The tiger has no use for them.

Blood sinks into the earth

and turns a dark red.

Shells in the drawer.

Muzzle velocity prepared.

Missiles cocked and ready.

We climb into the truck.

It has been a good hunt.

Tonight will be one of drink

and song.

I smoke before bed.

Laying quietly now,

I see the forest once again.

Hollows and ridges,

saddles and gullies.

A ghost, a specter,

haunts my sleep.

Black and hooded,

he waits for me up ahead.

I have no choice

but to move towards him.

"The Limb"

It has taken a while to find it, but pulling the "miss" from the forest floor, finds the 11-hand-long sharp is still good to use.

"The meat had been too far away but first meat he had seen in 3 days, and had to try."

Standing perfectly still to let the forest become alive again after his moving around, he looks slowly in all directions for a bush or tree branch, moving not quite right with the wind. Then, once again, he moves his head with his eyes closed, but this time only smelling the air, but there is nothing, not even smoke.

Shadows are beginning to form, and he can tell that the light and heat from above will soon be gone. He must forget meat and get to 'his place.'

His head slowly rotates, listening through the wind and leaves, for the roar. At first: nothing. He picks a direction, slowly walks a short way, stops and listens again.

Walk, stop and listen, sometimes returning to his original and heading in a different direction. Over and over again, he moves, stops, listens, and looks about, beginning to feel time slipping away and feeling that he must move more quickly if he is to get to "his place" before the darkness.

Finally, standing as still as he can so as not even to breathe, he hears a slight difference in silence from one direction and knows that it has to be the falls, but he can tell he is still a good many steps away.

With direction now set, he forgets meat and is no longer quiet when moving. The throw and three sharps are still in his right hand, ready, but now it is all sound.

The shadows lengthen, and the forest floor begins to rise ever closer to the base of the closest mountain. It is such a steep mountain, seemingly straight up or nearly so, but he knows what he seeks is at its base.

Three days out from his tribe, he knows he must find meat and soon return. His own supply of dried meat and wild berries are almost gone. Though he will only carry back a hind quarter or perhaps 2, it is still 3 full days of up and down the forest, and he must carry the load.

As the sound of the falls gets louder, it begins to dominate the forest and he can no longer hear the wind on the tops of trees move leaves about and knows he is close. Walking now, no longer mindful of what is around him, he begins to think of the falls, the power and the quiet, it always has brought him. Indeed, it was a gift to have been led to it, 3 dark sky brights, after the last cold.

After the find, he thought of telling others in the tribe about it, the magic of the place, how it made him feel, and how he slept so deeply. Hunters shared everything to enhance the success of all, but for some reason, he had not. The falling of great water, its sound, its light, and the small cave above on a rock ledge was "his place."

As the sound of the falls became a roar, he could see how the forest floor seemed to disappear ahead, and he knew the river was there.

Standing on the river's edge, watching the rapid flow, he knows he is above the falls and will soon be at "his place." Bending down, he cups some of the flow and drinks for the first time in over a day. The water is cool and clear, and he rubs some on his face and neck.

Rocks begin to dominate the forest floor, first just here and there but soon almost completely covering his path. A thought of a snake in his steps but never before, so he quickens.

And then, just ahead, he can see the river suddenly disappear, and on his side of the river, the rock ledge that he will now follow.

When he first found the river and then the falls, he had only stood at the falls in awe of the mighty sound and the rush of the water. A roar so strong it seemed to beat his hearing to death. Stronger than any sound he had ever heard, and even now, he does not know how, above the sound, he had even noticed a dark spot in the rock cliff and decided to get a closer look.

Slowly working the ledges of the rock face, he made his way along until the ledge widened and suddenly caved inward to form a depression, a place, in the rock wall.

Standing on the edge looking into the cut out in the rock, he noticed what appeared to be the remains of a small fire, and stepping in and stooping down, he made his way back until he reached the rear wall.

It was not a big place, but he could stand full at the back, and in front of him, the remains of an old fire and the floor seemed to be so sort of soft, deep bed of rock.

From the back, he could see the edge of the falls and the water flowing over, and it was everything to him: the rush of the water, the sound of the water rushing and then crashing below.

Now, here once again at the falls, he works his way along the ledge until he is in his place.

Laying down his throw, the sharps and the small pouch of dried meat, berries, and his long hair, he makes his way back out along the rock ledge to gather wood for a fire.

The light and heat from above was almost gone when he had made his fourth trip from the forest to his place and quickly set about spinning a rod in a piece of flat, dry wood to create the smallest of flames, to be fed by a hunk of his hair.

Adding small pieces of wood, the fire begins to grow and give off its own light and heat.

When he had started a fire the very first time, he had wondered where the smoke would go or if his place would fill with smoke and he would not be able to stay there, but like magic, the falls seemed to breathe in the smoke, and he never fail to not watch it rise up and then like a bird in flight, head straight for the mighty crash of the falls.

As his fire grows, the light and heat from above goes away and darkness overtakes the falls, and although he can no longer see it, its roar is not diminished in the darkness.

Sitting, leaning his back on the back wall, he pulls what little meat he has from a pouch and slowly begins to chew. Deer meat from one of the tribe hunters, and he quiets himself and thanks the hunter and the deer that has given its life so he may continue his.

As he eats, he feels himself begin to calm. The first time it had happened, he was taken aback and wondered if the place had some sort of demon that would suddenly appear and push him out and down into the falls below. But although his fear was intense for a moment, the sound of the falls pulled him back and calmed him in the strangest way.

Many times, out on a hunt, he had come out of dense mountain laurel into a small clearing and felt its power. Often, a single tree would sit on the edge of the clearing on a slight rise, and he would be drawn to the tree and would sit at the base for a very long time and be completely satisfied.

Here, now, in his place, he felt the same: satisfied, content.

The roar of the falls came and went in his awareness, but it was always there like some blanket, and when he lay down by the fire and fed it and watched the flames, it was as if the falls sang a song, and he always drifted off to dreamless sleep: a dead calm, quiet, empty sleep.

***

It was the quiet that arouses him, forces his eyes opening, and he can make no sense of it. The river, the falls, the roar, his place; he is no longer there, but instead, he is under an ancient, thick tree in a clearing. The light and heat is now high above, and he cannot grasp any of it. He sits up and quickly notices the throw and sharps are with him. "Did he leave his place at night and not remember? How could he not remember or even make his way along the narrow rock ledge in the dark." He sits and looks around, seeing or hearing nothing. He is alone, but he does not know where he is.

Nothing enters his mind. Not what to do or not do. And then, a noise from above and a limb of the old tree comes crashing down and lands at his feet.

The limb at his feet is not thick or very old but strangely has no branches or leaves off it. Neither is it dead but seems to have separated itself from the old tree and fallen directly to him. He looks up but sees no place it could have come from and there are many such limbs on this tree.

Still, without a thought, he reaches out, picks up the limb, holds it, looks at it, and wonders about it. It has a natural curve to it, and when he grasps it between his two hands, it seems to flex easily and then spring back into its fallen shape.

The sound of the falls is gone.

He sits, simply sits for a long time.

He finds his small pouch and inside the long hair he uses to keep the meat together as he carries it. Without a thought, he takes the long hair, knots it to one end of the limb, and then attaches it to the other.

He lays down the limb and long hair, finds the last of his meat, and slowly chews.

Once again, it strikes him hard that he cannot hear the falls.

He picks up the limb and long hair and moves it about in his hands, first this way and then that. "Why? What?"

Once again, he uses both hands to flex the limb, and as he does, he notices the long hair attached to each end will become loose or slack, and then when he releases the limb ends, the long hair snaps tight as he had attached it.

He flexes the limb and watches it snap the long hair back over and over again.

Then he picks up a sharp.

When he places the sharp on the throw, he could sling the sharp at a good distance and with some speed, but what if he could use the flex of the limb and long hair as a throw?

He looks at the sharp, but the longer he looks, the brighter the light and heat from above seems to get until he starts squinting and closes his eyes because the light hurts. Then he raises his hands and places them over each eye to stop the light from coming through. Then, in darkness, suddenly, the roar of the falls, and he drops his hands and finds himself back in his place.

He grabs his hair and pulls. He screams as loud as he can for a long time, and he shakes all over.

Slowly, the sound, the roar of the falls, lets him stop screaming, and his hands leave his hair and he sits totally lost in his place.

"A sleep-see? Had he had a sleep-see? Was the limb and long hair just a sleep-see?"

He has had sleep-sees before but never in his place. Now and again, he would sleep and see about something he had done the day before or perhaps talking to someone around a fire at night. And now and again, he would sleep-see himself as a child, learning to use a hand sharp to open some squirrel, rabbit or deer.

"But the limb, the long hair, was different: a vision?"

Now and again, he had heard one elder or another speak of having had a vision. Sometimes as a sleep-see or sometimes suddenly when the elder was alone in a special place, but he had always thought this was just old men who could no longer hunt, trying to show they were still important to the tribe.

As he watches the falls and listens to its mighty roar, he watches a small limb covered with leaves and sprouts come floating down the river and go over the falls.

"The limb, the limb in the sleep-see: could it throw a sharp?"

Then he was up and making his way along the rock ledge to the forest and begins his search for a perfect limb. At first, he picks up some limb off the ground, but when he flexes it, it snaps somewhere, and although he tries many, all break.

It has to be a fresh limb, cut from some tree, and the cut-and-try proceeded for a long time until he found one particular tree whose limbs would not break no matter how much he flexed them. And even after many flexing, they would always snap back to their original shape.

At first, he cut and tried straight limbs, but when he tried to attach the long hair, he could only get the long hair to stay attached by cutting away some of the tips of the limb, and even then, the long hair wanted to slip off at one end or the other.

The morning slipped to noon, and after having found more trees of the special limbs and after having cut many limbs that were as long as his sharps, hauls them back to his place to get out of the mid-day heat.

In his place, with the falls roaring away, he ties long hair to one limb after another, flexing it to see if the hair would not slip off and, in doing so, refines the cuts at the end of the limb and was now sure, the hair would stay on the limb but how to make the long hair-limb throw the sharp?

With the limb flexed and with just enough long hair attached, he could hold the limb in his left hand and pull the hair back with his right a long way, and when he let go, the limb snapped back to its original position quickly. But no matter how he tried to hold the limb, he could not seem to also hold the sharp in his right hand with the end of the sharp resting on the long hair and pull the sharp and long hair back together, far enough, without the sharp slipping away from the long hair.

The heat of the day was now oppressive, and he moves to the edge of his place for the cool mist rising off the falls and water below. Now and again, a leaf or another tree branch comes down river and goes over the falls to disappear in the churning, splashing, thundering water.

He begins to feel hunger but has no meat and has not seen any berries in the area. The limb would have to wait, and he takes his throw and sharps and starts to climb the ledge to the forest, but he pauses, returns, picks up the long-haired limb and places it over his head.

As he slowly moves about, looking for deer signs, he can hear squirrels chattering away at him, for they had the eyes of a hawk and could be very vocal when they saw something they did not like.

"Ah, squirrel. Not with this sharp. Squirrels are snares", and he has none and very little long hair left to construct one. "No, it will have to be a deer."

He begins to focus on the lay of leaves on the forest floor. He needs to find a deer trail. A run, a path, deer seemingly used over and over again to move from perhaps a hidden sleeping area to some feeding ground, and if he could find such a path, he could wait, hidden off to one side, and perhaps be close enough to take down one with his throw and sharp.

After his sleep-vision or whatever it had been, he keeps the sound, the roar of the falls, always near, more or less moving along the river bank, some distance away but not too far. Slowly, he moves further upstream until he comes to a narrowing of the river, and on his side of the river, there in the soft, wet dirt, right at the river's edge: deer prints. Deer prints pointing across the river to the other side, and prints pointing from the other side to his side. "Perhaps."

Looking about, he finds a downed tree stretched out full length, pushed over, root and all by some mighty wind that had visited from the wrong direction. Walking around the massive tree and roots, he finds a position he likes behind the tree's trunk so he would only have to make a limited throw of the sharp. "Now, if the wind direction holds and he was right about the path, the deer sign, all he has to do is wait."

In position, the forest returns with all the sounds of small animals and birds, unaware he is there, and he is startled by the sound of a woodpecker smashing away at the far end of the downed tree, obviously seeking the small things that had decided to call the tree their new home. "Everything has its place."

He stands, waiting for a long time, and then decides he could sit and watch, and if he is lucky, any deer from the other side, or even on his side, will pause at the bank and drink before continuing. He needs a good broadside shot, not too far away.

The woodpecker keeps up his hammering away and raising just enough, he catches sight of the bird. It is large, maybe three hands tall and red, and his hunger makes him wonder: "woodpecker meat?" He has never eaten woodpecker or been told, you could eat the meat of this big bird, but he does think about trying.

"Would be hard with a sharp," as although the bird is large, his throwing, or the throws of most hunters, were only made up close, and even then, mostly a miss or a minor wound, and the meat would be gone. "No, not going to risk a sharp." And with that, he feels the long hair of the limb itch his back, and he lifts it over his head and, once again, holds it in his hands and moves it about.

Standing, he places the limb in his left hand and then places the blunt end of a sharp against the long hair at the middle of the limb. He pulls the sharp and long hair, and as he pulls the long hair further and further back, the sharp always wiggles just enough to move away from the long hair.

Once again, he places the limb on the ground and takes up the throw and waits.

Shadows begin to appear as the light and heat from above move further and further over the edge of the close mountain, and when he thinks he must return to his place, he hears the sound of splashing water. Not a strong sound, but his eyes shift to the river bank and the deer sign, and there, standing in the middle of the shallow narrows, is a horned one. Not 20 hands high like some, but horned. "Must only take the horned. The mothers must not be killed, or there will be no more meat."

He places a sharp's blunt end into the throw, raises his arm, moves it backward, and readies himself. The horned one stands perfectly still in the river and stabs his nose into the air, smelling out the path ahead of him, but the winds are good, and the horned one does not smell the throw or the sharp.

Slowly, the horned one continues across the water, then out on the bank and a step or two into the forest.

Bothered by something, the horned one seems to be unsure. "Come on, move, come my way!" And the horned one begins to follow the path, the trail towards the throw and sharp, and when the horned one is no more than 10 or 15 steps away from the throw and sharp, he flings the sharp as hard as he can and sees it hit the horned one just above his front leg but below the heart and fall to the ground.

The throw is dropped, and with his hand sharp, he quickly is beside the struggling horned one, approaching the head and keeping clear of the thrashing horns, until he can grab hold by the horns, jabs his hand sharp deep into the horned one's neck and pulls and moves the sharp to cut the throat. As always, he makes eye contact with the horned one and watches life disappear. He always feels sadness and, at the same time, pride that he can now have meat to take back to his tribe.

Now, he must hurry as the scent of blood is strong, and although he had never seen any sign around his place, wolves can smell the scent of blood from very far away and probably live this side or the other of the high mountain. He would never be able to fight off a pack of wolves.

Grabbing the sharp to pull it out, he finds the sharp end has broken off inside, and he has lost a hand-long part of the sharp, but he could easily cut a new end and harden it, so he lays it aside and begins using his hand sharp, cutting the rear hind quarter off.

Moving his hand sharp with a jerking motion, he is able to peel back the hide and slowly cut his way to the bone and then cut around it until he pulls the hind leg and some meat above it off. He is now sweating, and darkness is coming.

Once more, he uses his hand-sharp to cut the horned one's hide along the backbone, deep enough so he can pull off enough hide to wrap the bloody end of the hind quarter and fasten with small sticks pushed through holes in the cover hide and the hind quarter.

Now, he must pull the horned one away from the killing spot so as not to ruin it for all other deer that might want to use the same path. The blood in the leaves will soon sink into the ground or be washed away when water comes from above, but what remains of the horned one must be pulled away and covered.

The horned one is not hard to pull by the horns, but hard enough over the littered forest floor and as the light fades, he knows he had dragged the horned one as far as he dares, and still make it to his place before darkness.

Covered with leaves and dead limbs, he looks the horned one in the eyes before turning away and back to the wrapped hind quarter, the limb, the throw, and sharps.

With the limb and long hair wrapped over his back, he hoists the wrapped hind quarter on his left shoulder, once again places the throw and sharps in his right hand and heads downstream to his place.

***

It takes several trips back and forth across the rock ledge to get everything in his place, before it became too dark to attempt another ledge crossing.

With the fire started enough that he could rest, he sits down on the back wall and once again listens to the roar of the falls.

"Meat." He can tell the day has taken it out of him, and although he is tired, he unwraps the hind quarter and cuts out a handful of meat to be dried by the fire.

As the fire flames the meat stick, its smell fills his place, and he thinks of sitting around with his tribe and how they all ate a fresh kill and were happy and smiled, and he felt a part of them.

But he really isn't much a part of the tribe. His father never returned from a hunt when he was still a small boy, and his mother did not survive the fierce cold, many colds ago.

Yes, he knows other hunters and likes some but not all, and seldom does an elder or any of the women ever notice him. Even those women that have not been chosen for bedding, ever seem to see him or give any sign they might be interested in sharing his bed.

And he is unsure if he wants a woman and a young one. Only more hunting and the tribe already has many women and children, requiring constant hunting to keep so many from starving.

"Does he really need to go back to the tribe? This place, his place, is all he needs. The meat is not plentiful but would be enough for him, and the falls and sound seems to give him much peace."

"The tribe is everything. Only together can one hope to have enough meat or survive an Ugly or wolf-pack attack. The tribe is everything."

He picks up the stick holding the flame-licked meat and tears off a piece that is turning black. He bites off a hunk, finds it dry enough to his liking, and slowly chews, feeling his strength begin to return, and his hunger go away. More is pulled from the flamed hunk and slowly chewed, and he begins to feel full and sleepy. He lies down beside the fire and watches the flames dance to the sound of the river until he can no longer hear the roar.

***

In the silence of sleep, a sleep-see soon begins and he is standing with other hunters in his tribe, holding the long-haired limb and moving it around and motioning to various parts but especially the cuts he had made on the ends of the limb so the long hair would not slip off: "Cuts to hold long hair!"

The roar of the falls comes rushing back, and his eyes open to find it is still dark and the fire not much more than smoke, but he knows now what he has to do, and grabbing what remains of his wood for the fire, he slowly adds it until he once again can see.

Picking up the broken sharp, he wipes his hand sharp on the outside of the hind quarter and begins to make small cuts in the blunt end of the sharp. He makes several small cuts, then slowly removes some wood between the cuts to make one large cut and places the broken sharp's cut end on the long hair of the limb. The long hair fits the cut in the sharp and now, he can pull the sharp using just the shaft of the sharp, and the sharp does not wiggle. He pulls back the sharp until he thinks the limb might snap, but it does not.

He knows, he just knows, but outside the light of his fire, the falls is still covered in darkness and he knows, he cannot cross the rock ledge until light.

Once more, he places the sharp into the long hair of the limb and holding the limb out away from his body, like one does using the throw, finds he cannot pull the long hair as far back and moves the limb closer and closer to his body until he is actually looking down the shaft of the sharp.

"He can see down the sharp! He could actually point the end of the sharp where he wants the sharp to go. No more slinging the sharp from the throw and hoping it would hit meat."

Oh, some of the hunters in his tribe are very good at throwing the sharp, and all hunters practice throwing almost every day. But few could make the sharp actually hit the pile of animal skins. Being able to actually point the sharp at meat should help every hunter!"

He stands up and sits down. He holds the long hair limb and, moves it about and then lays it down. He picks up the broken sharp, uses his hand sharp to make a new point, and slowly heats the end in the fire, hardening it. "Hardening it?" He does not know why the tip was always heated to harden. "Harden?"

The falls appears out of the darkness and as he watches, a new day begins. Not long after, he can easily see across the entire falls and above, is clear and going to be bright.

He gathers his pouch, puts some flame-kissed meat into it, the throw, takes up his sharps, the long-haired limb, and makes his way out of his place and into the forest floor.

Immediately, he places the broken sharp into the long hair of the limb, pulls the sharp back, and stares down the shaft. There is nothing to try to limb-throw his sharp towards. The sharp tip is hardened, but sharps did not stick in trees often, and most times, a tree hit breaks the sharp. Still, he must try it to see if the long-hair limb can throw a sharp.

Pulling the sharp back till the long hair almost touches his face, he releases the sharp, and it is gone so fast he is not sure what has happened. "Not as his feet." Stepping in the direction he has pointed the sharp, he does not see it. To mark the place he has limb-thrown the sharp from, he puts his pouch on the ground and then walks in the direction of his throw, looking this way and that for the sharp but finds nothing.

When he was well away from his pouch and beyond where he could have thrown a sharp using the throw, he still cannot find the sharp. Further still, this way and that, walking, searching, and looking back at his pouch.

The forest floor begins to rise as he walks, and looking back at his pouch, he tries to walk along the line he had seen looking down the shaft of the sharp, and then, ahead, still many steps away, he sees his sharp sticking up out of the ground, having just missed a dead tree stump.

Looking back at his pouch, the sharp had been thrown further than he had ever thrown one with a throw or any other hunters, at least during practice, he could remember.

He pulls the sharp out of the ground, sits, and stares back at this pouch.

He has to know, and sticking the sharp back into the ground where he has found it, sticking straight up to be able to see it perhaps, he quickly returns to his pouch, places another sharp into the throw, and stands such that he thinks he could throw this sharp near the one in the ground. He flings his right shoulder as fast and as hard as he can and watches the sharp move towards the long-hair sharp, but then hits the ground well short and to the left of the long-hair sharp.

Once again, he walks towards the hand-thrown sharp, and once there, he cannot believe how far the long-hair sharp has gone, and the hand-thrown sharp is not even in line with the long-hair sharp "meat."

A squirrel begins to chatter and then another. Birds stop their sounds, and the forest is on alert.

He looks around, first out a long way and then closer, but his eyes catch no movement. Sniffing the air, he senses something but is unsure what it is: something.

He goes to the long-hair sharp and pulls it out of the ground, then back to his pouch and hand throw.

Once more, he looks around him but sees nothing, but still, his nose is getting something. "Perhaps the dead horned-one has attracted?"

With the long-haired limb and his sharps in his right hand, he heads towards the river and his place, but perhaps the horned one is still where he left it covered, and he could take another hind quarter for the tribe.

He quickly finds the river but is well downstream from where he killed the horned one, and with a long-haired limb at the ready, he slowly and quietly makes his way along the river bank.

Now his nose is beginning to come alive with a terrible smell, and like the snap of the long hair limb when a sharp is released, he knows it is an Ugly and he freezes and looks and listens.

He came across a dead Ugly once out on a hunt, and it had a smell one could not forget. The Ugly appeared to have broken his leg and slowly either starved to death or simply died from lack of water. "And so, it was then as it was now."

Looking over the dead Ugly, he was glad he had not met him when the Ugly was fit and strong. Few run-ins with an Ugly ever ended well for his kind. And then, he found a hand-sharp beside the Ugly, and it was the best hand-sharp he had ever seen. It was so well-chipped and sharp. From that day, his hand sharp had been his only real possession.

"One Ugly or more?" "Perhaps forget other hind quarter and move away from the river for a while?"

When he reaches the rock ledge, his nose has lost most of the Ugly, and he is not sure that what he smells is new or simply that the smell has stuck in his nose from the first startle.

He sticks a finger up his nose, moves it about, wipes it on the ground, and repeats. Eyes closed, he slowly breathes in as he moves his head, and this time, the smell of the Ugly is gone.

Once in his place, he drops all he was carrying and makes several trips for firewood, although he wonders about a fire with an Ugly so close somewhere. Uglys should know the smell of smoke and might try to find where it was coming from. "Fire or no fire? No fire."

Seated along the back wall of his place, he feels safe again. No Ugly could ever find him here, and he begins to chew another hunk of flamed meat.

It was time to return to his tribe, if he could even find them. It had been four days since he left the gathering and it would be three more before he was even where the gathering, his tribe, had been.

They may have moved for any reason and he would have to find their trail, and follow it for however long it took. The gathering, the tribe was safe, and he had to return with meat and also share the long-haired limb, cut sharp, and show what it could do.

Darkness comes, and without a fire, he curls up on the back wall listening to the song of the falls and is soon in a dead sleep.

***

Usually awake at first light, he opens his eyes to find the heat and light, high above. "He has had a long, dark, dead sleep! The tribe, the gathering, he must start back, but first, make cuts in the blunt end of all of his sharps."

Chewing the last of the dried meat, he rises and slowly works the rock ledge until he is on the forest's river bank. The roar of the falls is too great for him to hear anything other than the falls, and his nose does not tell him anything.

He drops to a knee, takes a long drink of river water, and wipes his mouth. Then, feeling the urge, he empties his body, covers it in a large mound of dirt, leaves and sticks. "There must be no smell."

With his hand-throw now in his pouch slung over his back, hind quarter on his left shoulder, he heads away from his place. The long-haired limb and sharps in his right hand, at the ready.

Moving now without worry about the sound he makes; he moves away from the river and back towards the tribe. It is a late start, but he is much stronger now, having slept so long and no sleep-see to disturb him.

The morning passes quickly, and other than birds above and squirrels scampering up trees and hiding on the backside at his approach, he sees nothing of concern. Then, under a log ahead, he notices some tree food and stops to gather some to eat and also for his pouch. He had not seen tree food since he got to his place and now is glad to chew the woody leaves that stick off the downed tree, right at the ground. Not meat but something.

For a while, he sits on the tree, chews and listens for the roar of the falls, but he cannot hear it without really searching the silence.

A rustle of leaves and his eyes dart in the direction. There is an elk, more than a hand-throw sharp away, acting as if she has not seen him or gotten his smell. "What a meat that would be for the tribe!" He has eaten elk once, but it was a tribe-kill requiring many sharps, and even then, the elk had to be beaten over the head with rocks, many times, until it was dead.

He watches her move away, loads the hind quarter, gathers the limb and sharps, and begins toward his tribe again.

As he walks, a sweet smell comes to his nose, and he thinks of the bush that can have many pouches of sweet water and how he has often used the sweet water to quench a thirst, but now he is headed to the tribe and does not search out the smell.

As shadows begin to appear, he looks for a place to sleep safely but sees nothing. "No place is as safe as my place," and once again, he sees himself curled along the back wall and listening to the roar of the water.

If the tribe has moved on or does move once he is there, he does not know what he will do. The place is his place, and the roar and sounds have become more than familiar; a giver of sleep-sees or even visions.

Then, off to his right, he notices where a tree had once stood but now, at its passing, has left a hole in a rise, and although not his place, he could have a fire, put it out, and then in the hole in the rise, cover himself in branches and leaves and could at least rest or perhaps even sleep for a while: safe.

***

He awakes with a start as his nose tells him an Ugly is near and he does not dare move. Listening, he hears nothing, but the smell is there, and the Ugly has to be close. "What to do? He could try to wait in his hole until the Ugly was gone, but what if the Ugly stayed nearby? He could not stay hidden forever. Wait a while and then poke his head out, for a quick look?"

He waits and listens but still hears nothing until finally, he moves some branches that are over top him aside, pokes his head slowly up and looking around, sees nothing anywhere. This part of the forest is dense with trees, and although he cannot see the Ugly, he could be behind a tree or just over any of the small forest floor rises.

He slowly stands and then picks up the limb and the shorter sharp he has used before. He steps out of the hole, shoulders the hind quarter, and moves quietly in the direction of the tribe.

As he moves along, he begins to be less worried about the Ugly and more focused on stepping up his pace, and soon, the trees start to thin out, and there are more lying this way and that on the forest floor. He stops, sits on a downed tree, takes the hind quarter off his shoulder and rubs the shoulder with his hand.

The hide over the bloody hind quarter seems to be holding well, but he pushes a couple of small sticks deeper into the meat to make sure.

From his pouch, he lifts out the bladder of water and takes a short drink. On the way out to his place, he had found several small pools of water but has no way of knowing if he will find water returning and water has not fallen from above in days.

The heat is building and he knows he must move on. Putting the hind quarter over his shoulder, he grabs the limb and all his sharps and begins moving quickly.

There is a snap of a dead limb on the forest floor and a rustle of some brush and he swings his head toward it. Then, there, more than a hand-throw away, is an Ugly. Only one, but he is moving in his direction and quickly. The Ugly sees him.

Uglys do not use throws and sharps but have long, heavy spears they throw, but only when they are close enough to kill.

He places a sharp's cut end into the long hair, pulls back the sharp, looks down the sharp, places the point on the Ugly mid-body, and lets the sharp go. Although he cannot watch it as it moves to quickly, the sharp hits the Ugly in the right shoulder, and the Ugly cries out in pain and drops his spear.

Another sharp is put on the limb, pulled and pointed right at the Ugly, but upon seeing this, the Ugly stands for a moment and then turns around and begins running away.

He relaxes the pull on the long-haired sharp and tries to understand. Not only did he actually manage to hit the Ugly, but seems to have driven him away. He cannot remember ever hearing about any Ugly run-in that had not ended with one or more of his tribe dead or badly hurt.

Not only had the sharp, long-hair-strung and blunt-end cut, been quicker leaving his hands, but he also seemed to actually have some control over the path the sharp took.

Waiting, he listens and looks about for some sign of the Ugly, but there was none. He had driven off the Ugly but knows he cannot linger as there might be more than one around, and more than one could easily be headed for him.

***

By late afternoon, the smell of an Ugly is completely gone, and he feels comfortable finding a safe place for the night. But this time, he climbs a tree and up, a good many hands high, stretches out where the tree branches off into three large limbs. There will be no fire or meat, but up a tree, he might have a chance if Uglys are around and hunting him.

Shadows begin to appear, and the wind starts to pick up. Looking above, he finds water will soon fall, and it does.

The leaves of the tree stop some of the water, but not all and he is soon soaked. He tries to sleep but the water seems to pour over him as if he was under the falls of his place.

Usually, he did not like the wet, but this night, he thinks of his place, the water, the roar, and also of his tribe and how he so wants to show them his long-haired limb and what it can do.

He sleeps. A dead, calm, empty sleep, and when his eyes open, above is clear, and light and heat had taken away the darkness, and then he hears.

Looking down, he finds three tribe hunters at the base of his tree, looking up and around, and one calling out, "Ba" "O", "Ba" "O"

"The Nail"

I am an old man now, living with one of my daughters and her husband in a small one-room house in Rome, but once, I was a mighty Roman soldier.

Born in Rome to poor parents, my father had no trade and thus, had to work wherever and whenever he could. But we were Romans citizens and so much better off than slaves.

With no trade when I came of age to leave my father's house, I could think of no trade I wanted to learn, and having seen Roman soldiers throughout my childhood, being a soldier looked like what I wanted to do.

The only problem was that in those days, one had to know someone already in the army to even have a chance to get in. But I thought that if I could only get a chance to speak to the local garrison commander, with my strong body and being so tall, he might just take me in.

Then, one day, helping my father move stones for a man, I found myself near a Roman garrison and met two soldiers standing guard at the gates leading into the compound.

At first, when I told them I was there to become a soldier, they both laughed at me, but then the taller of the two turned to the other, "Why not let him in. He is the commander's type with that nice face and mouth and that nice body of his. Maybe the commander will give us some easy duty for throwing some fresh meat his way," and with that, the soldier who had just spoken opened the gate, went in, closed the gate and disappeared in the courtyard beyond.

A short time later, he was back at the gate and, holding it open, said, "Go right in, boy; the commander would love to meet you!"

Once inside the courtyard, I could see the commander in a small room, standing in front of a table with his metal tunic, helmet and sword on a stand behind him.

When I reached his room I stopped outside, spoke softly and he nodded for me to come in. "So, you want to be a soldier?" never taking his eyes off the table in front of him. "Yes sir." The commander looked up from the table and his eyes went up and down me once as if he was inspecting a horse to be bought or a slave. "Yes, I do see you are quite fit, but do you think you can follow orders, even if it means being killed or killing an enemy of Rome?" looking me directly in the eyes. I did not speak. With his eyes still locking with mine, "Ok, I will give you a chance. Tell the two at the front gate to take you to get your equipment and then you report to the training compound. But I will be checking on you, and if you embarrass me in any way, I will have your head on a spike in the courtyard, you hear me?"

The first year I was a Roman soldier, it was all I thought it would be. I was stationed in Rome and got to see my parents anytime I was not on duty. I spent most of my days just patrolling the streets of Rome, breaking up fights, or clearing the way for a Roman Senator or other Roman government official.

Then, in my 14th month, I was selected, along with 40 others, to go to the Roman province of Judea. We 40 were to relieve soldiers there that had served their time and were ready to come home. "Judea", I had never heard of it.

While a soldier in Rome, I had been collecting my pay, giving some to my parents, and saving for the day I could buy a small stall in the marketplace and perhaps sell vegetables I bought from farmers in the countryside. It would not be much of a living, but I would not have to work for another, like my father had to do.

Then the day came when the selected headed out to Judea, and I had no idea it was so very far away. It took weeks to get there with many long, hot, day marches and even had days on boats several times.

Once in Judea, I was sent with 4 others to the city of Jerusalem and settled into one of the two garrisons there. The garrison I was stationed in was mostly made up of local recruits, temple guardians and such, and I was to be more an advisor to them than an actual soldier.

At first, I could not believe my fate. Jerusalem was like Rome in many ways. Although smaller in size than Rome, it had many stone temples and was divided into sections with rich people in one and poor people in the other. But Jerusalem was rich with markets of all types and no slaves,

When I was in Rome and now Jerusalem, all I did every day was walk patrol with another soldier, usually a local recruit, making sure there was peace. As I did not know the language spoken in Jerusalem, it made it very difficult to settle any sort of argument, and usually, I just pushed people apart and waved my sword as some sort of threat.

Then, one day, while I was on patrol, a Roman soldier I had not seen before from the other garrison came running up to me and said, "There is a big disturbance in his district and that all soldiers were needed there immediately.

Since I had arrived in Judea, there had always been rumors that the people of Judea wanted to revolt against the Empire and get rid of all Roman presence in the region, but never believed it. These people were not war-like, and besides, what did they have to rebel about? We Romans did nothing but keep the peace and collect some taxes.

Following the other garrison soldier, running, he led me through one alleyway and then another, stopping briefly to talk with any soldiers he found and having them join our group. As we continued to run behind the lead soldier, after a while, I could begin to hear the many voices of a large crowd, which only grew louder and louder as we ran along.

Finally, rounding the corner of one building, there was this massive crowd of people in the street, overflowing into all the adjacent alleys, and they all seemed to be moving slowly in the same direction. As I got closer to the crowd, I could see, far up ahead, the tops of three wooden crosses being dragged through the street.

"A Crucifixion: there was going to be a crucifixion today, or rather 3!"

I had never seen a crucifixion but had heard this form of death was Roman punishment for crimes against the Empire. "Who had committed such a crime? How had I had not learned of it?"

The band of soldiers I was with, now some 10 or 12, took up positions along the trailing edge of the crowd just in case the crowd began to become violent.

Again, looking over the heads of those in the crowd, I could see that the crosses ahead were being dragged on a road leading out of the city, and I could hear people yelling and screaming at those carrying the crosses, but I could not see the criminals directly from where I was.

Slowly, as we moved along, the crowd began to thin out and slowly, but surely, I came closer and closer to those actually carrying or rather dragging their own crucifixion crosses.

Of the 3, I could see that one man had been scourged badly and had to be the worst offender, and with so much blood dripping from all his wounds, I wondered how he could even walk, much less carry the heavy wooden cross.

Finally, the soldiers at the front of the procession told the three men to drop them, and I, and the other soldiers with me, formed a ring around the crucifixion site to make sure those in the small crowd would not interfere.

One by one, the three men were dragged over to the crosses, which lay on the ground, and put into position with their heads at the top, feet at the bottom, and arms outstretched on the cross member.

Then, without warning, a Roman Centurion came up to me: "You. Nail that man's hand to the cross." "But sir," I responded, "I have never done that." "Soldier, you take the big nail over there, and you place it in the middle of his hand, and you hit it with the mallet until the nail is all the way through his hand and the wood. Understand?" "Yes sir," I responded, stepping forward and picking up 2 nails and a mallet.

Kneeling down beside the cross, the convicted man's arms had been tied with rope to the cross member, stretching them away from his body, and his hands, at each end of the cross member, had been placed palm up. I placed a nail in the center of his palm and began to lift the mallet to strike, but for some reason, I looked towards the man's head and found it turned towards me, eyes only half open from the beating he had endured and his lips, mouth, moving. He was trying to say something, but I could not hear him.

I lowered the mallet and leaned in closer to hear. And then, in a very low, weak voice, I heard, "Please." And then his eyes went closed and then, "Do not miss," and his eyes opened, and they pierced me, and I became frozen and could not move.

Faintly from behind me in what had become total silence, I could barely hear, "Soldier. Get on with it. What are you waiting for?" And then I remember being shoved to the ground and then nothing until I was back at the city garrison, told I was dismissed and to get out.

It took me a long time to get back to Rome, and as I traveled, I would hear about the crucifixion of what many people believed, was a holy, spiritual man. A man named Jesus. "Could it be the same? Could I have been there and seen him?"

Every time I sat with others and heard them tell what they knew of the crucifixion, I never said a word that I was once a Roman soldier.

Finally, after months, I arrived in Rome and my parents were very surprised that I was back from Judea so soon. Although I tried to explain what had happened to me that day, they never understood and thought I had been some sort of coward and had disgraced the family.

For years and years, no one in Rome knew of the crucifixion of this man, Jesus, and who cared about what happened in the outer provinces as long as they paid their taxes and did not revolt. But one day, my daughter came home from being out, and she had met this group of people who talked of the man, Jesus.

Jesus had lived in Judea and, at first, had been a carpenter and later a man who spoke as a rabbi to many now and again. He was crucified for trying to spread the idea that there was a kingdom mightier than the Roman Empire.

A carpenter! "Please, do not miss."

Many times, I have been tempted to speak to her of that day, that nail, but I never have.

"Was the man I saw, heard, this Jesus?" I have thought about it many times. "What did I see and feel in his eyes that froze me so that day?" The only answer I ever seem to get is: "too much." "His eyes held more, conveyed more than any eyes I had ever met before and now, since. "Holy man", I am not sure. "What is a Holy man? What is compassion?"

Musing: "Walt by the River"

River fish often place themselves behind rocks to escape the strong flow of the river and, facing upstream, simply wait for food to be carried down to them.

The first time I saw Walt, he was standing on a small sandbar, which jutted into the South fork of Virginia's Shenandoah River.

I was going down the river on a 2-day, 60-mile canoe trip with my youngest, 11-year-old daughter, and 2 of her friends, and my plan was to spend the night on the river at a campground I had found on a map.

It was just a guess, but by the time of day, I had begun to scan the river bank for the park and maybe tents, cars, people swimming in the river, boats, anything that would suggest a campground, but so far nothing and was getting concerned. I did not want to go by the park and have to spend the night on private property along the river. So finally, seeing a man standing on the sandbar was a welcome sight as he was the first human we had seen all day.

I called out to him, "Can you tell me where the camping park is around here? I think it should be near here." He called back, "You at it. Better stop soon or you will be out of the park." And drifting past the man, I quickly found a place where the river bank was not too steep, and soon, we were out of our two canoes and on solid ground again. It had been a long but very enjoyable day on the river.

Quickly, we set about pitching our two tents within feet of the river, unpacking the food, and starting a fire.

Once the girls had put down their sleeping blankets, they wanted to head out to the shower house we had spotted, and as it was still daylight and the park seemed empty of others, I waved them on.

As I watched the girls head for the shower house, I noticed, for the first time, an odd-looking panel truck parked not too far away and then a man sitting on a picnic table, alone, drinking something from a brown paper bag. "This might not be good. Little girls, out here in an empty park, and some strange man drinking what was obviously alcohol."

It was too late to get back into the canoes and head downriver. We had to stay here, so I tried to put the man, so close, out of my mind and prepared supper.

The girls soon came back from their showers, and we all proceeded to eat dinner, wash out our dishes and pans in the river, and then sat around the campfire for a while, talking about our day on the river. When it got quiet, the girls went into their tent to play card games.

I added some wood to the fire and sat poking it and watching it, and looking out over the river for a while, before turning my attention to the man on the picnic table. He was still there but now had his own little fire going. "What to do? Maybe I should talk with him, size him up, and warn him not to mess with us during the night if I had to." I got up and began walking slowly towards him. He was obviously lost to the flames of his fire and that brown bag he still held and drank from as I approached.

"Hello," I called out, and when he looked up from his fire, I saw it was the man I had seen on the sandbar. "Oh, It's you. Thanks for the help. I knew the park was around here somewhere, but was just not sure where." He did not say a word, and I continued to approach slowly. As I got closer, he looked me up and down, maybe sizing me up and then held out the brown paper bag, "Like a drink?" "No thanks, but would you mind if I sit a spell with you?" "Fine with me: gets lonely out here sometimes, name is Walt."

Walt was a short, thin man, maybe mid to late thirties, with a full head of hair buried under a painter's cap and a clean-shaven face except for a dense mustache. As I sat down, I noticed just beyond the picnic table, among the low branches of a large tree right on the river's edge, was a tarp hung overtop a lawn chair, a table made out of river driftwood and limbs, and pots and pans hung here and there.

"Yours" I asked, pointing to the canopy and odd collection beneath it. "Yeah, I have been here a while, and that is stuff I have collected out of the river or washed up on the bank somewhere near here." Walt took another drink from the paper bag.

"Here awhile, you not just camping?" "No" "Sort of a long story. You want to hear it?" "Sure, it's nice out here tonight."

"Well, see, I was living in Wisconsin with this woman in a nice house and had me steady work, and we were real happy, or so I thought. Then one day she comes home and says she wants us to move to California to be near her parents and wants me to drive her there, and so I do. But when we got to California, she started drinking and turned mean, and one night, she whacked me with a bottle and even bit me on the arm. Well, enough of that nonsense, and so I headed out and left her there.

I drove for a couple of days, just driving with no idea where to go. Then I thought maybe it was time to see my 2 boys. I was married once. My boys live in Berryville, just down the road, so I headed to Virginia. Made it here cross country on what money I had but had no real money for a hotel or anything, so I found this place, and it only costs me $5 a day or when the old man owner or his son comes by to collect the money which, is not all that often.

Anyway, I have been here for three weeks now. Right here, by this Old River and I like it. Fish for my breakfast, berries nearby are ripe, and deer come down to the river on the other side now and again to say hello. The sound of the river makes me want to sleep every night. River gives me all sorts of stuff like all that stuff under the canopy over there and the canopy too, for that matter, and even a watermelon one time, and nobody bothers me.

Not much of a campground, and not many folks coming and going. You are the first in a week or more. I haven't seen my boys yet. Not sure what I am waiting on. Somehow, I do not know what to do or where to go, so I just stay here.

It hurt me real bad when my woman friend turned mean in California. She was a lot older than me, but that didn't matter to me. I liked her, maybe even loved her."

With that, Walt became quiet and once again drank from the bag and stared at the fire.

Sitting next to Walt and hearing him talk, I felt a kind of peace, a calm, a quiet, I was not sure I had ever had. I wasn't sure that Walt was not the most at-peace person I had ever met. Perhaps the river's gentle, constant flow had somehow made its way into him?

I could hear the girls across the way and see their flashlights inside the tent, and I knew they were fine. "My turn," I thought.

"I'm going down river on a 2-day canoe trip with my daughter and 2 of her friends. Not a bad first day, but hot. Saw some snakes and stuff but never had to use my pistol." He never flinched or otherwise seemed to acknowledge my use of the word 'pistol,' which I really did not have with me.

I liked Walt, but I had no idea who he was and what he might be like drunk or if he had his own pistol or a knife, and drunk might get to trying something in the middle of the night.

"What did you do for a living in Wisconsin, Walt?" "I paint houses, store signs, stuff like that." He turned and pointed out his truck, which I had seen earlier but had not looked at closely. Now, in the flickering light of Walt's campfire, I could see a small panel truck, foreign-made, getting some age on it, and on the side was painted a large orange smiling 'Alice in Wonderland', Cheshire cat, and below it, neatly stenciled or painted, the words: 'Fat Cat House Painting' and a telephone number in Wiscola, Wisconsin.

Walt's campfire popped and hissed, and it made me think of the one I had going over by our tents and the girls, and looking over, I could see it needed tending.

"Walt, it has been nice to meet you, and thanks again for helping me find this place, but I have to go tend the fire. We have an early morning tomorrow with 30 miles more downriver." And then for some reason, "You know, Walt, it seems to me that you are in the right place. This is the right place to be right now." Walt never said a word. I got up and left.

That night, as I lay in my tent before sleep, I thought of Walt, alone by the river but somehow at peace: a strange, calm peace. For a moment, I pondered him being drunk and trying something, but I dismissed the thought and fell asleep to the gentle sound of the river.

The following day, I did not see Walt until we were boarding the canoes for the remainder of the trip. The girls were having trouble getting into their canoe, and although I was trying to hold the canoe steady, out of nowhere, Walt appeared and helped me with the canoe. Then, once I had gotten into my canoe, Walt pushed both canoes off the bank and out into the river.

As we left the river bank that morning, I watched Walt walk over to his picnic table and take his seat. "Another person I have met and will never see again!"

I didn't know it at the time, but I was wrong. I would meet Walt again.

***

After the 2-day canoe trip with my youngest daughter, three weeks later, I repeated the same canoe trip, but this time, with my son and one of his friends.

Having done the trip once, when I felt we had made enough distance on the river the first day, I began to search the river bank for the same campground I had used on the first trip and thought perhaps Walt's truck might come into view or his collection of river gifts on the river bank or maybe even Walt on that sandbar, but nothing.

The more we went downriver, the more anxious I became. I just had to find the campground and, only floating now with the river current, came around a small bend in the river and there, on the left, I clearly recognized the gentle slope bank of the camp ground.

As we pulled our canoes far enough out of the water so the current would not move them, I looked around for Walt and to where his river collection had been, but nothing. No truck either. But beyond the picnic table, further upstream and higher up the bank was a small tent. "Not Walt," I thought, and "the tent people, out and about somewhere for the day."

It began to finally cool from the heat of the day, and with tents set, wood gathered for the fire, and the boys playing in the shallow water at the river's edge, I relaxed a bit and had my second cigarette of the day.

As I prepared dinner, out of the corner of my eye, I detected some movement, and when I looked, there was Walt, walking off the dirt road that ran along the top of the river bank. "Where was his truck? Why was he walking?"

After dinner, the boys returned from their shower and after sitting around the campfire for a while, my son and his friend headed inside their tent for the night. I put more wood on the fire.

Looking over at the small tent to make sure it was, in fact, Walt, he had started a fire, and in the firelight, I could clearly see it was Walt. I watched him for a while, thinking he might come over to me, but my curiosity got the better of me, and I began walking in Walt's direction.

When I was close enough, I called out, "Walt, remember me?" Walt looked up and waved me in.

At first, he did not recognize me, but after telling him about our first meeting, we shook hands and we sat on his picnic table again.

It looked to me that Walt had gained some weight and apparently was no longer drinking, as the brown paper bag was nowhere to be seen.

"Where is your truck and all the stuff you had in that big tree over there?" "Well, I think it was the day after you were here last, well maybe 2 or 3, I don't remember, one afternoon it began to rain pretty hard, thunder and lightning. You know: a summer storm. Anyways, I crawled into my tent early and liking the sound of rain on my tent, fell asleep. Sometime during the night, the rain stopped and woke me up, and then, I don't know, later, another big storm and it really rained hard. I thought nothing of it as it had rained before and went back to sleep. Well, damn, if I didn't wake up to wet feet and dark, God Almighty, it was dark. Anyways, I opened my tent and the river was right there. I mean, it was right at my tent and moving real fast. I stepped out into the water and dragged my tent up the bank near my truck, but the water was still rising, so I packed the tent into the truck and drove up near the shower house. I didn't think the river would get me there, but I slept in the front seat just in case, and it rained and rained. When I woke up, the sun was out, but the river was still high up in the field here. Couldn't even see the picnic table and the river sure was moving, all muddy and full of stuff. Anyways, I stayed a while with my truck, but with the river still high, I drove into Berryville to see if I could make some money."

"River got into that field there?" "Yep, and now I know, more than once, been into the shower house, gets so high."

"So, Berryville: did you find some work? What happened to your truck?"

"Well, I got to Berryville, drove around looking at houses and find a couple that needed painting real bad and took a couple of door knocks but got a job painting this small one. So, I started work, preparing the wood, but I don't know, but someone must've thought I looked bad or something because they called the cops on me. Since I didn't have a license to paint in Berryville, had to pay a $50 fine but since I couldn't pay and had no mailing address, they put me in jail."

"Jail for no permit" "Well said I was a vagrant." "They don't do that anymore, do they?" "Well, they sure enough did. Said if I could pay a $50 fine, they would let me go but with no money, jail it was. At first, I didn't like it much. Never been in a jail in my life, but after a while, food was good, the place was clean, and the cot was soft."

"So, when did you get out? Did you call your ex-wife?"

"No, I didn't call her. See, I left her for my friend, that California woman, so my wife wasn't going to help me. Anyways, after 5 days, they let me go but said I owed them $100 for storage of my truck and, since I couldn't pay, could not have my truck until I did pay."

"That's crazy, Walt. Without your truck and no permit to paint, how are you supposed to come up with 100 dollars?"

"So, they let me out, and all I can think of is the river, the only place I know I can go and fella working the cells, he let me get into my truck and get my tent and says if I can get a real address, someplace to live, he knows someone that can help me get a paint license.

So, I start walking back to here and when I get on the dirt road that leads from the main road to here, this fellow in a pickup truck comes by and stops and asks me if I need a ride. Well, turns out he needed some help on his farm bailing hay, and I have been working there all this week. And today, he gave me $100 and asked if I could stay in this small house he has up off the road as it needed tending and he was too busy. You believe that?"

"Walt, that is amazing. I mean the flood, then jail, and now a place to live and maybe some work. It's crazy, just crazy."

Walt is silent.

We sat together for a while, my head full of his story. By the river, just by the river, but then the river floods, and he has to move. Move on downstream, I guess.

"Well, got an early morning tomorrow. Guy, that is his name, the fella I am working for, is coming to pick me up tomorrow, take me into town to get my truck, and then take me to the house he wants me to live in."

"Well, Walt, I am really happy for you: seems like things are moving again."

"Yep, I guess the river told me to move, and I did."

"Hope you get to see your sons soon."

"Me too," and with that, Walt got up and moved to his small tent.

***

The next morning, Walt was gone by the time we got up and out, and we headed down river again.

As we paddled our way towards the middle of the river, I looked back and thought of Walt and felt a little sad as I knew I would never see him again, but my mind seemed to continue to roll over and over, his story, his life by the river, the great peace he seemed to have.

The son that I took down the river is now almost 45, and over the years, out of nowhere, at odd times, Walt has come to mind, and my first meeting with him: by the river and at peace. A peace I still have never known. And for some reason, I always think of The Buddha, sitting, just sitting, and the world making itself known to him slowly.

Musing: "Miracles"

I am not a physicist or particularly intelligent, but I have always taken a real interest in science and cosmology and studied the mathematics of probability in college. However, with all that said, I don't get it.

Whenever I open my eyes, all I seem to see are impossible events, things all around me, which, from a probability point of view, or at least my understanding of probabilities, can only be described as miracles and impossibilities.

Now, I am aware that most folks do not see the world this way, and although I have never really been a protestor or one to carry a banner or flag and wave it for any one cause, I think I need to start a campaign to make people understand and see, what an incredible, miraculous place we call "living", really is.

Perhaps the first step to seeing what I see is to take a step back. If there ever was a case of not being able to see the forest for the trees, it is in the case of everyone taking the world around them for granted.

How many people give the weeds growing along a highway any thought or even notice them or a spider's web in a window or shadows?

But if all about us was once compressed into the space of about a grapefruit, and that is what scientists now say the initial point was of the 'Big Bang', then how did all the stuff around us come to be?

Doesn't it seem impossible that out of nothing but energy, even given 14 billion years or however the universe is old, would result in a spider web or a chrome bumper on a car, an oak tree, or the little finger on my left hand?

If you could stand at a point on that grapefruit and look out, you would say that the odds of a chrome car bumper ever appearing in the universe would be infinitely small. The Las Vegas odds would have to be billions and billions to one. I mean, how could energy that was not even tiny little stuff, like atoms, make its way into chrome bumpers or happy meals at McDonald's? Just not possible using any logic or probability theory, and yet, there's no denying that chrome bumpers or Happy Meals exist.

I reach for a set of headphones and the wire that attaches the headphones to the CD player, gets caught on the bed frame or the coat cuff on a doorknob as you exit. Could move either another 1 million times and would never get caught again, yet it happened. And what would be the Vegas odds of that happening? And yet, things like this happen all the time.

I watch a tree leaf let go from a limb and drift slowly down, only to land in a spider's web, which some enterprising spider has built in one corner of the garage. One leaf falls and hits a spider web and gets caught. 100,000,000 to one odds on that happening, and yet, there it is, right in front of my eyes: a miracle of impossibility.

Recently, in my science readings, I came across the concept if there is no physical law preventing an event from happening, then it can and might happen.

Ok. Then why don't I hit the lottery every time I play or get struck by lightning whenever there is a lightning storm?

Certainly, there is some "time" element to probability, and I understand that, but if I stand long enough in an open field, I could well be hit by lightning, although it might take many, many years before the first hit. But the fact that anything that is not physical law impossible could happen, does not take the edge off my amazement with this earth, sky, and living.

Think of any one thing; make it easy, like a hair comb. Suppose one of our space probes landed on some planet and immediately found a comb lying there on the ground. What a freak show that would be for all the scientists of the world trying to explain that one, and yet, right here, right now, you can get a plastic comb for a dollar just about around any corner.

If one steps back and looks at the comb, it would seem impossible that the universe could 'evolve', 'create', 'fashion', 'form', such a thing no matter how much time: just a miracle and only a comb at that.

I am not doing a good job of waving my banner.

Water is drawn up from the oceans and moved around the globe to fall on my lawn and nourish in the form of rain. Take some sun, dirt, heat, air and invisible chemical forces, and you have the miracle of an apple or pear. Again, step back. From just so much energy, after 14 billion years, an apple is hanging on a tree.

So, ok, one aspect of this must be "creationism" and "evolution."

One answer to all this, everything, is that God created it.

On the other hand, evolution says that from an organization comes more organization, and as the organization progresses, changes are made that allow for environmental adaptation.

To me, both schools of thought seem "miracle"-based: the immense improbability.

The banner: the flag, the cause.

Flip a switch and there is light. Coal dug from some deep mine, transported, burned, and converted to electricity, sent down wires strung along streets and into your house and connected to that switch and light at your command. Think of anyone 100 or 200 years ago and how improbable that would have seemed to them: light at the movement of a finger.

14 Billion years and it is all from something the size of a grapefruit. And from what I can tell, when this "grapefruit" exploded, expanded, had it been a little bit to 'hot', it would have expanded so fast that stuff could never have collected into stars and galaxies and planets or if a little bit, and I mean a little bit too 'cold', it would not have expanded fast enough to overcome gravity. It would have simply contracted back into the grapefruit thing again without forming the universe we now see all around us. Just a very

little bit of change one way or the other, and this place, all of it, doesn't exist. It is a miracle to me.

Some say it is no miracle at all, as lots of 'grapefruit things' around all the time, like firecrackers sharing the same fuse, going "off," with some too 'hot' and some to 'cold' and some just right like in the "Goldie Locks and the Three Bears" story and we in a "just right" grapefruit expansion.

OK. Sort of like, "give a million monkeys typewriters a million years, and they will eventually write all the works of Shakespeare." Ever heard that one? I have trouble believing it, but then again, I do not know of any physical law that rules it out, and thus, "they say" it is possible.

Waving the banner now for all it is worth.

Now, I know it is asking a lot, but step outside yourself for a moment and imagine being far, far away in the universe, distant from any star or planet, where it is very dark, very cold, and empty of everything. Now, hold there for a moment in the emptiness and nothingness of that space and time.

Now, bring yourself back. Back to the blue sky, clouds, trees, grass, weeds, birds, animals, rain, snow, wind, and yourself here, on this bright blue ball we call home, earth. Doesn't all this seem like the most complex place in the universe: so much complexity; so much diversity; so many miracles and improbabilities?

And we speak, communicate, write books to be shared, move about despite the laws of gravity, ponder all sorts of questions, peer into the depths of the universe, shake each other's hands, grow vegetables, ride subways, build subways, love each other and kill each other.

What a place this living is! Waving and waving my "Miracles" banner in the summer's sun. I am so happy to be here and you should be too.

It is a miracle that either of us is here, even for the few universe moments we have to breathe in and out.

Musing: "The Phone Call"

Doubt anyone will ever stumble, "trip", across these words and most readers will, after review, simply chalk them up as just another delusion, flashback of an old hippie. But I know what I know.

It was January 1, 2000. Yep, it was New Year's Day of the new millennium or what was often referred to back then, as the dreaded "Y2K."

Up at 6:30 and powering up my computer to see if it would actually come alive, after all the Y2K warnings, when the telephone rang.

"Who could be calling me so early?"

I did not want the ringing home phones to wake others in the house, so I picked up the telephone receiver.

"Ron?"

"Yes."

"Hey man, Happy New Year, 3000!"

"What?"

"I said, Happy New Year, 3000!"

"No, wait," the other end of the telephone line says, beginning to laugh, "It's only 2000 for you."

"What?"

And it is at this point that I think I recognize the voice on the other end of the phone.

And then the line is dead.

When the line dropped, putting down the receiver, I was" in a daze: had what just happened, happened?

"Perhaps a joke played on me by some friend: but the voice!"

And then a very strange feeling came over me. "Me, or a variation of me and perhaps an even better mankind, will see the year 3000, and that made me very happy."

So do not be surprised if one day, you get a landline or cell phone call, email, text message, chat, or communiqué from the future, and do not be afraid to admit it and share it.

We survive! We Do!

www.ingramcontent.com/pod-product-compliance
Lightning Source LLC
Chambersburg PA
CBHW032357310726
48973CB00007B/2048